ABOUT THE AUTHOR

John Charles Hall is a Business Consultant in the Horticulture Industry, helping small, medium and corporate organisations to grow their businesses; especially in the areas of business planning and development.

Having lived all his life in and around the villages of the South Downs and the West Sussex Coastal Plain, John has a great love and understanding of these rural communities. He has often wondered what might have happened had they been invaded and occupied during the Second World War.

John lives with his wife Anne in Felpham, West Sussex. They have three grown up children and Ash before Oak is his second novel following on from Under the Yew Tree.

Ash
before
Oak

JOHN CHARLES HALL

ISBN: 979 8 61 637324 3
Also available as an e-book

Book design by The Art of Communication www.book-design.co.uk
First published in the UK 2020

DEDICATION

'Ash before Oak' is dedicated to my wife Anne,
our grown-up children and their partners:
Laurie and Alicia, Rebecca and Alex, James and Lisa,
and our grandchildren: Ruby, Elias, Henry, Soraya,
Jerimiah, Freddie, Thomas, Oliver and Magdalena.

'Ash before Oak' is the second book
in the dystopian trilogy set in the second world war.
'Under the Yew Tree' was the first book
and the third is planned for publication in 2021.

ACKNOWLEDGEMENTS

Whilst writing Under the Yew Tree and Ash before Oak I have received a great deal of encouragement from my family and friends.

I am also very grateful for the professional support that I have received along the way. My special thanks go to: Sally Orson-Jones, Edward Couzens-Lake, Louise Hopkins, Chris Unitt and Christine Hammacott at Art of Communication.

FOREWORD

by Edward Couzens-Lake

Author and Broadcaster

The world as we know it grows smaller by the day. It is the one that Canadian philosopher Marshall McLuhan foretold back in the early 1960's when he coined the phrase 'global village' to describe the phenomenon of the world becoming increasingly interconnected as a result of the steady spread of media technologies across the planet.

Yet digital technology will never be master of all it surveys; because the very strongest of bonds come not from the proliferation of fibre optics, but from the very ancient and virtually indestructible bond that is brought about through a sense of community. Of people, not technology, working together. Creating, combining, sharing and exploring as one. A collective with a common goal. A goal that has purpose and is for the greater good.

Communities coming together can achieve great things. They can drag hope from despair, bring light from darkness and work together in order to defy the most ridiculous of odds. This is the community that lives in the small West Sussex village that is at the epicentre of John Hall's second novel about the everyday lives of people forced to live under German occupation in a world whose history is very different to ours.

Their peaceful rural existence has been shaken to the

core by the presence of enemy forces hell-bent on conquering and vanquishing this nation as ruthlessly as they have many others. South East England is already lost to Hitler's forces. How long before the inevitable and all of Great Britain is part of the Third Reich?

What chance does one village have against such military might? Perhaps none at all. Yet the one thing their enemy will have discounted is this village's sense of community. A people who come together; quietly and unobtrusively but united and with the common goal of defeating those overwhelming odds.

Everyone has their part to play, no matter how small or insignificant it might be. They are the tiny cogs that come together to provide the energy for the bigger ones. They may seem kowtowed and beaten, but they are anything but.

The opening pages of Ash Before Oak sees them coming to terms with the loss of someone who had brought them all hope. It was a loss that might have led to them submitting to their fate; but it made them stronger and more determined than ever to defy their foes and to offer resistance, resilience and, with it, renewed faith that this seemingly hopeless battle is still theirs to be won.

John Hall immerses you into their lives with all the narrative panache of a natural story teller. So much so, that you'll be there, on the front line, fighting alongside them.

Part of the greatest force of all. That of community.

ASH BEFORE OAK

"Ash before oak, we're in for a soak.

Oak before ash, we're in for a splash."

Traditional English proverb

Chapter 1

WHERE TO FROM HERE?

At first light, Alex set off for the path that he knew would take him through the woods to the top of the South Downs. Dressed in his everyday farm clothes, he walked at a steady pace, looking all around as he made his way along the well-trodden path. It was cold and the air was clear. Overnight there had been a heavy frost and the grass glowed in the early morning light.

Yesterday had turned out to be a disaster. As he walked, Alex ran the events of the previous day back through his mind. He knew that there would be others out early this morning looking for their friends. Last evening, as the shooting had started, and it became clear that the German troops were in the woods, the men of the Resistance had fallen back in as orderly a manner as they could. There was confusion throughout the evening and it was difficult to work out what was going on. By midnight, most of the men had made it back to the village and to the outlying farms and hamlets. Some reported that they had seen German troops coming out from the woods, whilst others said that troop trucks had been seen making their way back to their barracks on the south side of Watersham. It was clear that the soldiers had been hunting until late evening. Dogs had been heard barking and scores of shots had echoed through the woods for a long time.

The Resistance exercise which had been due to start during the previous afternoon had broken up before most of the men had reached the designated meeting place. It had long been standing practice for the men of the Resistance to "disappear" as quickly as possible if ever their meeting places were discovered.

On this occasion it took a long time as the whole area was swarming with German soldiers. Alex had to hide in a thicket on the edge of the woods before, after being certain that all was quiet, making a wide diversion back to the family farm. He didn't get in until midnight and, once safely home, lay awake for most of the night wondering who they had been shooting at.

He feared the worst.

Today, his plan was to follow the main path from the farm, up through the woods to the old drovers' trail and on to the top of the Downs. He dressed in his usual work clothes and packed some lunch and a bottle of tea into a knapsack that he hitched over his shoulder.

His family ran a small flock of sheep on the rough pastures further along the Downs, and if spotted by a German patrol, it would appear that he was a local farmers' boy, just going about his daily work of checking on the sheep.

Yesterday had been different. Yesterday, he had walked along the same path carrying a machine gun and a bag full of ammunition. His clothes had been different then too; like most of the men in the Resistance, he wore a khaki shirt, an old greenish brown jacket with leather patches on the elbows, dark trousers and heavy laced up walking boots. It wasn't quite a uniform, but it was the best that he and the rest of the men could do. When they were all together, you could tell that they were a paramilitary outfit, not just a ragtag group of rebels. The chances of running into a German unit in the woods were tiny… or so they thought.

After about thirty minutes of walking, Alex stopped at a point where the path entered the main part of the woods. He stood completely still for some time listening to the sounds of the countryside. He was only eighteen years old, but having spent all of his life on the farm, in the woods, on the Downs and in and around the small local villages, he knew every natural sight and sound. If there was something wrong, something out of place or something that grated with his senses; he would know. On this occasion he heard nothing that concerned him and he heard only the quietest of whispers coming from the trees as a gentle breeze brushed through the woods. Off to the east, a long way off, he could just make out the sound of cows mooing; a sound he knew so well. They seemed content, and for a moment, he imagined the herd ambling back out into the meadows after milking; steam rising from their backs as their warm bodies met the cold early morning air. He turned slowly on the spot to make sure that he was picking up every noise that he could. There was nothing to worry about.

As he stood listening, his thoughts turned again to the day before. How did the Germans know that the Resistance planned to meet in the woods that afternoon?

Before splitting up from the others and making his way home, Alex had managed a few snatched conversations with other fighters as they got away. It was clear from the limited information that he had, that it wasn't a simple coincidence that such a large group of German soldiers happened to be there at the same time as the local Resistance. It was also clear, from all the shooting and dog barking, that they had engaged with at least one of the Resistance fighters; but, had they caught anyone?

Alex wasn't sure what he was searching for or what he might find, but he felt compelled to look. He knew that other friends would be looking as well. He was fully aware that there was a strong possibility that German patrols would be in the woods too. With his local knowledge, he was fairly sure that he could keep out of their way, but even if he ran into one, why should they be suspicious of a farmers' boy on his way to check on a flock of sheep? What he was hoping for was to meet with his friends, out searching as he was; to exchange what little information they had and to try to make sense of it all. He looked all around before setting off again. He noticed how much darker it was in the woods and how much colder it felt.

He stopped again to button up his jacket and to turn up his collar. He opened his knapsack, took out his corduroy cap, and pulled it tight onto his head. Before setting off again, he looked back down the path and could just make out the weak early morning sun, sitting low beyond the outskirts of the woods.

Ten minutes later, his eyes had adjusted to the low light levels under the trees. He slowed his pace as he came to a spot where two paths joined that led further into the woods. He stopped and peered back down the other path and ahead along the new one. As he strained his eyes looking all around, suddenly, a cock blackbird took off from the ground only five paces in front of him, making its shrill alarm call as it flew away. The sudden noise made Alex jump, but he smiled to himself as he realised it was just a bird. Off to his right, there was another distinct noise; a sound he had heard many times before; a small group of deer moving off under the trees. He couldn't see them, but he guessed, from the sound of the cracking twigs, no more than about five fallow deer in the group. He stood still until all was quiet again and then headed off down the main path.

On the other side of the woods, about a mile to the West, Alan Benton and Bert Stubbs were making their way along a flint track that ran through the middle of the beech woods that would eventually take them to the top of the hill. They were taking it in turns to push a wheelbarrow, in which lay two long handled axes, a billhook, a hand bow saw and their lunch bags. If anyone wanted to know they were on the way to the top end of the woods to cut some fence posts. There was a large stand of coppiced chestnut trees there; perfect for the job. Like Alex, they too had got back late the night before, only just managing to avoid the German patrols.

Back in Watersham, Commander Henry Clay had already made an early morning visit to the Post Office, where he had a long conversation with Olive Tindall, the Post Mistress, and one of the postmen, George Marsh. He told them all that he knew about what had happened yesterday and that he was trying to establish if anyone was unaccounted for. He then made his way to the vicarage, where, after a quick chat with the vicar, he collected a large pile of the latest copy of the Parish Magazine, and then set off on his bicycle to deliver them around the village. At the bottom end of Church Road; there was a German truck parked, with about twelve soldiers standing on the pavement. Henry leaned his bike against a flint wall and worked his way along one side of the street, door to door, delivering the magazines. As he turned to go back up the other side, he had to walk past the soldiers to get to the houses behind them. As he walked away from the second door, Sergeant Matteus Weiss stepped in front of him. Henry and Matteus recognised each other immediately. They had seen each other many times since the Germans had occupied Watersham some months ago.

"Good morning Sergeant," said Henry.

"Good morning to you," replied Sergeant Weiss, "And

what are you delivering today?"

"Just the Parish Magazine," replied Henry, as he handed one of the magazines to the Sergeant. "Would you like one?" Sergeant Weiss flicked through the magazine, looked Henry straight in the eye and thanked him. "I'll read it later," he said.

The Sergeant stepped out of Henry's way, and as he did so, he said, "By the way, did you hear anything about what happened yesterday?"

"One or two people said that they heard shooting coming from the woods," Henry said as he pointed in the general direction of the woods.

"Yes," said Sergeant Weiss, "Some trouble over there, I think. Let me know if you hear anything, won't you?"

"Yes, of course, I will," said Henry as he walked on.

Sergeant Weiss and the soldiers watched Henry as he carried on up the road, delivering his magazines. As he rode back past Sergeant Weiss and the soldiers, he waved at them, and one or two waved back. Around the corner, in the High Street, there was another truck with a large group of German soldiers standing next to it. He stopped and leaned his bike against the front fence of number one and started to work his way along the street, posting the magazines through the letter boxes as he went. Half way back down the other side he had to pass the soldiers again, and as he did so, he realised that Sergeant Weiss was now talking to them. They nodded to each other and Henry carried on until he got back to his bike. As calmly as he could, he cycled past them and turned left into Cooper Street. He breathed a sigh of relief as he saw that there were no more soldiers there. He turned off of Cooper Street, dismounted and pushed his bike down an alleyway into the back of Rose Green Estate. He continued pushing the magazines through letter boxes until he reached number seven, at which, after looking up and down the street once more to check that no one was watching, he pushed his bike quickly through the gate, leaned it against the back of the hedge and knocked on the door. Mrs. Janet Brown opened the door, and without hesitation or speaking, ushered Henry inside and quickly closed the door behind him.

Janet and Henry hurried through to the kitchen towards the back of the house. Henry spoke first. "Did Jack get back okay last night?"

"Yes. He's safe. He's gone to work. He wanted everything to look normal this morning, but I know he was worried sick about some of the men. He said that there was a lot of shooting in the woods and he didn't know whether or not everyone made it back safely."

Janet placed her hand on Henry's arm. "What's happened Henry. Is everyone alright?"

"I don't know yet. I haven't managed to speak to many people yet; but there's no doubt there was lots of shooting in the woods last evening. Tell Jack to meet me at the usual time and place tonight. Hopefully, I'll have all the information by then."

Henry pulled out a Parish Magazine from his bag and handed it to her. "Here," he said, "take this in case I've been spotted. I'd better get straight off."

Henry saw no-one as he came out from number seven and he carried on delivering magazines around the village. He saw more German vehicles moving around as the morning went on. At Foxglove Cottage, he knocked at the door. Mrs. Washbrook opened it and stared coldly at him. Henry spoke first. "Morning Mrs Washbrook. Sorry to bother you. I just wanted to have a quick word with Tim if he's…"

"He's not here!" snapped Mrs Washbrook, "He didn't come home last night. I don't know where he's got to… and now you're standing on my doorstep. Where is he? I'm worried sick… he's only a boy… he shouldn't be mixed up in all this. Where is he?" Tears started to trickle down her face. "Where is he?" she screamed.

Henry jumped as she screamed, grabbed hold of her and bundled her inside, kicking the door shut behind him. Mrs Washbrook was crying loudly now, and as he tried to calm her, she slowly slid down the wall and sat on the floor in the hallway. Henry knelt down beside her.

"Listen," he said, "Listen. I don't know anything yet. I'm trying to find out and so are some of the others. We'll know more by this evening. I'll let you know as soon as I can find out where Tim is. I promise. I wish that I could tell you more, but I can't. We don't know what's happened yet."

Mrs Washbrook lifted her head, pulled out a hanky from her sleeve and wiped her face. Henry stood up and offered to help her up. She took his hands and pulled herself up, wiped her face again and blew her nose. "I'll never forgive myself… or you… if he's…" She couldn't find the strength to finish the sentence.

"We'll find him," said Henry. "Look, I'll have to press on. Alright?"

Henry stepped away from her and opened the door. As he left, he dropped a magazine on the hall table. Outside, he shook his head, before carrying on posting the magazines through letter boxes. He hoped and prayed that Tim Washbrook was okay. He didn't know how he would be able to face Mrs Washbrook if he wasn't.

By mid-morning, Henry had run out of Parish Magazines, and so he cycled back to the vicarage to refill his bag. He spoke briefly again to the vicar, who, despite trying, still hadn't heard any more about yesterday's events, but had heard that some villagers had been taken away by the Germans during the morning but he wasn't sure of their names. Henry stuffed his bag full of more magazines and headed back towards the High Street, where he called in to the Post Office again. As soon as Olive saw him coming, she waved him towards the kitchen, closed the door and started talking as they sat at the table. "The Germans... they... they carried several of their dead out from the woods last night. They also carried out one of ours." Olive looked at the floor and put her hands to her head.

"Who was it?" muttered Henry, dreading the answer.

Olive dropped her hands to her lap, lifted her head, but with her eyes tight closed, said, "They think it might be young Tim Washbrook."

Henry gave out a deep groan. "For God's sake no. No, not Tim. I've just been talking to his mum."

They sat in silence for a while staring at the table top until Henry sighed, pushed back his chair and stood up. Olive stood too. Henry stepped close to Olive and kissed her gently on both cheeks.

"Stay safe my friend... and stay strong." whispered Olive. "You too." replied Henry.

As Henry opened the kitchen door, George Marsh came hurrying down the corridor. Henry backed into the kitchen again, and George, breathing heavily, shut the door behind him.

"Joseph Carter!" he blurted. "He hasn't made it back to the farm and no one's seen him since he left there yesterday to go to the woods."

Henry grabbed the back of a chair to steady himself. He suddenly felt sick and light headed. "Joseph? Not Joseph as well, surely?" Olive stepped closer and put her arm around him.

"Did you hear anything else George?"

"They're all pretty sure that the body taken from the woods was Tim Washbrook." His voice faltered. "But as I say, no one has seen Joseph. I haven't heard of anyone else that's missing. There's several out looking through the woods now, but there's still lots of Germans about."

"Thanks George," said Henry, "I'd better get off to see what else I can find out."

Henry didn't finish delivering the magazines, but rode

straight back to the vicarage. As quickly and succinctly as he could, he explained to the Reverend Timothy Streeter all that he needed to know, without telling him his fears about Joseph Carter. They agreed that the vicar would go to the German barracks and see if they would confirm whose body they had taken from the woods. If it was Tim, Henry needed the vicar to deliver the terrible news to Mr and Mrs Washbrook as soon as possible. If it wasn't Tim, Henry needed to know whose it was. The vicar didn't hesitate for one moment.

"I'll get straight to it." he said. They shook hands and Henry made his way back home to see if any further messages had been left for him while he was out.

In the woods, Alex had criss-crossed many of the paths that he knew well and some that he'd never come across before. He hadn't seen a soul or heard anything unusual since leaving home.

Just past an old dell, he came across a long-fallen tree. He straddled its trunk, sat down, took out a bottle of tea from his knapsack and drank. The tea was cold, but milky and sweet – just the way he liked it. As he clipped the lid on and slid the bottle back into his bag, he noticed spent bullet cases laying on the chalky earth near his boots. He looked around to check that no one was watching, stood up, looked around again, and then, quickly bent down and scooped up five cases. He blew the chalk dust from one of them and smelt it. It was fresh and he recognised it as a standard issue British Army .303 bullet case. He dropped them into his bag and quickly set off again along the path through the trees. About twenty paces further along, he came across another identical spent bullet case. He turned and walked back to the fallen tree. Looking closer, he could see that the earth on one side had been scuffed, as if someone had been lying there. The penny suddenly dropped. Someone had been lying there, using the fallen tree as cover and firing towards the dell that he had just walked past. There was very little doubt that the man had been one of the Resistance fighters; one of his friends… probably one of the people he was looking for now.

He walked back towards the dell. There had certainly been a lot going on here. Much of the thin and weak undergrowth had been trampled and in a chalky area he found three more spent bullet cases; this time though, not ones that he recognised. He also found part of what looked like a bloodied dog collar. He made his way back to the fallen tree again, and on closer inspection could see where pieces of bark had been shot away. Alex looked around once more and then set off down the path, wondering what else he was going to find.

Alan Benton and Bert Stubbs were making steady progress up the flint path, and wherever they had come across a crossing, they had stopped and checked to see whether they could find any evidence of recent disturbance. They had found plenty of deer droppings, and one pathway smelled to high heaven of fox scent, but there was no sign of recent human activity. Any animals that might have been nearby would have soon run away at the sound of the approaching wheelbarrow. Ahead, they could see it was becoming lighter as the beech woods opened out to well-grazed grassland near to the top of the South Downs. Although the grass was still white with frost, and the air was cold, it felt much warmer as soon as they walked out from the woods into the sunshine. There was a pile of beech logs stacked up out in the open where they found a good spot to sit for a while, facing the sun. They had a few bites to eat and a quick drink and then stood ready to move on again. As Alan bent down to lift the handles of the wheelbarrow, he looked back towards the woods; just in time to see a figure emerging from under the hanging branches of the beech trees. Alan waved at Bert and they both ducked back down behind the logs.

"What is it?"

"There's someone coming."

Alan peered around the corner of the logs, and as soon as Alex emerged into the sunshine, he could see who it was. "It's okay." he grinned, "It's Alex."

They stepped out from behind the logs and waved. Alex stopped for a second, and then waved back and quickened his pace to join them. They shook hands and hugged each other in relief. But then, stepping back, Alex cleared his throat. "Have you found anything or seen anyone?" he asked. "Have you heard from any of the others?"

Alan and Bert shook their heads. "No, nothing," replied Bert.

"I found some spent shells in the middle of the woods; British and German, I think. It looked like quite a bit was going on there recently, alright. But apart from that, nothing. I haven't seen anyone all morning. I was pretty sure I would bump into a German patrol at some time… but no, nothing." He looked back towards the woods and then spoke again, "Did you hear if everyone got back okay last night?"

"No." Bert shook his head uneasily, "We haven't seen or heard from anyone else."

Alex frowned. "What's with the wheelbarrow and the axes then?"

"Like you, we weren't sure who we might run into; so, we thought we'd claim that we were up here to cut fence posts from the chestnut coppice behind the yew trees. In fact, we must do that before we make our way back down again. We still might run into trouble."

Alex pointed towards the brow of the hill about three hundred yards to the south. "Let's have a look over there first, then you can cut some fence posts while I have a quick look down the other side."

They walked to the brow and then, leaving the wheelbarrow, they spread out to search along the scrubby open top. Alex's flock of sheep looked up as they spotted the three men coming towards them. He stopped and watched them for a while, but again, didn't spot anything unusual. They looked surprisingly well in the weak December sunshine. Out in the open, the air temperature had just managed to get above freezing and some of the frost was beginning to disappear. They walked east for nearly a mile, spread out over a span of about one hundred yards; looking all around, and paying special attention to any scrubby and bramble clumps that they came across. They found nothing of interest and turned around, repeating the exercise in the opposite direction. When they got back to the wheelbarrow; they stopped to chat for a while, still trying to make sense of what had happened last night.

Eventually, Alan said, "Right then. Come on Bert. Let's go and cut some chestnut stakes."

"Okay," said Alex, "I'll have a quick look down the slope and then I'll come and find you."

After half an hour, Alex had found nothing and made his way towards where he knew that the chestnut trees grew. He could hear the others cutting and chopping and it didn't take him long to find them. He helped them for about twenty minutes, by which time they had twelve stout chestnut posts in the wheel barrow; each cut to exactly five feet nine inches and each with a perfect pencil point at one end.

"I'll take the first push if you like," said Alex, as he picked up the handles of the wheelbarrow and set off. It wasn't too heavy and he knew that once they reached the flint track, it would be downhill all the way.

"Just a minute!" shouted Bert, "Let's go down through the yew trees. There's a better path that way."

"Good idea." said Alex.

They headed down towards the yew trees. As soon as they reached the yews, they were back under heavy shade again, and could feel how much colder it was there. Frost still clung to the large patches of moss that grew so well here and to the odd tufts of grass that managed to survive under such a canopy of dark branches. As long as the great yew tree roots that, every now and again erupted from the ground, were avoided, pushing the wheelbarrow here was definitely easier. Alex stopped for a breather, and Alan and Bert, walking slightly further back, stopped too and looked up through the great branches. After a while, Alex stretched his back, and as he bent to take the handles again, something caught his eye in the distance.

"What's that?" he said, pointing towards the largest yew tree.

Alan and Bert looked towards where Alex was pointing and seeing that there was definitely something there, they joined Alex and quickly walked on. As they got closer to the tree, they slowed their pace as they realised that the something was in fact a man.

"Bloody hell…" shouted Alex, "… it's Joseph."

Alex dropped to his knees in front of Joseph and touched his colourless face. He was stone cold. He felt for a pulse and leaned in close, hoping against hope for some sign of life, some shallow breath, a faint noise, anything. There was nothing.

"He's dead…" said Alex.

Alan pointed at the belt pulled tight around Joseph's leg and his bloodied trousers.

"He's bled to death." Alan mumbled, tears starting to run down his cheeks. "He's been shot… struggled all the way up here… sat under the yew tree… fucking freezing cold… and bloody died… just bloody died all on his…" He turned and walked away. Bert walked after him.

Alex wiped his own tears away now and sat back on his haunches, his hands to his face, staring at the mossy ground between the roots. He spoke quietly as he sniffed and wiped more tears away. "What happened mate?" He briefly looked back at Joseph's face and then back at the ground. "How did they get you?" He looked again at Joseph hoping for an answer. No answer came. "For Christ's sake mate. If they can get you, they'll get all of us."

Bert trudged back to where they had left the wheelbarrow, wheeled it back to the yew tree, and unloaded the newly cut fence posts, axes and saw. As gently as they could, the three men lifted Joseph's body into the wheelbarrow. Alan picked up the bow saw and then hitched Joseph's rifle and bag over his shoulder. Bert carried the long-handled axes; one in each hand. Alex took charge of the wheelbarrow and the party moved off in total silence.

Not a word was spoken until they reached the start of the flint path. "Look," said Alex as he set the wheelbarrow down, "We can't go down to the village. We're bound to run into the Germans that way and they'll take Joseph away from us. Let's get him straight back to his family."

"You're right," said Bert. "Come on. Let me have the wheelbarrow."

Alan nodded in agreement and they set off towards Hill Farm.

Chapter 2

HILL FARM

It took more than an hour for the sad little group to reach Hill Farm. They had taken turns to push the wheelbarrow, and fortunately, they hadn't run into a German patrol. As the barns in the farmyard came into view, Alex called a halt and Alan put the wheelbarrow down and straightened his back. They were all tired.

Alex spoke, "We can't just push Joseph up to the Carter's door," he said. "I think it would be best if you both hold back a bit when we get close to the house. I'll knock on the door, try and get everyone together and do my best to prepare them. I'll then wave you forward."

Alex looked at Alan and Bert for reassurance. "What do you think?" he said.

Bert and Alan nodded their approval. "Yes," they said in unison, "that sounds about right."

"It's coming up to lunchtime," said Alan, "with a bit of luck, they'll all be inside."

They moved up closer to the house and stopped by the

corner of the large barn, within view of the kitchen door.

"Right." said Alex, "I really don't know how I'm going to do this. I hope I can get the words out."

Alan and Bert patted Alex on the back as he set off slowly towards the house. He stood for a moment by the door without knocking, taking deep breaths to calm himself. Still trembling, he knocked. Lily, Joseph's little sister, opened the door and broke into a huge smile as she saw that it was Alex, Joseph's best friend.

"What's up Alex?" but then the smile fell away as she looked into Alex's eyes.

"Is everyone inside?" Alex said as Lily stepped back to let him in to the kitchen.

Lily spoke again as panic started to rise up through her body, "Where's Joseph? What's happened? Where is he? Is he…?"

Granny and Grandad Carter and Mrs Carter were already in the kitchen, and as they stared at Alex, the boy's father Charles joined them from the back room.

"Hello Alex." he said cautiously, instinctively knowing that something was wrong. "Any news?"

"Can we all sit down?" said Alex as he pulled back the nearest chair.

Everyone shuffled to their usual places around the kitchen table. Mary, Joseph's mum, put her hands up to cover her mouth as she sat down.

"It's terrible news,'" said Alex looking down at the table. "It's the worst news… I don't know how to tell you… but… Joseph is dead. We've just found his body in the woods."

For a few seconds there was absolute silence, and then Mary started to make a deep strange noise that Alex had never heard before. It was primeval; like a wild animal calling out in pain. The sound filled the room and then, as Charles pulled her in close, the sound descended into gentle sobbing.

Lily managed to speak "It can't be Joseph though," she

said, "that can't be right. Not Joseph … I don't think that… that's not…"

Lily suddenly stood up, pushed her chair back and walked over to the kitchen window, staring out into the distance. George and Catherine hugged each other, gently weeping.

Charles looked across at Alex and asked, "Where is he? Where's Joseph?"

"He's outside," replied Alex. "We've brought him home."

Charles gently separated himself from Mary, stood up and made his way around the table. Alex stood too as Charles reached him. "Let's bring him in then."

"Yes of course. But will you come outside with me first?" replied Alex. He was worried about the state that Joseph was in. They hadn't had time to clean him up, and he wanted Charles to see Joseph first and to decide what to do. Charles and Alex stepped outside and Alex waved to Alan and Bert. Without hesitation, and feeling some relief, they wheeled Joseph's body towards the house. As they approached, Alex took Charles by the arm and walked him down the garden path to meet them. Ten yards from the house, Alan stopped and put down the wheelbarrow. Charles leaned forward, reached out a hand and gently touched Joseph's face. Slowly he sank to his knees, reached out for Joseph's bloodied hand and pressed it to his face. "Dear God!" he gasped, his tears mingling with Joseph's dried blood, "What have they done to you?"

Lily was still watching from the kitchen window. All her feelings told her to run to Joseph, but she knew not to; she knew that she would have to wait for her dad to bring Joseph to her. She gripped the side of the cold hard sink tighter still.

Alex leaned down and spoke quietly to Charles, "Should we bring Joseph to the house? What do you think? Will it be alright, or shall we…?

Alex didn't have time to finish his sentence as Charles replied firmly, "Yes, yes, of course. Let's get him inside."

Charles stood up and walked slowly towards the kitchen door. Alan pushed the wheelbarrow with Alex and Bert walking on either side. Lily ran to open the door as they approached and called out softly, "They're coming."

At the doorway, Charles spoke quietly to Lily. "Lily, my love. Go and fetch one of the grey blankets from the front room. There's a good girl."

Then, pointing to the kitchen table, he said "Let's clear those few things off from the table, shall we?"

Quickly and quietly, they cleared the table and pulled the chairs back to the wall as Lily returned with the blanket. Mary stepped forward, and between them, Lily and Mary laid the blanket across the table and then clung on tight to each other, both looking towards the kitchen door.

"Right," said Charles, as he turned to face the men outside, "Let's bring Joseph in, shall we?"

The three men picked Joseph's body up as gently as they could and carried him through the door to the table. The family stood back as the men laid him carefully on the blanket. They stepped away, back towards the door, as the family closed in around Joseph's body to touch him.

They were all crying now.

Bert opened the door and the three men stepped outside. "God, that was awful," said Alex, as they wiped their eyes and moved a little further down the path.

After about five minutes, the door opened and Charles came to talk to them. His eyes were red and he struggled to speak.

"Thanks," he said. "Thanks for what you've done today boys… thanks for finding Joseph and bringing him home to us." Charles looked directly into the eyes of each man. "You're good boys. I'm so glad it was you who found him." He patted each man on his arm. "I don't know what… I don't know…" His voice trailed away and he stared down at the path.

Alex placed his hand on Charles' shoulder "There's no

need to say anymore now Mr. Carter. We know that Joseph would have done the same for any one of us. Now listen, you go back in with your family. We'll get back to the village. We need to let others know what's happened."

"Thanks again for your help boys," replied Charles as he turned to go.

Bert took hold of the handles of the wheelbarrow and set off for the village. Alex and Alan followed.

Chapter 3

ALEX AND JULIA

On the way back to the village, the three men cut through the lower woods. They met no one. As they walked, they discussed who they needed to talk to got back. Alex said that he would prioritise Commander Henry Clay, in addition to the Vicar and the Post Mistress. Between them, Alan and Bert divided up four or five each of the more senior men in the Resistance, knowing that they in turn would be able to spread the word quickly. The thing that they talked about most was; how had the Germans known that the Resistance were in the woods yesterday? They were all convinced that someone must have betrayed them.

As soon as they reached the outskirts of the village, the men shook hands and split up. Bert headed straight for his workshop, to get rid of the wheelbarrow and tools, before starting on his list of contacts. Alex and Alan headed off in opposite directions, with Alex aiming for Commander Clay's house first. He took a circuitous route, all the time keeping an eye out for German patrols. He could see a staff car parked half way down the High Street, with two Officers alongside it on the pavement. Fortunately, they were facing the other way, so he was able to slip down a footpath that led to the side entrance to St Mary's Primary School. Following the path that skirted around the school, he reached the small housing estate where Commander Clay lived.

He checked that there was no one around as he walked up the path to the Commander's house and knocked on the door. Mrs Clay answered the door and beckoned Alex in as soon as she saw him. "Hello Alex," she said. "Henry's out the back. Go on through."

Alex thanked her and went straight down the hallway, into the kitchen and out through the back door. He could see Commander Clay through the window of his workshop across the other side of the small lawn. The afternoon light was already beginning to fade and the small lamp over Henry's work bench was just bright enough to show through the window. Henry was a mechanical engineer by trade, and before the war he had run a very successful engineering business. His business was much smaller now, but he still employed a handful of mechanics in a fair-sized industrial unit on the outskirts of the village. If he was at home, he would usually be working on some small project or other in his garden workshop for a friend or neighbour. Engineering to him was as much a hobby as work and everyone knew that he could turn his hand to most things. Very few people knew that he was the leader of the local Resistance.

Henry looked up as Alex opened the door to the workshop. "Alex," he said as he put a screwdriver down on the bench and wiped his hands on his overalls. "What news?"

"It's bad news, I'm afraid," Alex said. "Joseph's dead."

He waited a few seconds for his news to sink in and then continued, "We found him – that is, me, Alan and Bert found him, up under the yew trees. Up the top on the far side of the beech woods. You know the spot."

Henry leaned hard back against the shelves opposite his work bench and grabbed hold of an upright post to steady himself. He was speechless for a while and then collecting his thoughts, said "Jesus Christ. What a blow. Oh God. Did you get him home to the Carters?"

"Yes," replied Alex. "We managed to get him home." "I must go and see them," said Henry. "First Tim and now Joseph. Is it all worth it Alex? I'm beginning to wonder… I really don't know…"

"There's tea in the pot!" called Mrs Clay. "Come into the kitchen, why don't you?"

Henry opened the door. "Coming!"

Henry and Alex made their way back from the workshop to the house and sat down at the kitchen table.

"Young Joseph Carter's dead, love," Henry said to Mrs Clay.

Margaret looked up as she was about to pour the tea. "Not Joseph too! It was bad enough losing Tim Washbrook! But Joseph as well… My God… Those poor boys… those poor families."

She turned, walked away from the table, pulled out her handkerchief and wiped her eyes.

Henry stood and poured the tea and the two men started to discuss what arrangements needed to be made. After a while, Margaret calmed herself and sat back at the table.

At about four o'clock, Alex left the Clay's house and set off for St Mary's Vicarage.

Reverend Tim Streeter answered the door. "Alex," he said, "Come on in my boy."

By the look on Alex's face, he already knew that something was wrong. Alex followed the Vicar into the office where he sat in his leather chair and indicated to Alex to take the chair facing his.

"What's up Alex? Not more bad news I hope?"

Alex leaned forward slightly and spoke quietly. "The

worst news Vicar, I'm afraid to say. We found Joseph Carter's body in the woods this morning. Me, Alan and Bert. We got him back to the Carter's farm around midday."

There was absolute silence for what seemed to Alex like an age as the Vicar tried to come to terms with what Alex had just told him.

Eventually the Vicar managed to speak, "For the love of God. Poor Joseph. The poor family. What's the world coming to?"

"Do you think that you will be able to go to the Carters' farm straight away?" said Alex.

"Yes. Yes, of course," replied the vicar. "Is there anything else that I need to know?"

"I don't think so," said Alex. "Except to say that I ought to warn you that Joseph's body is in a pretty bad way. He was shot several times and he'd been out all night in the woods. Under the yew trees in the freezing cold. We think he bled to death."

"Thanks," said Reverend Streeter. "I'll let my wife know what's happened and get on my way to Hill Farm without delay." They stood and shook hands.

"Look after yourself Alex and for God's sake be careful, won't you?"

They walked back towards the front door. "I'll do my best."

Alex opened the door and set off towards the Post office. The Reverend Streeter stood holding the great oak door for a while, watching Alex make his way down Church Road. He then looked away and went off to the kitchen to find his wife. The light was going fast as Alex reached the Post Office.

As soon as Olive Tindall spotted him, she lifted the hinged counter top and waved him through.

"Go on through to the kitchen," she said. "I'll see if George is still around." Out the back, in the sorting office, Olive found George putting the front wheel back on his upturned postman's bike.

"That's the second puncture I've had this week," he said as he looked up to see Olive approaching.

"All fixed?" said Olive.

"Yes," replied George, "and I hope that's the last one for a while."

"Can you come into the kitchen for a minute? Alex has just arrived."

"I'll be right with you," replied George.

George followed Olive back to the kitchen. She slid the kettle from the side of the range to the central hot plate as she made her way to the table and they all sat down. George and Alex shook hands as they did so.

"What's the news?"

"Only more bad news, I'm afraid," said Alex. "Really bad news. We've lost Joseph Carter. He's dead. They shot him late yesterday. We found his body this morning. Me, Alan and Bert."

Olive and George stared at Alex in disbelief as he filled in the details, and as he finished telling them all that he knew, the kettle came to the boil and Olive rose to make some tea, wiping her eyes as she did so. George stood up and walked around the room, pulled out a handkerchief and blew his nose.

"God," he mumbled. "I never thought we would lose Joseph. He was one of our best." He blew his nose again and sat back down. Olive brought the teapot, milk, sugar, tea cups and saucers to the table and let out a deep sigh.

"That's two young lads in a day," she said. "I wonder how many more of us those bloody Germans will kill before this is all over?" She wiped her eyes again and then spoke to Alex, "How did Henry take the news?"

"Pretty badly."

Olive poured the tea as Alex turned to George. "George, first thing in the morning, can you tell the other postmen exactly what has happened, so that they can let everyone else know as soon as possible?"

"Of course, I will," replied George. "I'll also call in to see the Carters myself on my rounds tomorrow."

"What else can we do?" said Olive. "Nothing much for the moment."

They talked for a further ten minutes whilst they drank their tea and then Alex said, "I suppose I need to get going on my way home now. It's been a long day, a bad day, and my family will be wondering where I've got to."

"Yes," said Olive. "Your folks will be worried sick. Off you go."

Alex said his goodbyes and made his way back out to the High Street. He noticed straight away, parked under a street light about fifty yards away, there was a German troop truck. There were soldiers milling around it and the tail gate was down. He walked steadily on and as he came to the truck, he crossed to the other side of the road to get around it. Some of the soldiers watched him closely as he walked by and he nodded at them and one or two of them nodded back. As he drew level with the back of the truck he glanced inside. A cold shiver ran down his back as he spotted Bert sitting between two soldiers. For a split second, he and Bert made eye contact, but then each man looked away. Alex walked on, any moment expecting a soldier to call him back, but no call came. As soon as he was out of sight, he cut back through a side street and made his way towards Commander Clay's house. Henry himself answered the door this time and was surprised to find Alex standing there.

"You're back a bit soon lad," he said. "Come in."

"No, I won't, thanks – listen," said Alex. "I've just spotted Bert sitting in the back of a German truck in the High Street. They must have picked him up for some reason. I thought they might stop me, but they didn't. That's all I know and I need to get home. I don't know if there's anything we can do?"

"Leave it to me," said Henry. "You get off home."

With that, the men shook hands, and Alex hurried off into the dark evening.

It was another hour and a half before Alex made it back home to join his family, and it took him a further hour to explain what had happened and to answer their questions.

After a quick wash and brush-up, Alex sat down with his family for supper. His mum, Sarah, had cooked shepherds' pie; Alex's favourite. As with most meals these days, there wasn't as much meat in the dish as there was before the war, but the extra mashed potato filled the space well enough and, as always, even at this time of year, there were still fresh vegetables from his dad's garden. Carrots and onions came from the dry store, next to the coal and wood bunkers adjoining the house. Throughout the meal, the conversation was about Joseph Carter, Tim Washbrook and their families. Mostly, it was about the Carter family, as they all knew each other so well. They were both farming families and through the generations, they had grown up, gone to the local school and lived together in the same community. Losing Joseph was almost as bad as losing one of their own.

By the time that ten o'clock came around, Alex was exhausted. After yawning and stretching his long arms above his head, he stood up from the kitchen table, wished everyone a good night, and headed upstairs to bed. Although he was dog tired, he couldn't get off to sleep. Over and over again, he ran the events of the past two days through his mind. There were two images that refused to leave his mind. The first was of Joseph, sitting dead under the yew tree where they had found him that morning. The second was of that brief glimpse of Bert sitting between the two German soldiers in the back of the truck. He was worried sick about Bert and he wondered if they had taken him away.

It was well past midnight by the time he finally drifted off to sleep.

At half past two, he awoke with a start and in a cold sweat. He sat bolt upright. Has anyone told Julia? Did she know yet that Joseph is dead? He couldn't believe that they might have missed her from their lists of people that needed to know. He knew immediately what he would have to do. He reached out for his alarm clock, set it for six thirty, lay down again and eventually fell back to sleep.

Before anyone else was up and about, Alex quietly let himself out through the back door, pulled his bike out from the lean-to by the side of the house and headed for Watersham. The only person that he saw in the village was Peter Terry, delivering milk to houses along the High Street. Peter was surprised to see Alex cycling through the village at that time of the morning, and thought that he might stop for a chat; but he just waved as he cycled on by.

At seven o'clock, Alex knocked on the front door of Julia's house. After a long wait, Julia's mother answered the door. She was wearing her dressing gown and half hid herself behind the door as she peered out to see who was there.

"Alex!" she exclaimed, recognising him at once as one of Julia's friends. "What brings you here at this time in the morning?"

"Hello Mrs Adams. I'm sorry it's so early, but is Julia in? I urgently need to speak to her. In fact, if Mr Adams is in, I'd like to speak to you all. Can I come in?"

Mrs Adams hesitated slightly and then stepped aside and waved Alex in. "Of course," she said. "Of course. Come on in. I'll call the others." she left Alex in the kitchen and ran back upstairs to find her husband and Julia. After a while, Mr Adams joined Alex in the kitchen.

They greeted each other and Mr Adams opened the damper on the range chimney, riddled the grate, filled the kettle and placed it on the hot plate.

"They'll be down in a minute," he said. "Please – have a seat. Do you want to tell me what this is all about, or would you rather…?"

Alex interrupted him before he could finish. "Thanks, Mr Adams, but if you don't mind, I'll wait until Julia and Mrs Adams have come down to join us."

A few silent minutes ticked by until Mrs Adams, now fully dressed and closely followed by Julia, came into the kitchen. Alex stood and managed a strained smile.

"Hello Alex," said Julia, as she walked up to him and touched his arm. "What on earth are you doing here this time of the morning? Is Joseph with you?"

Alex reached out and took Julia's hand. Something he hadn't done since their primary school days. Julia suddenly felt fear fly into her mind and she started to tremble.

"What – what's happened?" she mumbled. Alex reached out and took Julia's other hand.

"Julia. Julia, listen," he said softly. "Joseph is dead."

The room answered with total silence. The only discernible noises were that of the kettle purring on the stove and the ticking of the clock on the kitchen wall.

Alex, looking straight into her eyes, said, "We found him yesterday, under the yew tree, above the beech woods. They shot him the day before. He'd – he'd been there all night, Julia. We think that…"

Alex stopped talking as Julia let go of his hands and sank to the floor on her knees, a strangled noise coming from her throat. Mr and Mrs Adams rushed in to comfort Julia and guided her to a chair. Julia's sobbing grew louder as she leaned against her mother. The kettle began to whistle and Mr Adams quickly walked over and slid it away from the heat. Julia's sobbing quietened, as her mother dabbed at both Julia's and her own cheeks with her handkerchief. Mr Adams stood leaning against the towel rail that ran along the front of the Rayburn, staring at the wall. Eventually, Mrs Adams

managed to speak. "Did you get him back to his family?"
"Yes," said Alex. "We got him back to them. He's at Hill Farm now."

Julia looked up at Alex, and in between sobs, she managed to speak again "Alex… I need to see him… will you take me to him?"

Alex nodded. "Yes; of course, as soon as you like."

"Can we go now? Please? I need to see him."

"For goodness sake have a cup of tea before you go," said Mrs Adams.

"Yes," said Mr Adams, shaken from his thoughts, "It won't take a minute. I'll make it now."

Julia slowly stood "I'll fetch my warm coat."

She and Mrs Adams left the room, Mr Adams busied himself making tea whilst Alex sat and waited in silence. A few minutes later, they returned. Julia was wearing her winter coat and walking shoes. Mr Adams poured tea and they drank it in silence. As they finished, Mr Adams said "I'll get your bike and bring it round to the front, love."

Alex and Julia made their way to the front door.

As they cycled away from the house, they passed Peter Terry, who, having finished delivering milk to houses in the High Street, was now delivering on the housing estate. He looked up as they rode by and waved. Alex waved back, but they didn't stop. Peter watched them for some time until they disappeared from view.

They cycled along at a steady pace; Alex in front with Julia following, until they were about half a mile from Hill Farm, when Julia called Alex's name. "Alex! Alex – stop a minute, will you?"

Alex immediately looked back over his shoulder, slowed down and pulled over to the side of the road. "What is it?"

Julia stopped right next to Alex and put her hand on his arm.

"Tell me more," she pleaded. "Tell me everything. I

want to know. I need to know."

Alex started to explain everything that had happened over the last couple of days, but after a few minutes, he stopped and looked down the road. Julia followed his gaze, and in the distance, she saw a truck coming towards them.

"Quick," Alex urged, "Push your bike away and put your arms around me."

Without hesitation, Julia did what he said, and they stood on the side of the road embracing. The German truck passed by, and as it did, the soldiers sitting in the back cheered and waved as they saw the young couple together on the side of the road. For good measure, Alex pulled Julia in closer and kissed her on her forehead. The soldiers cheered again as the truck went on its way. Once it was out of view, Alex slowly released Julia from his arms and she straightened her coat.

"I'm sorry," he said, "I thought it was the best thing tobdo."

"Well, it seems to have worked. They've gone now."

They picked up their bikes and pushed them along the road for the next few minutes, as Alex carried on telling Julia everything that he knew of what had happened.

They cycled the last few hundred yards to Hill Farm, pushed their bikes down the garden path, leaned them against the side of the house and knocked on the door. Granny Carter answered and seeing that it was Alex and Julia, immediately opened the door wide and ushered them in.

"My dear Alex and Julia," she said. "Come on in my loves."

Lily was with her dad by the main barn when she saw Alex and Julia arrive, and the two of them walked straight over to the house to meet them. Julia had managed to stay calm until now, but broke into tears as Lily and Charles walked through the door. Charles opened his arms wide and Julia gladly allowed herself to be wrapped in them. She buried her face into his chest and sobbed. Charles held her tight and stroked her hair; like a parent comforting a child who has fallen and grazed their knees.

"Shush, shush …" tutted Charles gently. "Shush, shush…"

After a few minutes, Julia managed to calm herself again and her sobbing slowed. She noticed as she breathed against Charles' now wet shirt, that he smelt just like Joseph. Charles looked down at her as she pulled slowly away and looked up at his face and whispered, "Can I see him now? Is he here?" Charles took her hand and slowly led her from the kitchen to the front room. There, in the middle, standing on a trestle table, was an open topped pine coffin. Julia hesitated for a moment, until Charles put his arm gently around her and helped her to reach the table. She looked into the coffin as Charles stood even closer to her now and squeezed her hand. Julia reached out and touched Joseph's cool white face and stroked his cheeks.

"I love you Joseph and I always will," she whispered, as she leaned forward and kissed his face.

Chapter 4

TREACHERY

L ate the next day, Bert Stubbs walked back into Watersham from the German barracks. He had spent the previous 24 hours there, under the supervision of the loca German Commander, Captain Muller. On and off through that time he had been thoroughly interrogated. No violence had been used, but there had been real threats of violence, and although Bert had expected it to happen at any moment, it didn't. Captain Muller was not a member of the Gestapo, and Bert suspected that he was a decent man but he knew that his masters needed answers to their questions about the local Resistance.

When he had time to think, he wondered why they had picked him up? What did they already know about him? Had he been betrayed? If they only knew how much he hated them, how much he wanted them all dead; especially since the loss of Joseph and Tim, they would do well to kill him now. Throughout the ordeal, he managed to stay relatively calm, and didn't give anything away. Captain Muller and the other officers seemed relatively content with his answers and believed him when he said that he had no interest in the war, didn't want to get into any trouble and certainly, didn't want to have anything to do with the Resistance.

As Captain Muller escorted Bert to the main gate, he said "Don't forget Mr Stubbs, we will be watching your every move from now on. You will let us know if you see or hear of anything suspicious, won't you?"

Bert looked straight into the Captain's eyes and replied "Yes, of course. If I come across anything suspicious, I'll be sure to let you know."

Captain Muller watched as Bert made his way through the gate and up the road towards the village. He saw one or two people that he recognised as he walked along the street towards his cottage, but other than raising his hand and touching the tip of his cap, he didn't attempt to engage with them. He was glad when he reached home and went straight to the kitchen, throwing off his cap and jacket and rolling up his sleeves as he reached the sink. Turning the tap on and running the water until it felt icy cold, he grabbed a glass from the draining board, filled it and gulped the water down. He then leaned over the sink and allowed the cold water to run over his head. It felt good. After a while he turned off the tap and straightened himself up, reaching for a towel that hung by the side of the kitchen range. He wiped his face and rubbed the warm towel through his hair. When he turned around and opened his eyes, his wife, Alice, was standing in front of him. Without a word, they embraced and stood swaying gently in the middle of the kitchen.

"We didn't know where they had taken you," whispered Alice. "Commander Clay's wife managed to let me know that Alex had seen you with the German soldiers and she told me about Tim and Joseph. I was so frightened, I didn't know what to do. Thank God you're alright. I didn't know…"

"I'm back now and I'm still in one piece. They kept me

at the barracks... interrogated me all through last night and today. I'm so tired now, I can hardly think straight. I hope I never have to go through that again."

They kissed and then separated. "Why don't you take yourself straight up to bed and get some rest? You can tell me all about it later."

"I think I might just do that. I'm completely whacked." They kissed again and Bert walked slowly towards the stairs, and then stopped and turned. "We need to let people know that I'm back and that I'm alright. Could you nip straight down to Commander Clay's house and let him know?"

At 7:00 o'clock the next morning, Commander Henry Clay knocked on the back door of Bert and Alice's house. Worried that the Germans might be watching, he had walked along the twitten that ran close to the back of the house and climbed over a fence into their garden. Alice opened the door and waved Henry straight in.

"How is he?"

"He's still in bed," replied Alice, "but he seems to be alright – just tired. I'll see if he's awake."

"Thanks." said Henry, "I know how difficult it is for everybody, but I really need to speak to Bert if I can."

Alice went off to see if he was awake whilst Henry waited in the kitchen. A few minutes later, she came back down stairs with Bert close behind her.

"Good to see you mate," said Henry, as he and Bert shook hands. "Thank goodness you're alright."

"Yes. I feel a lot better now having had some sleep, but I don't want to go through that again. I have to say, I was pretty frightened at times. You just don't know what they're going to do. Thank God it was the Army Captain and his Officers and not the Gestapo. I doubt I'd be back here now if it had been the Gestapo."

Henry and Alice listened to Bert's story of what had happened from the moment that he had been picked up in the

49

village until they released him. They all agreed that it seemed strange that they had picked on him for interrogation.

"Yes," said Bert, "It was as if they knew exactly who I was. The sergeant with the soldiers in the street called me by my name – "Mr Stubbs... he said, ...very strange."

"Once they got me to the barracks, they wanted to know what I had been doing for the last couple of days, where I had been and who I had seen. They seemed to believe me when I said that I was on the farm the day before and that I'd been cutting fence posts in the woods after that. Obviously, I didn't tell them anything about what else we'd been doing, or anything about finding Joseph. They asked some very odd questions though. They wanted to know who I knew at the Post Office, who my friends were, did I think any of them were in the local Resistance, what had been going on in the woods and did I know Tim Washbrook? I managed to skirt around most of their questions fairly well, without giving anything away, and when it came to Tim, I said that I'd heard that he had been found dead in the woods, but I didn't know any more than that."

Bert paused for a while and then looking straight at Henry said, "How do you reckon they knew so much about me? That's what worries me."

Henry had been thinking about that as well. "Exactly." he said, "Sounds to me like someone's been tipping them off." Henry stayed talking with Bert and Alice for some time before taking his leave and walking back towards the centre of the village. As he walked, he thought back over the events of the last few days. Since Bert had been picked up for questioning, he was now more concerned than ever. How did the Germans know that his men would be in the woods the other day and what made them pick on Bert? He was heading for the Post Office, but seeing a German staff car parked outside, he kept walking and made his way to the Vicarage instead.

Peter Terry lived on his own in a small farm cottage about two miles from Watersham. The cottage was next to the dairy farm from where he collected the milk every day for his milk round. At 7:00 o'clock that evening, Peter was surprised to hear a knock at the door. He put down his newspaper, lifted himself from his fireside chair and went to see who was there. Just as he reached the front door, he heard the sound of the backdoor opening. He turned and walked quickly towards the kitchen. Before reaching the kitchen, Alex Miller appeared in front of him.

"What the? Oh! It's you Alex. What the heck are you doing here?"

"I'll explain in a minute," replied Alex, "but first, would you like to open the front door?"

Peter hesitated for a moment and then turned back towards the other door.

"Yes," he said, "Who else have you got with you?"

Alex stayed in the kitchen doorway with Alan Benton standing outside by the back door. Peter opened the front door to find two more men standing there: Charlie Stewart and Tony Smith.

"What are you lot playing at then?" said Peter, starting to feel very uncomfortable, "Some sort of game is it?"

Peter looked at Alex and then turned and looked at Charlie.

"It's not a game," said Alex.

Charlie Stewart motioned for Peter to move back and then followed him along the small hallway to the sitting room. Tony Smith shut the front door and waited in the hall. Peter stood with his back to the fireplace as Alex joined them. "What's up then lads?" Peter said nervously, his voice cracking slightly.

"That's what we want to know," replied Alex as he stepped slightly closer to Peter. "A little bird tells us that you've been working with the Germans. Is that true Peter?

Have you been telling tales?"

Peter started to feel very frightened and his hands started to tremble. His throat felt incredibly dry and he suddenly blurted out, "I didn't really mean any harm! Nobody got hurt. I mean, I just told them about some general stuff – no detail or anything."

"Do the names Joseph Carter and Tim Washbrook mean anything to you?" said Alex as he took another half a step closer to Peter.

"Well," answered Peter, now even more flustered at the mention of the two names. "I can't say that I really knew them very well. I mean I know their families of course. I deliver milk to their houses most days. I hear that the Germans killed them. Is that right?"

Peter suddenly felt sick and spoke again. "Surely, you don't think that's anything to do with me? I wouldn't have told them… I mean… I never told them anything about what was going on in the woods. I didn't know for sure what you lot were up to. How could I… I mean… you must believe me."

Alex raised his voice and shouted straight into Peter's face. "They're both dead because of you and your big rotten mouth! Shot dead in the woods by the Germans! But it might as well have been you who killed them. It was you who told them about our movements that day wasn't it?"

Most of the colour had drained from Peter's face as the realisation dawned on him that this was very serious and getting more serious by the minute. "Bloody hell," he said, "I had no idea. Honest! No one told me… they didn't say that anyone would get hurt! I wouldn't have said anything if I thought this would happen! I..."

Alex interrupted before he could say any more. "And then there was Bert Stubbs – wasn't there Peter? You told them that you thought Bert might be a member of the Resistance, didn't you Peter?"

"Look! I didn't really know whether or not he was

part of the Resistance! I just guessed – I just guessed from watching him and seeing what he was doing. You know, from his movements and that. I didn't say that he was definitely part of the Resistance… I mean… I mean I didn't know. Did I? How could I?"

"Follow me outside Peter," demanded Alex.

"Why?" muttered Peter, desperately trying to think straight, and to think of a good reason why he shouldn't do what they wanted. Were they going to beat him up when they got him outside?

"Just bloody do it!" shouted Alex.

Charlie Stewart moved around and stood behind Peter as Alex turned and walked slowly out from the sitting room. Charlie pushed gently but firmly at Peter's arm, and Peter, feeling frightened and confused, stumbled from the room. Charlie walked behind and as soon as Alan Benton saw that they were all in the hallway, he joined them. Tony Smith opened the front door and stepped to one side to let them all pass. It was very dark outside. Alex continued on towards the cow sheds that, as their eyes adjusted to the dark, they could just about make out, some thirty yards further on.

On reaching the first barn, a strong scent of cow dung, straw and hay drifted towards them on the gentle evening breeze. Cattle could be heard moving around in the neighbouring barn.

As they all walked further on, Peter suddenly stopped and said, "What are we doing? Where are you taking me?"

"Just walk on a bit further," said Charlie, "and you'll see."

Peter edged forward until his feet came up against some straw bales.

"Just turn around now and sit down on the bale," said Charlie.

Peter did as he was told, and as he sat down, there was suddenly light as torches were turned on, one behind him and one shining straight in his face. He automatically raised a hand to shield his eyes, and as he did so, a hand reached around from behind him and something wet was pushed firmly over his mouth and nose. Peter recognised the strange smell instantly – it was chloroform. He tried to pull the cloth away from his face, but as he struggled, more hands came to hold him down, and a few seconds later, his whole body relaxed as he fell unconscious.

After a while, he started to regain consciousness. He felt nauseous, his head was swimming, and for a moment, he couldn't remember where he was or what was going on.

"Just stand up here a minute will you Peter?"

Peter couldn't understand what was being said to him or who had said it.

"Stand up!" snapped Alex, and Peter reacted immediately and tried to stand. Helping hands arrived from all directions, and with some difficulty, he managed to stand. He tried to balance himself better by stretching out his arms, but struggled, as his hands were tied behind his back. The men were quick to steady him.

"Now, turn around and step up here," commanded Alex. Torches showed the way, and Peter, still not sure what was going on, turned and stepped up onto the straw bale. Hands reached out again to support him and as he struggled to find his balance, he felt something being slipped over his head and then around his neck. His head was lifted slightly as the unseen rope was tightened and tied off somewhere to the side. The supporting hands suddenly left him. Alex called out "One, two three!" and the bale on which Peter stood was suddenly pulled away.

He dropped like a great soaking wet sack of grain; his neck snapped and for a few seconds his legs twitched, then he was still. As his body swayed gently from side to side, the rope made an eerie creaking noise as it rubbed against the wooden beam over which it hung.

Charlie shone his torch at Peter's face and Tony shone his at Peter's hands, as Alan stood up on the bale and undid the string from Peter's wrists. Peter's arms swung back to his sides and the rope creaked even more.

"Looks like suicide to me," said Alex, as the men turned and walked back out into the night.

Chapter 5

MR AND MRS GEORGE GOLDBERG

George Goldberg and his family had lived in the village since the early thirties. Their children, Sarah and Mark, attended the village primary school, and they were all well known in the local community. George worked as a tailor in a menswear shop in South Street, Chichester, whilst his wife Marie, was a cook at the local primary school. George and Marie had grown up in Bavaria, but when things started to get difficult for Jews in Germany, along with many others, they had managed, with a lot of help from family and friends to get to England. George, being a highly skilled tailor, had no difficulty finding a job, first in London, and then in Chichester. They were very happy living in Watersham.

When Commander Henry Clay first heard rumours that the Goldberg's had been taken away by the Germans, he didn't really register the seriousness of the event. He thought, like others who knew about it, that it was the usual cock-up. Someone had messed up somewhere. The wrong name or wrong address; some sort of administrative mess.

The Germans were always doing it – picking up the wrong people. Chances were, they'd be brought back home the same day, and a German officer would be there as they arrived, offering profuse apologies for their terrible mistake.

It was only when Henry heard the next day that the Goldberg's hadn't returned home that he became alarmed. Just after ten o'clock, he called at the post office, to see if anyone there had heard anything. Olive waved Henry over and he followed her through the back of the post office to the kitchen.

"Any news on the Goldberg family?"

"Yes" said Olive, "One of the young lads was riding his bike nearby when they led them out to the truck. He heard one of the German soldiers say that they were rounding up all the Jews in the area."

"That can't be right surely?" said Henry, "It doesn't make any sense... I mean... what's being Jewish got to do with anything?"

"I don't understand what's going on either" said Olive, "What can we do?"

"Are there other Jewish families in the village?" asked Henry.

Olive stood and walked around the kitchen. "Let me think," she said, "What about the Freemans at the far end of the High Street. Are they Jewish?"

"I'm not sure," replied Henry. "But we'd better let everyone know what's happened."

Henry made to leave, and as he opened the door back into the Post Office, he turned and said quietly to Olive, "I'll see if I can find out where they've taken them."

He hurried off down the street and headed straight to the Vicarage where he was greeted by the Vicar. "Come on in" he said, "You look a bit flustered," henry followed the Vicar into his study. "What's up?"

"Tim," replied the Commander, "I've just come across something very sinister going on in our village. The Germans.

They seem to be rounding up Jewish families. Have you heard anything about it?"

"Rounding up Jewish families?" stuttered the vicar. "My God. There's been rumours for some time in the Church about Jews being rounded up in Germany and other countries; but it's always been difficult to understand what's really been going on. He paused for a while, and then, leaning towards Henry, he said, "Are you sure? I mean – if this is true – well – it's outrageous."

"I'm afraid that it seems to be true. Can you get a message out to your colleagues in the Church, to see what they know?"

"Yes, of course. Where do you think they're taking them?"

"We don't know at the moment, but I'll find out and let you know as soon as I can."

"I must get on," said Henry, as he stepped towards the study door.

They shook hands and Henry headed home. As he walked by the Green Tea Rooms, he noticed Captain Muller, standing just inside the door, talking to some other German Officers. He slowed his pace, stopped, turned around and leaned against a wall, looking back towards the door of the café. After a few minutes, Captain Muller and his fellow officers stepped out on to the pavement. Henry walked straight up to them.

"Good day gentlemen," he said, "Captain Muller, could I have a word please?"

Captain Muller stepped away from the other Officers. "Certainly, Mr Clay. How can I help you?"

Henry lowered his voice and leaned in closer to the Captain. "Do you know why the Goldberg family has been taken away, and where they have been taken?"

Captain Muller's expression changed immediately. He moved his position slightly so that his back was to his fellow Officers and placed his hand on Henry's arm.

"It's a bad business. We have orders to round up Jewish families and certain other people. They are being taken to a camp near Brighton. I know that you will understand that I have my orders and I have to follow them."

"But this is outrageous" replied Henry, "These are innocent people. They're just ordinary civilians ..."

Captain Muller interrupted Henry. "Listen" he said, "I've already told you. We have to follow orders, and let me give you some advice – don't get involved."

Captain Muller let his hand drop from Henry's arm as he stepped back.

"I must go" he said, "I'm sorry."

The Captain moved back to join the other Officers and they walked away. Henry stood where he was for a while, trying to make sense of what was going on. After a minute, he turned and headed for home.

The next morning, Henry walked round to the Vicarage to speak again to the Vicar. Mrs Streeter joined them in the kitchen and asked, "Did you find out anything?"

"They're definitely rounding up Jewish families," said Henry as they all sat down at the kitchen table.

"They're taking them to somewhere near Brighton. Captain Muller told me."

"My God," replied Mrs Streeter, "This is beyond the pale. What on earth do they think they're doing? I've read about this sort of thing in the Daily Express, but I had no idea that it was happening here."

"Did Muller say anything else?" said the Vicar.

"No. Only that he was just following orders. I could tell that he was very uncomfortable about the whole subject and clearly didn't really want to talk about it."

Mrs Streeter banged the table with her fists, "Oh yes. They're bloody good at just following orders aren't they... the whole miserable lot of them! I wonder how many more they'll kill before they're satisfied?"

Tim jumped to his feet and threw his arms around his wife as she began to cry and turn away. "We all feel the same you know" he said, "We all know that they're evil. It's just knowing how best to deal with them that's so difficult. We have to try to stay calm and do our best behind the scenes. You know how much Henry and his boys and girls are doing; the risks that they take every day. We've already lost a lot of good people and I'm sure we'll lose more yet; but we're not beaten you know. The Germans have only got a foothold here so far. They haven't managed to break through the front lines to the north. It's only a matter of time before our lot make a counter attack and push them back to where they came from. Then we'll see what's what."

The vicar took his handkerchief from his pocket and handed it to his wife. She wiped her eyes and they both sat back down.

"I'm sorry about that Henry," she said, "I'm just so angry and frustrated about everything at the moment. There seems to be no end to it. I know it's hard for everyone."

"That's alright Margaret," replied Henry, "It is hard. Hard for us all; but Tim's right you know. We'll get through this. We'll beat those buggers in the end."

Margaret wiped her eyes again and then said to her husband, "You've got some good contacts with various churches in Brighton; haven't you?"

"That's right. I'll start making some enquiries straight away."

"That would be much appreciated," said Henry.

After leaving the vicarage, Henry made his way straight to the Post Office to meet the Post Mistress. As soon as Olive saw him come through the doorway, she beckoned to him to join her in the sorting office. He nodded to the young woman behind the counter. Elsie slid down from her stool and lifted the counter flap to let him through. Henry smiled at Elsie as he walked through to the back office.

"Anything new on the Goldberg family?"

"Not much" replied Henry, "but we know that they've been taken to some sort of collection point in Brighton with other Jewish families."

"Didn't we hear something like that from other occupied countries?" she said, "I thought that was just a rumour. Why Brighton though?"

"I don't know why they've chosen Brighton. Maybe it's because it's the biggest town around here and it's fairly central? It's probably some sort of collection point... a staging post, before moving the poor devils on to somewhere else."

"So, what do you think they're doing with them? The Nazis I mean. What do they want them for? Slave labour back in Germany or some such?"

"I just don't know Olive. But you can be sure it'll be bad news. Clearly Muller doesn't want to talk about it; but I'm sure he knows what's going on."

"Listen," said Henry, stepping slightly closer to Olive, "I need to get a message out to a few of the men. Can you get your postmen to spread the word first thing tomorrow morning?"

"Of course. Which men and what's the message?"

He told her what the message was and to which men it should be relayed, and after exchanging news on some general village gossip, he thanked Olive for her help and made his way back to the High Street. Ten minutes later he was back home, in his workshop at the bottom of the garden, looking at maps of Brighton.

The following evening, Mrs Streeter called at Henry's house. Henry opened the door, but before he had time to greet her and invite her inside; she leaned towards him and whispered. "Message from my husband. His contacts tell him that there's a large old warehouse right next to the railway station at Brighton. They're holding them all there."

Henry whispered back, "Thanks," and before he could say anything else, Mrs Streeter turned on her heels back towards the street and called out, "Can't stop. Bye," as she hurried away.

At ten minutes to midnight, Henry stood waiting under the overhanging branches of some spindly ash trees, about twenty paces east of Barnham railway bridge. It was very dark, overcast, damp and cold. A stiff breeze was blowing from the west, straight along the railway track, making it feel even colder. He pulled up the collar of his heavy jacket and peered down the line back towards Barnham Station. One dim orange light showed where the empty platforms were. Apart from the sound of the breeze, all was quiet. From off to his right, somewhere behind the ash trees and the thick brambles that interlaced with the rusty wire fence, he could hear the sound of others pushing through the hedge. One by one, Alex Miller, Alan Benton and Bert Stubbs joined Henry on the edge of the railway line.

"Well done chaps," said Henry, "Spot on time."

"Bloody cold out here," replied Bert, "Any chance we could get in somewhere warmer?"

"I hope so," said Henry, pointing towards Barnham station, "There should be a freight train pulling out from a siding down there somewhere shortly. Hopefully heading for Brighton."

"Good!" said Alex as he rubbed his hands together, "Are you taking us for a night out?" They all laughed, knowing that would be the last thing that they would be doing this night.

Henry spoke again. "When the train reaches us here, it should still be travelling quite slowly, so we should be able to get into one of the freight cars without too much trouble. The one to look out for will be the eighth car after the coal tender. Its doors won't be locked. I've had someone make sure of that earlier this evening."

He turned and faced Alex. "Alex. You're the youngest and fittest of us four, so, you can be the first up to jump up and open the doors for us. Alright?"

"Shouldn't be a problem. That is, as long as the eighth car is the right one!"

They all laughed again and peered back down the line towards the station.

Three minutes later, the unmistakable sound of a steam engine stuttering into life could be clearly heard coming from somewhere near to the station. At the same time as the new sounds rang out, the wind carried the distinct smell of coal smoke to them.

A few more minutes went by before they could pick out the outline of the steam train moving very slowly through Barnham station.

"Get ready" called out Henry, "and spread yourselves out a bit. We don't want to be tripping over each other as we try to jump on board. Alex, you stay here and we'll all move down the line a bit, about twenty yards apart. Mind out that you stay under cover as long as you can though."

Henry was right. The train was moving very slowly, making it fairly easy for Alex to jump on to the running board, yank open one of the doors, and climb into the car. Holding on with one hand, Alex held out his other hand to help the others up. As soon as they were all safely on board, he slid the door closed again, leaving a narrow gap for them to see out, and for what little light there was, for them to see inside their temporary home. Looking around, they could see that, apart from some large open topped wooden crates filled with machine parts, they had the freight car to themselves. The air smelt of a strange mixture of dust, grease, coal smoke and steam. They could hear the engine working harder and the train gradually picking up speed.

"Right," said Henry, "Time to let you know what we're up to tonight."

The faster the train went, the noisier their new home became, so they stood closer to Henry to hear what he was saying.

"There's a place somewhere near to Brighton station where the Germans are holding some of our people. We need to see if we can help to get them out. There's men, women and children in there... whole families in some cases. We need to do what we can."

"How close to Brighton station will we get? I mean; when will we get off the train?" asked Alan.

"We'll be able to see when we're in Brighton. So, as we approach the station, and the train slows down, we'll jump off as soon as we think it's safe enough. OK?"

"Sounds reasonable," replied Alan, "but how do we know which building they're in?"

"Yes. Good point," said Henry, "I'm not sure of that. We'll have to check out all the large buildings next to the station."

Alex, Alan and Bert remained quiet for a long time; each man wondering just how many German soldiers might be on patrol around Brighton station in the middle of the night. The four men were wearing manual working clothes, and between them, in their back packs they carried hand tools: spanners, wire cutters and wrenches. Their work sheets showed that they were railway engineers based at Barnham station. Explaining why they were wandering around Brighton station in the middle of the night might prove a little difficult, but they hoped that situation wouldn't arise, and if it did, they were sure that they would be able to talk their way out of it.

Alex knew the line well, and so, although the light wasn't good, as he saw each station go by, he was able to judge where they were and let the others know.

"We're only about five minutes away now."

Two minutes later the train began to slow down. Alex

opened the door slightly further to get a better view. As the train rounded a slight bend, he could see ahead of the steam engine towards the town. The train slowed further and it became easier to judge just how fast they were going.

"Don't forget," said Henry, "after you jump, throw yourself flat on the ground until the train is out of sight. We don't know if there are any soldiers on the back of the train."

Alex looked around once more, gave the thumbs up and jumped. He landed safely, fell sideways and stayed as still as he could. The others followed, one after the other, also falling sideways, but managing to stay still. The train carried on and once it was far enough away, they all stood up, retrieved their backpacks and brushed themselves down.

"Everyone alright?" asked Henry.

"I think we're all a bit bruised," said Bert, "But not too bad."

"Right" said Henry, "Let's get off to the side and see if we can find this building."

They walked in single line along the railway track. Stepping from one sleeper to the next wasn't too difficult and soon the station came into view. Their train was stopped in a siding just back from the main platforms. Men were moving around, opening doors and preparing to unload.

"Let's see if we can get away from the railway line and find a footpath" said Henry.

He found a gap in the hedge, and on the other side of the fence, he could see a well-worn path. Turning to Bert and pointing at the fence, he said, "Cut a hole through here mate." Bert quickly extracted the heavy-duty wire cutters from his back-pack, and whilst the others looked on, quickly cut through the mesh fence. Henry held the flapping wire back as the others stepped through and then Alex held it from the other side whilst Henry climbed through. There was good cover along the pathway for some distance; the railway fence and hedge on the one side and a mixture of wooden fences and hedges on the other side. They made good progress until the path petered out about two hundred yards from the first platform. There was plenty of activity on the far side of the station where the freight train was being unloaded, but all was quiet on the main platforms. Henry and his men watched until they were satisfied that there was no one about on their side of the station, and then as naturally as they could, all four strolled along the track towards the main platforms. On reaching the first one, they ducked behind the fence that bordered the back of the platform and made their way to a twitten that ran between two sets of industrial looking buildings.

They emerged from the path into a dark lane. All the street lights were off, but the natural light was just about good enough to confirm that they were in amongst a mixture of poor housing and old warehouses. Non-descript sheds rose out of the gloom along both sides of the lane; locked wrought iron gates fronting most of them. Parked in the lane and behind the wrought iron railings were an assortment of trucks, each with painted lettering on the door panels stating the name and specialist trade of the Company to which they belonged: Barclay, Smith & Co. – Timber Merchants and Frank Ide & Sons – Quality Bakers. They walked unhurriedly along the street, peering at the frontages of the buildings.

"What the hell are we looking for?" whispered Bert to Alan.

"No idea," replied Alan, "But I expect we'll know it when we see it."

As they finished speaking, Henry stopped suddenly and waved his arm to indicate that they should move across between two of the parked trucks. Henry pointed further along the lane and, peering out from behind the first vehicle, they followed Henry's gaze, to see the faint orange glow of a light at the entrance to one of the larger buildings.

"I wonder why that's the only light here?" said Henry in

a low voice.

"Difficult to tell from this distance," replied Alex, "We need to get closer."

Checking all around and moving in single file behind the row of trucks, they eventually came to a point that was very close to the main entrance of the building with the solitary light. Standing either side of the double front doors, were two German soldiers. They were facing each other, rifles hitched over their shoulders, and clearly engaged in conversation.

"That's probably it," whispered Henry.

Safe from view behind the last truck, they discussed tactics for a while, and then quite nonchalantly, stepped out as a group, chatting away as they walked down the middle of the lane. The soldiers turned to look as they heard the four men walking by. Alex and Bert waved at the soldiers, and seeing four workmen on their way to or from work, waved back. About fifty yards further on, and out of sight, they left the lane and followed a rough path next to a fence that enclosed the neighbouring building. By pushing through a scrubby box hedge, the men came to another fence that ran along the opposite end of the building that the soldiers were guarding. It was even darker here, but peering through, Henry could see a single doorway in the gable end.

Henry called to Bert, "Cut through here mate," he said, pointing at the fence.

The mesh fence wasn't very tall and was made of thin wire. Bert made short work of it; cutting through its full height, so that Alan and Alex were able to easily fold back both sides. Henry and Bert stepped through whilst Alan and Alex stayed where they were. Gingerly, Henry tried the door handle. To his surprise, the door opened by an inch and a weak shaft of light spilt out onto the damp grass and across to where Alan and Alex stood. Instinctively, they both stepped out from the light and into the dark cover of the hedge. Henry pulled slightly harder on the door to see if it would give anymore, but had no luck. Looking up and down the leading edge of the door, he could see the problem. There was a chain holding the door fast on the inside.

"Cutters," whispered Henry to Bert, "Just here, look. There's a chain holding the door."

Bert moved over near to where Henry was standing, pulled out the long-handled cutters from his back pack, gently slipped the business end through the door and clamped them onto the chain.

"Ready?" he said. "It's going to make a bit of a noise."

Henry nodded and held the door handle as firmly as he could.

Bert whispered, "One, two, three," and squeezed the handles of the cutters.

There was a loud noise as the chain links parted and part of the chain clanked against the door. Henry quickly and quietly pulled the door to, and followed Bert back through the gap in the fence to join the others standing under the cover of the hedge. For five full minutes, they stood as still as statues; each man with his eyes fixed firmly on the dark door.

Inside the building, a number of adults, sleeping on the floor nearest to the door, had been awoken by the sudden noise of the breaking chain, and now sat up, wondering what the noise was. In the dim light they looked at each other.

Harry Wiseman spoke quietly to the man nearest to him. "Did you hear that?" he said.

"Yes," he replied, and then after a few seconds, "What do you think it was?"

Harry shrugged his shoulders and looked across the sea of sleeping bodies towards the front of the building. He was pleased to see that there was no indication of anything going on up there and no sign of German soldiers either. The only sounds were that of people snoring. Harry looked at his pocket watch, turning its face towards the light, so that he could just about make out the hands.

"Just gone half past one," he said to himself.

Henry walked slowly back to the door, gently pressed down the handle and pushed it open far enough to be able to see inside the building. Henry flinched as the smell of stale air, urine and body odour hit him. Seeing Harry staring straight at him and the group of sleeping bodies on the floor all around, he immediately raised his fingers to his lips, so that Harry and the others who were awake would know to be quiet. He then turned and gave the thumbs up signal to his men. Alan, Alex and Bert immediately stepped up to join Henry by the door as he pushed it further open. Henry carefully stepped over some still sleeping children and spoke quietly to Harry.

"How many people are in here?" he said.

"Over one hundred," replied Harry, "But who the hell are you?"

"It doesn't matter who we are," replied Henry. "We're here to get you out."

Harry and some of the others looked towards the door as Bert and Alex stepped inside.

"Do you know if George Goldberg and his family are here?" asked Henry.

"There's a Goldberg family in here somewhere" replied Harry, "but don't ask me whereabouts."

"Right" said Henry, "Now, we need to start to get as many of you out as possible, so get your family members together, pick up what you can carry and move away as quickly as possible."

Harry didn't need telling twice. Within minutes, all six of the Wisemans were awake, on their feet, picking up their belongings and out through the doorway. Outside, Alex quickly briefed Harry as to the lie of the land and pointed in the direction of the station.

"If I were you," he said, "I'd go around behind the station, get down to the railway lines and head north. You need to cover as much ground as possible before day break. There are no trains going north or south at the moment; so, you'll be alright. As soon as it starts to get light, you'll have to get away from the railway line and take cover in the woods. Somewhere around Crawley, you'll run into British Forces. That's where the front line is. Good luck."

For the next thirty minutes, in almost total silence; men, women and children poured out from the rear of the building into the dark night. Henry, Alex, Alan and Bert spoke quietly to each adult as they trooped by; reassuring them and giving them broad instructions as to which way to head.

The third to last group were the Goldberg family.

"My God!" said George Goldberg, as he recognised Henry, "Henry! Henry, it's you. Praise be to God! Thank you, thank you… Thanks be to God that He has sent you."

George dropped his bags, threw his arms around Henry and hugged him tight. Mrs Goldberg and their children looked on.

"Come on now George," said Henry, easing himself from George's grasp, "You can save your thanks for when you've reached safety. You need to get going. You need to be as far away as possible before morning comes."

George patted Henry on his arms once more, picked up his bags and stepped through the doorway. Henry looked back across the floor of the empty building at the few remaining discarded bits and pieces: two or three blankets, a single glove, a broken umbrella and an assortment of cardboard boxes and shopping bags. He wondered how long it would be before the soldiers opened the front doors and realised that everyone had gone. As quietly as possible, Henry stepped back through the doorway, pulling the door shut behind him as he did so. The men quickly slipped their back packs on and marched off towards the station. Within minutes, they were overtaking many of the families with young children who were struggling to keep up a good pace. Henry and his men encouraged them onward as they themselves hurried along the path. When they came to the end of the rough pathway that ran along the back of the platforms, they stopped and watched, as one family after another, walking in single file and staying as close to the fence as they could, made their way to the relative cover and safety of the hedge that they could just about make out in the darkness ahead of them.

Alex looked across to the far side of the other platforms. All was quiet; just a few soldiers standing around near to the ticket office. He thought that there was a very good chance that everyone would get away from the station without being spotted. It was very dark where they were at the moment and there would be at least another four hours of darkness before first light. With a bit of luck; even the slower ones should have covered about ten miles to the north by then. If they could hide up somewhere during the following day, most of them could make the Crawley area during the following night.

"Right," whispered Henry to Alex, "Time for us to get going too. Come on."

Again, in single file, the four men hurried along to the distant hedge and then pushed on as quickly as they could for about a mile. Where the railway-track forked, the men stopped, and then they ducked through the hedge, slid down a grassy bank and stepped across the rails to the far side of the tracks and disappeared into the gloom. After striding along the sleepers for a further ten minutes, Henry stopped and spoke to his men.

"Listen," he said, "We have to get to the railway bridge at Shoreham. That freight train unloading at Brighton will make its way back to Barnham in a couple of hours, and they all slow down to a walking pace at Shoreham bridge. That's where we have a chance of getting on board."

"Will it be the same routine as earlier?" asked Alex.

"Yes," replied Henry, "Eighth car. No padlock."

With that, Henry, Alex, Alan and Bert, set off at a quick pace. Each man marched on in deep thought and Alex found himself thinking about the families making their way north along the railway line.

We've all been lucky so far, he thought to himself, but for how much longer would their luck hold? How long would it be before they discovered that the building was empty? When the alarm went up and German patrols started searching the area; how many of the families would be caught and how many would make it to safety?

It was approaching five thirty as they reached Shoreham bridge and no sign of first light. Henry and his men sat on the edge of the board walk that ran along the side of the railway crossing.

"I wonder how they're all getting on?" muttered Bert.

"Should be well clear of the town by now," replied Alan. "It's about three hours since they got away; so, some of them might be as far as eight or nine miles to the north by now. The trouble is that no one knows for sure what's up the line from Brighton. For all we know, there's a full division of Germans camped next to the railway line to the north, with road blocks and full border control and everything. We just don't know, do we?"

Alex looked over at the others, "True," he said, "But at least they've got a chance. God knows where they'd have ended up if we hadn't got them out. I still don't understand what the Germans think they're doing?"

The men were tired now and they sat on the board walk quietly dosing, keeping their thoughts to themselves. At almost exactly six thirty, they heard the first faint, but unmistakable, sounds of a steam train approaching from the east.

"That sounds like our train," said Henry, "Get ready."

All four men got up and walked quickly back about thirty yards to where a line of young macrocarpa trees stood. They spread themselves out and stood back under the hanging evergreen branches. As the train came into view, it started to slow, as Henry said it would. Staying under cover, they counted the cars as they noisily clanked by. As the eighth car reached him, Alex stepped out from under cover, jumped onto its running board, pushed open the doors and stepped inside. As soon as the others jumped up to join him, he slid the doors to an almost closed position. Shortly after clearing the bridge, the timbre of the steam engine began to change and the train picked up speed. The men took turns to look out through the small gap between the doors, trying hard to identify each station as they passed through. After about forty minutes, the train began to slow again as it approached Barnham station, and as it came up to the bridge, the four men jumped down and hid in the hedge until the train had passed. After a short while, they pushed through the hedge and stepped down into the field on the other side. The men shook hands with each other and then at two-minute intervals, they set off for their homes. Henry looked back towards the eastern sky as he walked across the fields towards Watersham. Dawn was just beginning to break. In the middle of the field, he stopped and stared into the distance. His thoughts turned back to George Goldberg, his family and all the other families that were heading north along the Brighton to London railway line.

"Good luck," he muttered under his breath as he turned for home.

Several miles north of Brighton, the Goldbergs, along with others, climbed the railway embankment and made their way into the woods. It was very dark there and difficult to make out the outline of the pathways; but slowly, they continued on their way. Other families left the railway line and walked along the small roads that meandered through the South Downs with most not quite knowing where they were headed. Occasionally, at the sound of a vehicle, they would quickly duck down behind trees, hedges and scrub that lined the road, waiting for the engine sounds to disappear before continuing on their way. Some families continued to walk north along the railway line with the Bernstein and Weizmann families leading the way. As they passed some railway gates, a German soldier suddenly appeared on the roadway behind the gates. He was pointing his rifle at them.

"Halt!" he shouted.

The Bernsteins and the Weizmanns stopped immediately and turned to face the soldier, by which time, three more soldiers appeared by the gates. Further back down the track, others ran and jumped into the rough vegetation to the sides and quickly disappeared into the undergrowth.

Lights suddenly came on around the gates and two of the soldiers pushed them open and walked towards the families.

"Go over there!" shouted one of the soldiers, indicating with his rifle which way they should go. Joseph and Sarah Bernstein walked slowly through the open gate and stood next to another soldier, as he indicated for them to stop, near to the back of a truck that was parked in the road next to a signal box. Their young children, Alexander aged ten and Maria seven, followed them and stood close to their parents. Mrs Bernstein was trembling and pulled the children in close to her.

"Up!" said the soldier, pointing with his rifle to the back of the truck.

Mrs Bernstein firmly pushed the children towards the steps that hung down from the back of the truck and Alexander and Maria quickly climbed up and looked back as their parents climbed up to join them. The Weizmann's also had two children; Andrew aged sixteen and Peter fourteen. They followed the example of the Bernstein family and walked slowly to the back of the truck; but suddenly, and without any warning, Andrew pushed the soldier standing nearest to them, hard back. The soldier fell backwards over the kerb stone, lost his balance and crashed to the pavement. Andrew and Peter took off down the road like hares as Mr and Mrs Weizmann screamed and shouted after them.

"Stop! Stop! What the hell … for God's sake stop!"

The two other soldiers stepped out into the road, raised their rifles and fired several times each. They only stopped firing as Mr and Mrs Weizmann crashed into them, knocking them both off-balance. By this time, the first soldier had picked himself up and hit out at the Weizmann's with the butt of his rifle. They both fell to the ground, blood pouring from a deep gash on Mr Weizmann's forehead. As Mrs Weizmann started to try to stand up, the soldier swung the butt of his rifle up hard, catching her under the chin. She was knocked out cold and fell back, prostrate onto the tarmac. Mr Weizmann crawled on his hands and knees to her side and placed a hand under her head, blood dripping from his face onto her hair. Two of the soldiers walked quickly down the road to where the still bodies of the boys lay. One of the soldiers rolled Peter over whilst the other stood close by with his rifle aimed at Peter's head.

"Dead" said the soldier, as he straightened up and walked over to where Andrew was laying.

The two soldiers repeated the procedure.

"He's dead too," muttered the soldier.

As they stood looking at the two boys; the lights of a car appeared from further down the road, and half a minute later, it slowed and pulled up next to them. The small Nazi flag fixed to the bonnet of the car fluttered in the gentle breeze as a German officer stepped out.

"What's happened here?" he said, as the two soldiers saluted.

The senior of the two soldiers explained what had happened.

"… and then these two tried to escape," he said, looking down at the two bodies.

"I see," said the Captain, as he walked off towards the gates. "Most unfortunate."

The soldiers followed on and stopped as Corporal Lange lowered his rifle and saluted.

"Stand easy," said the Captain in a quiet voice, as he pointed at Mr and Mrs Weizmann. "Who are these people?"

"They're the parents," replied Corporal Lange, his voice trembling. "They tried to help them get away; tried to stop Dieter and Hans from shooting. I had to knock them down."

"Well," replied the Captain, looking down at the Weizmann's. "You certainly knocked them down alright, didn't you?"

The Captain looked over at the truck as he saw some movement there. "And who's in the truck?" he said to no one in particular.

The Corporal stepped forward and said, "That's another family, Sir."

"Any trouble from them?"

"No, Sir. No trouble at all," replied the Corporal.

"Good," said the captain. "These are almost certainly some of the prisoners who broke out from the Jewish detention camp in Brighton earlier tonight."

"I thought that the older ones looked different," said the soldier.

"Right," said the captain as he turned back to look down at the Weizmanns. "Get these two over to the side of the road."

Two of the soldiers laid their rifles down in the road, grabbed hold of Mr Weizmann by his arms and dragged him across the road. He had lost a lot of blood and didn't seem to know what was going on. They then did the same with Mrs Weizmann, and laid her, still unconscious, next to Mr Weizmann.

"Here," said the captain, handing his Luger pistol to the Corporal. "Finish them off."

The corporal took the pistol and looked the Captain

straight in the eyes.

"Is that an order captain?" he said.

"It certainly is," replied the captain in a raised voice. "Do your duty man."

The Corporal saluted, turned and walked back over to the Weizmanns, leaned down so that the pistol was only a few inches away from Mr Weizmann's head, flicked off the safety catch, closed his eyes and pulled the trigger. Mrs Weizmann opened her eyes at the sound of the gun shot and looked over at her husband. The Corporal leaned over her, took aim, closed his eyes again, and once more, he pulled the trigger. Without looking directly at the bodies, he straightened himself, put the safety catch back on, turned and walked back to the Captain and handed the pistol back to him.

"Your orders have been carried out Captain!" he said.

"Good man," replied the Captain, "Now, get all these bodies into the truck and take them, with that other family, back to the detention camp in Brighton. You can explain to the officials there that these people are escapees from their camp and that these four were shot as they tried to escape. If the officials have any further questions please refer them to me: Captain Weber SS."

"Certainly Captain," replied the Corporal as he saluted, turned and marched over to speak to the other soldiers.

Captain Weber walked slowly back to his car and climbed in, giving instructions to the driver as he did so. Everyone watched as the car turned and drove away.

Half an hour later the soldiers had loaded the four bodies into the back of the truck and with the Corporal driving and the other two sitting in the back, they set off for Brighton. The Bernsteins sat perfectly still and quiet on the wooden seats, trying with all their might not to look down at the bodies of the Weizmanns that lay at their feet.

Some hours after the break of dawn, with the early morning light filtering through the bare branches above, a group of Jewish families walked straight into a British patrol.

"Where the hell are you lot from?" asked Sergeant Adams, as he stood on the path in front of them, pointing his Thomson machine gun off to one side, but with the safety catch off.

"We've escaped from the detention camp in Brighton," replied one of the women. "The Resistance got us out last evening. There's over a hundred of us… but we're spread out all over the countryside. God knows if they are all safe… please don't hurt us. We're all so tired… we've had just about enough of this…" The woman burst out crying, dropped her bag and fell to her knees. Two other women who had been standing behind her stepped forward immediately and bent down to comfort her. One of the men now took a few careful steps towards the soldier, looked back at the bedraggled group behind him and said "Are we safe? Please God; tell me that we are safe?"

"You're safe," replied the Sergeant, lowering his gun and pushing the safety catch back on, "What's your name?"

"George Goldberg," he replied weakly, as he stepped closer and rested his hand on his wife's shoulder, "And this is my wife Marie. Our children, Sarah and Mark are with us too."

Sergeant Adams moved forward, bent down and offered a hand to Marie.

"You all look worn out to me," he said, "Let's get you back to our base. If you're lucky; there might be some breakfast left."

Chapter 6

THE HEART OF THE VILLAGE

On the middle Saturday of November, a joint funeral for Joseph and Tim was held at St Mary's Church, Watersham. Local people from all around turned out; villagers, farmers, whole families. They spread out and stood quietly amongst the head stones and watched as the two coffins stood supported on planks above the freshly dug adjoining graves that awaited them. The late morning air was still and cold and the weak winter sunshine cast long shadows across the scene from the three ancient yew trees that grew between the church and the grave yard. In the silence many people were gently weeping.

Seeing so many mourners gathered, the Reverend Streeter lifted his head and raised his voice as loudly as he could, so that everyone could hear.

"We shouldn't be here today, should we?" he started. "We should be going about our everyday business: ploughing the fields, tending to the animals, chopping wood, preparing food... or going for a walk... all those everyday things thatwe take for granted."

Captain Muller and two of his fellow officers stood together, next to the base of one of the yew trees; each holding their hats in front of them, having removed them as they passed through the lych-gate along the path that lead to the church. None of the villagers stood near them

"But here we are…" continued the Vicar, "… here we are at the funeral of two young men. Two young men who belonged to the heart of this village and who should have been going about their business today with the rest of us. Two young men – Joseph and Tim – with their whole lives before them. Two young men shot dead in our own woods by occupying forces." The Vicar paused for a few seconds and the resounding silence deepened across the grave yard. There were a few strangers in amongst the crowd. Most people took no notice of them, and thought nothing of it: but Commander Henry Clay took notice.

The Vicar continued, "Their lives will not have been lost in vain, and Watersham and England will never forget them."

The German officers all had a good understanding of English, and the Vicar's words were not lost on them. Captain Muller, in particular, felt the depth of the meaning. Since arriving in Watersham, he had grown to like the village, the surrounding area and its people. He was sure, that in different times, he would have been friends with the locals and he and his family would have been welcomed. Although he knew that it was the soldiers under his command who had killed these young men; he felt deep sorrow and wished that none of this was happening: the funeral, the constant conflict and the occupation itself. He hoped that the villagers knew that under his German uniform, he was a good man.

The Vicar spoke again "One day soon, this evil occupation will come to an end, and God willing, peace and normality will return. Whether Joseph's and Tim's families will ever be able to forgive, I don't know. I wonder if any of us will ever be able to forgive this wickedness, this evil?"

The German officers turned and quickly walked away.

Most of the people edged closer to the site of the graves as they realised that the Vicar was working his way towards the final words for the committal of the bodies to their final resting places.

There was silence again as the crowd settled. The vicar stood between and just in front of the coffins now and he bent down, his fingertips gently touching and stroking their smooth beech wood lids.

"Ashes to ashes, dust to dust…" and as he spoke, Joseph and Tim's mothers began to sob and soon the church yard was full of crying so that very few could hear the final words spoken by the vicar. He stepped back to allow the men to lift the coffins and to very slowly lower them on ropes into the graves.

Throughout the funeral service, Henry had kept an eye on the two strangers. As the crowd made its way from St Mary's to the village hall, he lost sight of them. He stopped for a while and looked up and down the street, but not being able to spot them again, he carried on to the hall. Alex Miller and Bert Stubbs were standing outside the main door and Henry stopped to talk to them. "There are strangers here," he said.

"You can't know everyone," replied Bert.

"No," said Henry, "But I'm sure they're not villagers.

There's something about them. Keep your eyes open."

The hall was packed to start with and after an hour, the crowd began to thin out, and Henry, Alex and Bert managed to have a few words with the Carter and Washbrook families. On their way out, they chatted briefly to a few more people and then made their way to The George. Bert was first to the bar and after exchanging pleasantries with Carole, the barmaid, he ordered three pints of best bitter and waited whilst Carole pulled the pints. He carried the glasses across to the table in the corner where Henry and Alex had chosen to sit. "Cheers," they all said, "Here's to young Joseph and Tim." They sipped their beers and sat in silence for a minute. A few more locals came in, and after a while, the pub was doing some good business. Half way through their pints, two strangers walked over and sat at the table next to them. As they finished their pints, Henry said, "My round gentlemen," picked up the empty glasses and headed off to the bar. Hoping to catch Carole's eye, he leaned forward and waved an empty glass in the air. She was busy serving at the other end of the bar, but nodded to show Henry that she had seen him. Henry straightened up, and as he did so, he felt someone standing close to him. He turned to see one of the strangers standing by his side. "Henry," he said, "Meet me back up at the graveyard in about twenty minutes." The stranger didn't wait for an answer, but walked briskly to the door. His friend followed him.

Henry waited for the fresh pints and made his way back to the table. "Well, well," he said, "Did you see that? One of our stranger friends spoke to me at the bar. They want to meet us at the graveyard."

"Yes," said Alex, "I noticed one of them follow you to the bar. Do you think it will be safe to meet them?"

"Nothing's safe anymore," replied Henry, "but I think we'll risk it."

After fifteen minutes, they had finished their pints and Henry said "Right then. Let's go and see what our friends want with us."

The late afternoon light was even weaker now as they reached the church, and the shadows cast by the yew trees reached the far side of the graveyard. Standing next to the freshly back-filled graves were the two strangers. As Henry, Alex and Bert approached, they stepped out onto the main grass path that ran through the centre of the grave yard.

"So," said Henry, "What can we do for you gentlemen?"

"Major John Blackman, Royal Hampshire Regiment." replied one of the strangers, as he offered his hand to Henry.

"Blooming heck!" said Henry. "Pleased to meet you. What brings you here? You're taking a hell of a risk, aren't you?"

"This is Sergeant Tony Haskins," replied Major Blackman.

Henry introduced Alex and Bert to them and they all shook hands.

"Yes." continued the Major, "It gets more difficult to move around by the day. Do you think that we're safe talking here?"

"Listen," replied Henry, "Let's go into the church.

I doubt that anyone will disturb us there at this time on a Saturday afternoon."

Henry led the way and the others followed him to a side door. The door was open as usual and they made their way to the vestry, where the last of the afternoon light struggled to find its way through a stained-glass window. The shafts of light picked out tiny particles of dust that hung in the air and there was a distinct smell of musty old books.

"Okay," said Major Blackman, "First of all, I want you to know how sorry we are that you've lost some more good men. We know how difficult it is for the Resistance, and we know that you've all made huge sacrifices; but it's worth it. You're doing a great job keeping the enemy busy. The more you harass them, the less time they have to think about pushing out and on through the rest of the country."

Commander Clay interrupted, "What progress have they made then? I mean, we get occasional messages and we listen to the BBC when we can; but, as you know, we have to be careful. If they catch anyone with a radio, there's big trouble. They often take people away. It's difficult to know what's true and what isn't. The Germans haven't reached London, have they?"

"No, no," replied the Major, "They're bogged down in the South East. Every time they try to move further out, we attack them. In fact, although you might not have seen or heard much of us here in Sussex, there's plenty of action on the front line. They've really only got the very southern bits of Kent and Sussex under their control. What with the regular forces hitting them hard on the front line, and with you chaps, keeping them tied down here, they've bitten off a bit more than they can chew at the moment. On top of that, the Royal Navy and Air Force hit their supply ships in the Channel every day. They've lost a lot of ships."

"It's great to have some good news at last," said Bert. "So, what can we do for you today?" asked Henry. "Well." replied Major Blackman. "We need you to step up your activity. We're asking all Resistance fighters in the south east to step up – immediately. It's the start of a big counter offensive, and the big chiefs reckon that the Resistance fighters are the key to it."

Major Blackman paused for a moment to allow Henry and his men time to understand the importance of what he was saying. He knew that what he was about to ask would be the most that anyone had asked of them since the occupation.

Alex was the first to respond, "So, what exactly is it that you expect us to do?"

"Just about everything," replied the Major. "We need you to go into total offensive mode. Starting tomorrow. We need you to disrupt them as much as possible, whilst we push in from the north and west."

"What about all the other Resistance units?" asked Henry.

"As we speak," said Major Blackman, "other officers like me are contacting Resistance leaders right through the whole region and having the same conversation that we're having now. The whole thing will kick off in a few days' time. Your people will need to be monitoring the radio around the clock."

Henry turned and spoke to his men, "We'll have to get messages out to everyone this evening and fix a meeting for our key people." He then turned back to the Major. "What about additional ammunition and supplies?"

Major Blackman pulled an envelope from his jacket pocket and handed it to Henry. "Here. They'll be dropping extra supplies at these coordinates at 3:00 o'clock on Monday morning. You'll need to get a couple of trucks up on the Downs to pick them up."

"Right," said Henry, "Anything else?"

"Yes. We need to agree a specific meeting place where we can debrief each other. It needs to be at a specific time and place. 23:00 hours on Wednesday evening. Let's agree the meeting place now. Obviously, you will need to share this information with a few key men in case the worst happens. I'll do the same, so that we can be sure that the meeting takes place, even if one or both of us can't make it."

Sergeant Haskins produced a map of the local area, opened it, and tilted it towards the window so that they could see it better.

"There." Henry, pointed at a spot at the far end of the beech woods. "There's a group of large yew trees there. You can't miss them. That's where we'll meet."

Major Blackman and Sergeant Haskins studied the map for a while and then the Sergeant folded up the map.

"Right," said the Major, "We'll see you there on Wednesday evening."

The five men chatted for a few more minutes and then filed back out through the side door of the church. They shook hands and Major Blackman and Sergeant Haskins set off across the graveyard towards the school. Henry, Bert and Alex discussed immediate plans for a while and then each man set off to pass on instructions to their colleagues.

Alex got back to the farm just in time for supper and explained to everyone that he would be going away for a few days. His family knew better than to ask where he was going and what he would be doing.

At 05:00 the next morning, he left the house with a large pack full of provisions on his back. As well as some spare clothes, he had packed a water bottle and enough food for a few days; including: bread, ten cooked sausages, a large chunk of cheddar cheese, some of his mum's fruit cake and a bag of apples. He also packed a bottle of cold sweet and milky tea. After collecting his rifle and ammunition from its hiding place inside the granary, he set off on foot towards the meeting place. At about the same time, many other men were setting off for the same destination. It was very dark, there was a light drizzle falling, but the air was still. In the distance, a fox barked.

During the night, Alan Benton and Tony Smith in a cattle truck, along with Charlie Stewart and Jack Brown in a furniture removal lorry, had found the two drop off locations for the additional ammunition and other equipment that Major Blackman had promised. They had each split their loads into two, so that they were now stashed in four separate locations in the woods.

Chapter 7

THE ARUN BELLE

Henry was amongst the first to arrive at the five-ways path junction in the middle of Hangar Wood. By 06:00, twenty five heavily armed men gathered and waited for instructions. "Listen up men!" called out Henry. "Whilst it's still dark, we'll push on for a bit, and then we'll stop and I'll tell you what we're going to be up to today."

They headed east along the Downs for about two hours, then dropped down to the flood plain of the River Arun, before following it south. On reaching the west bank, they stopped. "Take a break," Commander Clay said quietly.

The men were glad to stop. They sat, well hidden in amongst a great clump of willow. As the weak light of early morning began to break, they could make out the battlements of Amberley Castle about three hundred yards away. At a similar distance, but off to the north, a small herd of fallow deer were grazing.

Everyone took advantage of the break to have a bit of breakfast and a drink. Most of the men had tea in their water bottles and were carrying bread and cheese in their packs. The men chatted quietly as the early winter morning tried its best to start the day. It wasn't a particularly cold morning for the time of year, but it was clearly going to be a grey day. There was no breeze, the cloud was low and a heavy mist hung over the river.

After about twenty minutes, Henry told his senior men what the plan was, and they moved amongst the men to pass the word: they were headed for Ford airfield.

"Are we going to move on in daylight?" said Alex. "Sort of…" replied Henry, with a smile.

Thirty minutes later, a large sail barge came into view, heading down river on the morning tide. As it reached their position, it pulled over towards the river bank. As the barge brushed against reeds and came close to the bank, two men jumped off, one from the front and one from the back. A third man threw a rope from the back and then ran along the edge of the barge and threw another from the front. With little fuss, they tied off the ropes to the base of the willow trees and secured the barge to the side of the river bank. The third man was quick to push a gangplank out and the two men grabbed hold of its end and slid it across to the bank.

Henry stepped out from the willows and spoke to the bargemen.

"Well done," he said, "Anyone would think that you've done that before."

The three men shook Henry's hand and slapped him on his back.

"Good to see you again," they said.

The bargemen were brothers: Jack, Thomas and Edward Searle. They were all in their forties, lived in Pulborough and had been working on the River Arun all of their lives. Two or three times a week, they would sail their barge, Arun Belle, up and down the river plying their trade from the port of Littlehampton, via Arundel and Amberley, to Pulborough and back again. This morning, they were riding the tide back down to Littlehampton. They had little cargo on board, mostly building bricks, bound for a customer in the town; but on reaching the wharf, they would load with the usual wide range of materials and provisions for the businesses in Pulborough.

Henry waved his men out from under the cover of the trees and onto the barge. One by one, they ducked beneath the tent-like canvas that covered the cargo, sat down and made themselves comfortable.

"We're in the Royal Navy now boys!" quipped Bert Stubbs.

As soon as everyone was on board, the Searle brothers cast off, pushed away from the bank with their poles and the Arun Belle gently drifted off again down-stream. As had happened on countless occasions before, the Searles skillfully guided the barge under the central arch at Houghton bridge. Children on their way to school stopped on the bridge and waved to the bargemen and the Searles waved back.

The stretch of river from Houghton to Arundel was quiet. A grey heron stood motionless in the mouth of a small drainage ditch that joined the river at South Stoke, watching the barge sail by. Two immature swans paddled out to join the barge, but then quickly fell back to the shelter of the reeds to the side. The Searles concentrated on keeping the barge in the middle of the river whilst Commander Clay and his men talked quietly amongst themselves under the tarpaulin covers that stretched from side to side.

Through the mist, the Arun Belle glided silently past the Black Rabbit Inn, and then the towering walls of Arundel Castle came into view. At Arundel, a solitary German soldier stood on the bridge and watched as Jack Searle steered his barge through the central archway. Looking back, Edward Searle waved at the soldier, but the soldier gave no response. Two minutes later, the Arun Belle had disappeared into the river mist that enveloped her again.

One mile further downstream, the brothers steered the barge towards the small boardwalk that led to the Ship and Anchor pub at the hamlet of Ford. As soon as contact was made with the wooden uprights, Thomas and Edward jumped from the barge and quickly secured their ropes to the heavy cast-iron rings set into the sturdy oak posts. The ebbing tide pulled at Arun Belles' sides, but she was held firm against the boardwalk. Jack joined his brothers as they walked up the steps that led to the top of the river bank where they stopped to look around. The mist from the river was still thick, but they could clearly see the outline of the pub and its outbuildings about forty yards away. There was no one about.

Jack made his way back to the barge to tell Commander Clay that it was all clear. Henry said something to Alex, and he quickly jumped up, stepped off from the barge and walked up the steps to join Thomas and Edward. After a quick look around, he waved at Henry and a minute later, Bert Stubbs joined him on the top of the bank. Alex stayed where he was, whilst Bert made his way down to the nearest outbuilding next to the pub and opened the door. He quickly checked that the building was clear and then waved back at Henry. Within a few minutes, all 25 men were safely inside. Having watched the last of them disappear, the Searle brothers returned to their barge, cast off, and sailed on down the river towards Littlehampton. Commander Clay checked his watch: it was nearly nine o'clock.

"Right," said Henry, as his men made themselves comfortable on whatever they could find to sit on. "We're going to be here for some time, so make the most of it, but be quiet. We'll be moving out after dark. I'll be speaking to the team leaders shortly about exactly what I need each team to focus on this evening and then they will explain to you separately what your duties are. Okay. That's all for now."

Henry called the team leaders over and they moved to the far end of the building to talk. Alex Miller, Bert Stubbs, Alan Benton, Tony Smith, Charlie Stewart and Jack Brown stood in a circle with him. "Okay lads," said Henry, "Here's the deal. We're going to hit Ford Airfield tonight."

"Thought so," murmured Tony under his breath.

Ford Airfield had been taken over by the Luftwaffe within days of the RAF leaving during early October. In the weeks that followed, the Germans had set up offices in the old buildings and the airfield was being used as a main supply base for the immediate area. In addition to Luftwaffe air and ground crew, there were large numbers of administrators based at Ford, as well as over 200 soldiers.

Henry outlined the broad plan to his men and then explained to them what basic tasks he expected each small team to carry out. Twenty minutes later he was finished, and the leaders made their way back to explain to their men what was required of them. Most of the men were familiar with the general layout of Ford Airfield, but a few were not, and so the leaders had to explain to individuals how one part of the site related to the other, and especially, where the main buildings were located, relative to where they were sitting right now. The relevance of this was not lost on any of them, as they all understood that this would be their way out, once the attack had been completed. The plan was to pick up the Searles barge again on the incoming tide.

After quiet had returned to the barn, Henry walked back amongst his men.

"I just need to repeat a key point to you all so that there's no misunderstanding. The barge will be waiting for us at midnight. It can't wait, that would be too dangerous. It will cast off at five minutes past midnight. If you're not on the barge, then you'll have to look out for yourself and make your way back as best you can."

The rest of the day passed by slowly. The men entertained

themselves by chatting, snoozing, snacking from their lunch bags and sipping cold tea. From time to time, individuals would make their way to the back door, check that all was clear, and wander outside for a pee. By five o'clock, with the mist still hanging, what was left of the day's dim light faded and darkness fell. It felt very odd, sitting in the pitch-black barn, and with each quarter hour that went by, the chat diminished and their moods changed as each man thought of what was to come. For some of the men, this would be their first engagement with the enemy.

At precisely ten o'clock, Henry stood up and made his way to the front door of the building. He cracked the door open as quietly as he could and peered out. The dimmest of lights struggled to show itself through the nearest pub window, but there was no sign of movement anywhere and all seemed quiet.

"Right," said Henry quietly to Alex, who was standing nearby, "This is it; off we go."

Alex spoke to the men nearest to him and the message was passed quickly down the line. Within a couple of minutes, everyone was outside and formed into their respective groups. Two minutes later, the groups had divided and quietly disappeared into the mist and dark. The two or three old men drinking in the pub saw and heard nothing.

Alex Miller and his team had the furthest to go and headed for Ford Lane. Alex knew that the lane ran along the northern edge of the airfield and that if they followed it nearly to the end, they could turn south and find their target. Three hangars sat at the far side of the airfield, and recent intelligence told them that on most nights, three German planes were parked there. What security there might be; they didn't know.

Bert Stubbs and his men were heading in the other direction. They were following the river a little further south, and then heading for Climping church, near to the south-east corner of the airfield. That's where the fuel dump was.

Alan Benton was following Alex with his team, but would turn into the airfield near to the north-east corner where there was a mixture of service buildings.

Tony Smith and his team headed out to the main road and then, walking in the field under the cover of a tall hedge, made their way towards the control centre to the south.

Charlie Stewart led his group south, staying close to the river; then, turning west, they cut behind Church farm until they reached the southern edge of the airfield. There were a number of aircraft hangars spread out along the southern boundary and that was where they were headed.

Jack Brown and his men had a completely different role to play. Their instructions were to stay near to the main road and spread out near to where the old canal used to run. This was strictly a defensive position in case they needed to give covering fire as the teams made their way back to the river. Henry decided at the last minute that he would stay with Jack's team.

By half past ten, Alex and his team reached the hangars on the far side of the airfield. They hadn't seen anyone as they made their way along Ford Lane and there didn't appear to be any guards anywhere. For several minutes, they circled the hangars, just making sure that there was no one else around, then they slid inside the first open ended hangar. They had rehearsed this sort of thing many times before; in the woods and at farms near to Watersham. Alex and Josh Phillips stood guard by the entrance, Eddie Harman shone a small torch at the Messerschmitt 109 that stood before them, and Alfie Sugden stuck the explosives to the fuselage and carefully connected the detonators and timers, setting them for exactly 45 minutes. All four men moved on to the second hangar, where they found another Messerschmitt 109, and went through the same procedure. The third hangar was empty, apart from a fuel bowser and three large portable generator sets. Eddie shone his torch as Alfie used up the last of his explosives on each of the pieces of equipment.

"Let's go," whispered Alex.

As quietly as they could, they cut back behind the hangars, and headed towards Ford Lane.

The other teams had also reached their targets and were busy setting explosives and timers. Each one making sure that they were set for 45 minutes. Each team realised that they couldn't set them all to go off at exactly the same time, as it depended on so many factors, such as how long it took each team to get to their targets and what problems they encountered when they got there. This was exactly the problem that Charlie Stewart and his men had come across. As they reached the first of the hangars on the southern boundary, through the misty gloom, they could hear voices.

"Quiet!" whispered Charlie, as he brought his men to a halt. They knelt down behind a truck, parked some twenty paces from the corner of the first hangar, and listened. There was a faint light emanating from the front of the hangar, and after a while, the sound of laughing came from inside.

"There's several men in there," whispered Charlie, "Let's work our way along and have a look at the others."

Spread out, and half doubled, they made their way down the far side of the second hangar, and on reaching the open front, Charlie peered inside. There was no one around. He waved his men forward and they all disappeared inside. Ken Whitman shone his torch, and there in front of them was another plane. "What sort's that?" he whispered to no one in particular.

"It looks like a trainer to me," whispered back Charlie, "A Focke-Wulf 190."

The men were finished setting their explosives within three minutes and all moved off to look at the third hangar. Again, there were no guards around and Ken shone his torch at the key points on the side of another the Messerschmitt

109, as Bill Bryant fixed the explosives. As he finished with the last one and went to set the timer, Ken's torch failed.

"Don't move!" said Ken, as he tapped the torch and switched it off and on several times.

"It's no good mate. You'll have to guess the settings on the timer. I daren't strike a match in here."

Ken found it much easier walking back towards the entrance, as the arc of the roof stood out clearly against the night sky, even though it was still dark and misty outside.

Bill twisted the lever on the dial around to its fullest position, and then slowly wound it back to where he guessed the three-quarter position was. Holding his breath, he felt for the switch on the side of the timer and flicked it on; breathing out slowly, he heard the clock start to tick.

"Right!" he said, "That's enough excitement for one day. Let's get out of here."

Charlie and his men retraced their steps and headed back towards the river.

All around the airfield, the five teams had set their explosives, and were making their way back. At the old canal crossing, Commander Clay, Jack Brown and their team were spread out along the roadside, under cover and listening for signs of any trouble. At about ten past eleven, headlights appeared through the mist from the north, and a very noisy German truck drove past them, slowed and turned into the main entrance of the airfield.

"Routine," said Henry to himself.

All was quiet again until ten minutes later; when Alex and his team arrived back at the main road. He spoke briefly to Henry, who was waiting by the small lane that led back to the river, and then set off with his men to the boardwalk. Shortly afterwards, the others arrived safely back and headed for the river.

At just after eleven thirty, Henry walked along the road and told Jack Brown and his men that they could also make their way back to the river. He followed them down the lane, and as they reached the front of the pub, the noise of a massive explosion reached them from the far side of the airfield. Birds clattered out from the trees all around, dogs started to bark and within seconds, shouting could be heard from the airfield. All the men had instinctively dived for cover as the explosion had gone off and they now looked back towards the airfield as the low dark cloud and mist reflected an orange glow across the sky.

"Shit!" said Henry to Jack Brown who was lying on the ground next to him, "That one's gone off far too early!"

The men were back on their feet as quickly as they could and headed for the river bank. As they disappeared into the gloom, faces appeared at the windows of the Ship and Anchor, as the landlord and his family looked out to see what was going on.

The Searle brothers were still twenty minutes away from the mooring at the Ship and Anchor, sailing the Arun Belle up river with the incoming tide. The three brothers stared at each other as the sound of the explosion reached them, wondering what they might find when they got to the rendezvous point. Small secondary explosions followed from the same part of the airfield, the sky continued to glow orange and new noises could now be heard as soldiers, airmen and ground crew rushed to tackle the flames and move vehicles away.

By the river bank, Henry peered into the mist that still swirled above the waters of the now fast flowing river. He hoped and prayed that the barge would arrive on time; but there was no sign of it yet. He turned and held his arm out towards the glowing sky. He could just make out the hands on his watch: ten to midnight.

Most of Henry's men were spread out and lying down on the river bank, with five or six crouching on the boardwalk itself. Tucked in by the old stables, Jack Brown and his team had taken up defensive positions, facing back down the lane.

Jack was at the northern end of the building and George Stubbs was at the southern end. Harold Blake looked out over a low wall that adjoined the rear corner of the pub, and Fred Andrews was positioned about ten paces further back, looking out from behind an old well house. They all stared back down the lane, hoping that no one would come.

The sound of vehicles on the move was clearer and closer now. Henry Clay wondered how long it would be before the Germans started to scour the area and to send patrols out to search by the river. It must have occurred to them by now that the devastation around them was sabotage and not some unfortunate accident. As he peered out across the water for the tenth time, the second explosion reverberated across the fields and another great flash of orange lit up the sky. As he turned to speak to Alex, the third explosion rang out.

Midnight arrived, but there was no sign of the barge. Henry and his men were becoming anxious as one after the other, the explosives all around the airfield detonated. Jack Brown and his team continued staring back down the lane and listening out for any noise that might indicate the enemy approaching. With so much noise coming from the airfield, it was difficult to tell whether or not anything was heading their way. Suddenly, out of the mist, the headlights of a vehicle appeared. The truck advanced very slowly down the lane and stopped in front of the pub. The engine cut and the headlights went out. Jack Brown and his men waited in the dark and listened. They couldn't see much, but they could clearly hear the German soldiers climbing down, their boots scraping the gravel path. Jim Sullivan, the landlord of the pub, stepped away from the windows.

At five past midnight, the Searle brothers brought the Arun Belle alongside the boardwalk. Thomas and Edward jumped from the barge and tied the ropes off as quickly as they could. Henry waved at the men nearest to him, and one by one they started to board.

Sergeant Helmut Lange spoke to his men as they stood near to the back of the truck. The driver and his mate climbed down from the cab and joined the others. Sergeant Lange pointed towards the pub and six soldiers split from the group and walked quickly towards the front door. On reaching the porch, one of the soldiers lifted the heavy cast iron knocker and banged it firmly. Even with the noises of continued explosions coming from the airfield, the sound of the knocking rang out clearly.

Jim Sullivan jumped as the knocking reverberated through the old pub. He grabbed his dressing gown and peered out through the landing window. He couldn't see much; just the glow of the fires coming from the airfield. He felt his way down the dark stairs and just as he reached the front door, the German soldier gave three more loud knocks. "Alright, alright!" shouted Jim, "Hold your horses! I'm coming!"

He unbolted the door, held it ajar and peered out.

The first soldier pushed passed him and said in broken English "English soldiers. English soldiers here?"

"There are no English soldiers here!" answered Jim as he followed the soldier into the main bar in the pub. "The English army left us months ago. You drove them all away; remember!"

The German soldier pushed him back again as the other soldiers stomped into the pub and spread out to search.

Jim called after them. "There's only me, my wife and the kids here! Don't frighten them."

By the truck, the remaining soldiers were talking and milling around; nervous from the sound of explosions and other noises coming from the airfield. Two had moved slightly further away; closer to where Jack Brown and his men were hiding.

Down by the river, most of the men had climbed on board the Arun Belle, and Henry was getting ready to give the order to cast off.

The Searle brothers were becoming more anxious by the second as they too realised that they couldn't wait much longer. In the distance, sounds of muffled explosions continued to drift in from the airfield. There was the distinct smell of burning in the air now, and, mixed above the dark mist that still swirled around, there was a strange glow in the sky.

Alex Miller was now the last man on the river bank. He was lying flat on his stomach, peering towards where he knew the pub and its outbuildings were. He couldn't see anything beyond ten paces in front of him. He knew that the German truck had stopped near to the pub and guessed that German soldiers were nearby. He also guessed that Jack Brown and his men were in hiding near to the outbuildings, holding their fire and hoping that the soldiers wouldn't come their way.

Henry called quietly to Alex, "We'll have to go! We daren't wait any longer!"

The Searle brothers started loosening the ropes of the Arun Belle and then leaned back to hold her steady with just one loop of rope around the oak posts of the board walk, fore and aft. The incoming tide was gathering in strength and was doing its best to rip the barge away from her moorings.

Back at the Ship and Anchor, the soldiers clattered their way back out through the front door and re-joined the main group. There was a brief discussion, and then suddenly, Sergeant Lange called out in a loud voice, "Right! Search those buildings and have a look around the back!"

The German soldiers spread out immediately and headed towards the out-buildings. Jack Brown could just about make out some movement coming towards him and he could hear the sounds of heavy boots on gravel. It was too late and too dangerous to move back to a new position and so he braced himself against the brick wall and waited. As the first soldier appeared out of the mist, he opened fire in a sweeping fashion with his Thompson machine gun. Within a split second, the other members of his team did the same. Several soldiers fell to the ground as they were hit by a hail of bullets. Sergeant Lange and the remainder of the soldiers dived for cover and started to return fire.

"Cast off!" shouted Commander Clay, and the Searle brothers whipped the ropes in and pushed the Arun Belle away from her moorings. The incoming tide took her immediately and she headed up river.

As bullets flew around, Fred Andrews was hit in the head and fell back dead. The others were trying to move towards the river, but with the visibility being so bad, they were all struggling.

Alex sat on his backside, slid down the grassy bank, and headed towards the buildings. He stopped when he reached a large oak tree.

"This'll do," he muttered to himself.

Jack was the first to join him. Out of breath, he swung himself behind Alex and quickly changed the magazine on his gun.

A salvo of bullets whistled through the branches of the tree above their heads and then there was silence. Within seconds, Harold Blake and George Stubbs appeared next to them and they all ducked down.

"Where's Fred?" whispered Alex.

"I saw him go down," replied George, "I don't think that we can do anything to help him now."

"Damn it!" said Alex, "Right! Let's see if we can get out of here. The barge has already left, so we'll have to look out for ourselves."

The four men clambered up the river bank, and then, half doubled up, they ran along the footpath as fast as they could, heading towards Arundel – the crack of shots ringing out behind them and the sounds of chaos from the burning airfield drifted to them through the dark mist. At the Ship and Anchor, Sergeant Lange, having realised that the enemy had slipped away and that the danger had passed, picked himself up from the gravel path and called out to his men.

"They've gone! There's no point chasing after them. We can't see where the hell we're going," he Shouted, "Now, check for casualties and let's get everyone back to the truck as quickly as we can."

He swore as he walked back towards the truck and suddenly became aware of a throbbing pain is his left arm. He hitched his rifle over his right shoulder and felt his arm. The jacket sleeve of his uniform was soaking wet. He brought his hand up close to his face. Even in the poor light, he could see that it was covered in blood.

One of his men called out to him. "Sergeant! There's a dead Englishman over here!"

"Good," replied Sergeant Lange. "Get his body back to the truck. We'll take him with us. He might have some ID on him."

Sergeant Lange then pointed back towards the Ship and Anchor.

"Fetch the pub landlord! He can come with us too!"

Once Alex felt that he and his men were far enough away, he stopped running and walked quickly down the side of the river bank to a small stand of willow trees on the edge of a meadow. He waited until the other two joined him. They were all exhausted and breathing heavily.

"I think it will be best if we get away from the river now," he said, "As soon as the visibility improves, they're bound to start looking up and down the banks, and we certainly don't want to go anywhere near Arundel. They're bound to have extra patrols out."

As soon as they had all got their breath back, Alex led the others down the side of the meadow until they came to a five-bar gate that opened up to the main road, about half a mile south of Arundel. They listened for a while, and then being certain that they were alone, crossed the road and walked quickly along a cart track on the other side. Fifteen minutes later, they reached the relative safety of Binsted Woods.

Ahead of the Arun Belle, the bridge at Arundel suddenly loomed up through the mist. The Searle brothers had steered her under the bridge hundreds of times before, in all weathers and at all times of the day and night, and always with the flowing or ebbing tide. Although the German sentries who manned the bridge had only been in England for a short time, they were used to seeing the Arun Belle sail by. She was as familiar to them as the river itself. The Searle brothers waved at the soldiers as they ducked under the bridge and sailed on up river. Two of the German soldiers waved back. Commander Henry Clay and his men kept quiet and hidden under the covers of the sail cloth tarpaulin that covered the hold.

About ten minutes later, the barge passed by the Black Rabbit pub. The mist was slightly thinner now and the Searle brothers could make out four German troop trucks lined up outside the pub. Several German soldiers were standing right on the edge of the river bank, looking straight at them. One of the soldiers waved at them as they sailed by and George Searle waved back.

Visibility improved again as they made their way up river; past South Stoke, and up to Houghton Bridge. There was no sign of anyone about as they cleared the bridge and headed north. As they rounded the next bend in the river, the mist lifted completely for a minute and the Searles could see the familiar outline of Amberley Castle again across the fields. The brothers started to slow the speed of the Arun Belle and George lifted the edge of the tarpaulin, bent down, and called quietly to Henry, "Two minutes."

Henry and the men nearest to him started to get themselves ready to stand. The men furthest along the barge soon got the message, and they too started to rouse themselves. Henry stood, ducked out from under the tarpaulin cover, and accepted the helping hand of Jack Searle as he stepped up to the edge of the barge. One by one, his men made their way out from under cover, until they all stood ready to disembark. The barge slowed even more and the Searle brothers steered her towards the grassy bank until she was rubbing against the waiting reeds. Jack Searle was the first to jump off, closely followed by his brother George; both holding a short coil of rope. Within seconds they had everything under control and the Arun Belle came to a complete stop. Henry and his men disembarked and knelt down by the stunted willow trees that grew just back from the river bank. With no fuss, as the last man jumped clear, Jack and George Searle stepped back onto the barge, dropped their ropes on deck, picked up the barge poles and pushed her off from the bank. Frank Searle steered the Arun Belle back to the centre of the river where she was immediately carried on again by the running tide. Henry and his men waved at the Searles and the brothers waved back as she slipped back into the darkness.

"Right," said Henry, "Now, let's get away from the river as quickly as we can. Follow me. I know a path up ahead that will take us to the cover of the woods."

The men were all glad to be back on dry land again and to be on the move. They walked for about ten minutes further along the river bank until they came to a stile.

"This is it," said Henry, "We'll cut across the field from here and get to the woods."

A short while later, they reached the cover of some large beech trees, their great branches hanging over the edge of the grassy flood plain. For the next twenty minutes, they walked up hill amongst the trees, finally reaching flatter ground. Henry stopped. All the men were breathing heavily from the exertion of climbing the hill, and they were pleased to take a break.

Henry waited for a few minutes until he got his breath back and then he spoke again.

"Okay, now listen. The top of the hill is about fifty yards

further on. We'll make our way up there in a minute and then we'll split up. It'll be better for all of us if we each find our own way back home. It'll be safer."

The men weren't at all surprised at this latest instruction from the Commander. They often trained this way, carrying out a night exercise and then splitting up to make their way home.

At the top of the hill, still under full cover of the great beeches, Henry shook the hand of each man and wished him well, as one by one, they set off into the night.

At the west end of Binsted Woods, Alex called a halt to his small group.

"Time to split up again," he said.

He patted each man on his back as they set off, one after the other, into the night. Alex waited for a further five minutes and then turned and headed towards Binsted Church.

Back at Ford Airfield, things were quietening down, as fires were being brought under control and order was being restored. Sergeant Lange stood near to the back of the truck and watched as three of his dead soldiers were transferred to stretchers and then carried off to the main hall. Injured soldiers were helped down from the truck and they were also steered towards the dim light of the hall doorway. The last to leave the truck were two German soldiers carrying the body of Fred Andrews on a stretcher. They too headed towards the hall and Sergeant Lange followed closely behind.

"Put him down here!" he called out, pointing to a wooden table top.

The soldiers slid the stretcher on to the table and stood back. Sergeant Lange stepped forward immediately and started going through Fred's pockets. Apart from a used handkerchief, he found nothing. He looked at Fred's neck. No chain. No ID.

"Turn him over!" shouted the Sergeant.

The two soldiers struggled for a while, but eventually managed to turn Fred's body over. Sergeant Lange checked Fred's back pockets.

"No fucking ID!" screamed the Sergeant. Blood was dripping on the floor from the wound in his arm and he leaned against the table and lowered his head as he started to feel faint. "No papers. Nothing!"

"Bring the pub landlord in here."

Two minutes later, Jim Sullivan found himself standing in front of the table that held the body of Fred Andrews.

Sergeant Lange called to the soldier standing nearest to him.

"Help me off with my coat," he said.

The soldier saw immediately that there was a ragged hole in the Sergeant's coat and that blood was running down his arm. He carefully eased the coat from the Sergeant and stood back. Another soldier gently rolled up the Sergeant's shirt sleeve to a point above the gaping wound. Sergeant Lange pointed towards a towel that was hanging on a hook behind the door.

"Cut that up into strips and tie it tight around my arm," he said.

Jim Sullivan watched as the soldiers did what the Sergeant asked. The blood stopped dripping almost immediately as they tightened the tourniquet on his arm, and Sergeant Lange wiped his bloody hands with what remained of the towel.

"Fetch a medic!" called out the Sergeant, "And let the Intelligence Officer know that we might need his assistance here."

Jim Sullivan didn't understand German and missed the point concerning the call for the Intelligence Officer. Jim felt cold. He was only wearing his dressing gown over his pyjamas and slippers on his feet. He stared at the lifeless body lying on the table in front of him.

Sergeant Lange walked around the room, his arm throbbing. He eventually stopped walking and stood facing Jim across Fred Andrews body.

"What is your name?" he said to Jim in a slow controlled voice.

"Jim Sullivan," Jim replied without hesitation, "I'm the landlord of the Ship and Anchor."

"Yes." said the Sergeant, "And you know who this man is don't you? What's his name?"

"I can't help you there I'm afraid," replied Jim, "I've never seen him before. He's not one of my locals you see."

"Oh really!" shouted Sergeant Lange, "So you have all these English soldiers in your pub and you say that you don't know who they are? You say that they're not local. Do you really think that I am going to believe that?"

Jim looked around the room at the other soldiers there and then rested his eyes again on the body on the table. He was frightened. He was more frightened now than he had ever been in his life before.

"Let me ask you again before the Intelligence Officer gets here. Who is this man and where does he come from?"

Jim immediately understood the significance of the threat of an Intelligence Officer becoming involved. He put his hands up to his face and wiped them slowly down across the sweat that was beginning to break out.

"No, no! You don't understand! Those men were not in my pub and I didn't know they were out the back. You can ask me as many times as you like who this man is, and I will give you the same answer. I don't know his name! I've never seen him before! I can't help you."

Sergeant Lange stepped back from the table and walked around the room again. He stopped by the door, and hearing someone approaching, opened it with his good hand. A medic entered, carrying a large first aid bag.

He took one look at the Sergeant's bloody arm and said

"My God, that's a serious wound. You'll have to come with me. We need to get you to a hospital."

Sergeant Lange spoke to his men. "Keep Mr Sullivan here until the Intelligence Officer arrives. I'll be back as soon as I can."

The medic helped the Sergeant put his coat back on and they both turned to leave. Sergeant Lange then hesitated at the door, turned and walked back to face Jim Sullivan.

"Mr Sullivan," he said in a low voice, "You need to think hard about what answers you might give when the Intelligence Officer comes to see you. He and his men are not part of the regular army you know. They play by different rules."

Jim didn't know much about the German army or German Intelligence Officers; but the message was clear enough.

"But I don't know who this man is," he replied nervously, "I don't know anything about any of this stuff. You have to believe me!"

"It doesn't matter what I believe," said the Sergeant as he walked back towards the door, "It will be what the Intelligence Officer believes that matters."

Sergeant Lange stepped out into the night air. It was cold and the throbbing in his arm was getting worse.

Feeling more fearful now, Jim looked around the room at the German soldiers guarding him and then back at the body of Fred Andrews laying on the table. For a few seconds, the thought of making a run for it crossed his mind. But what would be the point? They would probably catch or shoot him before he got far; and anyway, they knew where he and his family lived. He felt tears in his eyes as he thought about his wife and children.

"What a bloody mess," he muttered to himself.

On reaching Binsted Church, Alex walked quietly down the footpath until he reached the main door. He turned the heavy ring handle and pushed the door open. The ancient hinges creaked as it swung open and a tawny owl called out from the oak tree that stood in the corner of the churchyard. Alex turned and looked towards the tree. In the dark, he could only just about make out its shape and he couldn't see the owl, but he knew that it could almost certainly see him. As he stepped through the doorway, the owl hooted again. Alex gently closed the great door behind him.

It was bitterly cold inside the church and pitch black. Alex shuffled slowly forward and reached out until his hand came into contact with the back of a pew. Using it as a guide rail, he was soon able to find his way to its end, turn around and slide in. The pine timbered seat was hard but it was good to be able to sit down and rest for a while. He laid his rifle and kit bag down, pulled his collar up, folded his arms and closed his eyes. Within a minute, he was fast asleep.

He awoke with a start. He had no idea how long he had been sleeping, but it was still pitch black. He listened in the darkness and cold silence. For a minute there was nothing; and then he could hear the unmistakable sounds of fluttering in the roof space above him. Bats, he thought to himself, and smiled.

He reached out for his kit bag and rifle, slid back out from the pew and felt his way back to the doorway. He hitched his rifle and bag over his shoulders, reached down and turned the door handle. The hinges creaked again as he opened the door and he stepped back outside, closing the door quietly behind him. He looked towards the oak tree, expecting the tawny owl to call out again, but there was no response. He walked through the church yard, taking care not to bump into the head stones, until he reached the stile steps that bridged the flint wall boundary of the church yard. He climbed over and set off down the path that led down to the stream that he knew as the Avis. As he walked across the short wooden planked foot bridge to the other side, the tawny owl called out once more.

Alex stopped for a moment, and looking back towards the oak tree where he knew the owl was sitting, he said to himself, "Yes, I know you've been watching me. Good night."

Half an hour later, he arrived back at the family farm, hid his rifle and kit away, let himself into the house as quietly as he could, took his boots off in the kitchen and hung his jacket over the back of a chair and made his way upstairs to his bedroom.

As the first weak light began to spread across the grey early morning sky, Tony Smith peered out from behind a wooden fence, looking towards the centre of Watersham village. Like all the others, he had split up from the rest of his team some hours before and had made his way back to the village via a circuitous route. His carpenter's workshop was down one of the side streets, which was where he wanted to get to, to hide his rifle and kit. He watched for some time to check that no one was watching, and as the light improved, he broke cover and made his way towards his workshop. He looked back as he turned the corner into Cooper Street, and as he faced forward again, standing only twenty yards in front of him were three German soldiers. They saw him before he saw them and as he instinctively turned on his heels to run, one of them shouted.

"Halt!"

As he ran back around the corner, he dropped his kit bag and slipped his rifle from his shoulder. He was running as fast as he could, desperately looking for somewhere to hide. He looked back over his shoulder just as the German soldiers rounded the corner. He made about another seven or eight strides before the shots rang out. Several shots whistled by, but three hit him in his back, sending him sprawling in the middle of the road, his rifle sliding on ahead on the tarmac, as if still trying to get away. Tony's blood trickled across the street and pooled against the kerb stones. By the time the German soldiers reached him and rolled him over, Tony was dead.

Chapter 8

RADIO WAVES

Julia had been at the radio station in the hideout since early afternoon. The light from her oil lamp was poor and the air quality was foul. She was day dreaming; thinking about Joseph. Two months had already gone by since he had been shot and killed by the Germans and Alex and the others had found his body in the woods, and nearly three months since she and Joseph had lain together under the yew tree. She looked down and felt her stomach through her coat pockets. There was nothing showing yet; but she knew that she was pregnant.

"God knows what sort of world you're going to come in to my love," she said to herself.

She needed to get outside for some fresh air. She looked at the pocket watch that lay on the table. It was 19:30 hours and she was sure that it would be completely dark outside by now.

She pushed her chair back, stood and leaned down to extinguish the flame in the lamp. Pitch blackness instantly fell around her. After standing still for a few seconds, she felt for her coat on the back of the chair, lifted it up and slipped it on, struggling for a while to do up the buttons with her cold fingers. She felt again for the back of the chair and then slowly made her way towards the ladder that led up to the main hatch door. She met the wall of the hide-out, adjusted her position and reached out to touch one of the steps on the ladder. She stepped up and on reaching the hatch, listened for half a minute, and on satisfying herself that all was quiet outside, she lifted the wooden top a few inches and peered out into the late autumn evening. It took a while for her eyes to adjust but, although it was dark, visibility was good compared to the absolute blackness of her den. She looked out as far as she could see into the woods. Nothing. No one and no sign of movement anywhere. Just the comforting sound of the night breeze running through the great beech trees that stood all around. Very slowly and with great care, she pushed the hatch back to its full extent, climbed the last few steps and stood on the ancient earth bank in which the entrance to the hideout had been dug. She gently lowered the hatch back to its closed position and checked that the camouflage branches were in place. Looking around again, she walked deeper into the woods, taking in great gulps of fresh air as she did so.

She felt much better now that she was out in the fresh air. She stood still for some time, enjoying the solitude and the peace. After a while, the cold air had an effect on her and she squatted next to the nearest tree to relieve herself.

The main message that she had received over the radio was clear. Her contact at HQ had told her to stand by at 20:30 hours for an important announcement. It would be 'Code Red'. She had never received that sort of message before, but she knew from her brief training that 'Code Red' was the highest category message that they ever gave out, and that they were as rare as hens teeth. When her opposite number at

HQ had used that phrase, a cold shiver had run down Julia's back. That was half an hour ago and the radio had remained silent since.

She was apprehensive and the extra adrenalin running through her veins was making her more alert than ever. The breeze continued to blow gently through the tops of the beech trees, but every now and then there would be a lull, and other more distant noises could be heard coming from deep within the woods. Tawny owls hooted and a roe deer gave out three sharp barks in the distance. There was the faintest smell of wood smoke in the air and as she looked up through the almost bare branches, she could make out stars twinkling in the jet- black sky. Julia pulled up the collar of her coat, checked that all the buttons were done up and thrust her hands into her pockets. She was feeling the cold. She looked up at the stars and thought of Joseph again.

She walked around. Time felt like it was dragging, although without a lamp or torch, she couldn't see exactly what the time was. Even if she had a torch with her, she wouldn't have dared to switch it on. She couldn't stand it anymore and made her way back to the entrance to the hideout, stepped onto the ladder and climbed down a few steps and pulled the hatch back down. Very gingerly, she climbed down the last few steps and felt her way back to the desk. She found the matches, lit the oil lamp, adjusted the wick and pushed it towards the back of the desk. The two accumulator batteries reflected the light from the lamp from their glass cases around the underground chamber. She checked the time. 20:05 hours.

Julia walked around the room, looked in the cupboards, checked the stores and returned to her chair. 20:12 hours. She stared at the brick wall behind the desk and watched two woodlice making their way along the mortar pathways. She wondered where they were headed. Did they know where they were going, or were they just wandering aimlessly?

She looked away and gave out a sigh of frustration, walked around the room several more times and then sat back down again. 20:17 hours. She knew not to turn the radio on too soon. Battery life was precious. She straightened the note pad on the desk for the tenth time and checked the points of the three pencils that stood in a clay flower pot next to the radio; eventually choosing one and laying it across the pad. She stared at the wall again and tapped her fingers on the desktop. At precisely 20:25 hours, she pulled the headphones on, cleared her throat and turned the radio on. After a few seconds, the radio gave out a satisfying gentle buzzing sound and she knew that she was ready.

Julia checked her watch for the umpteenth time. 20:29 hours. At a few seconds past 20:30 hours the buzzing sound increased and ten clear pips at one second intervals were delivered to her ears: pip … pip … pip … pip … pip … pip … pip … pip … pip … pip … There was then just the sound of buzzing static again for a few more seconds, followed by a very slow and clipped male voice.

"This is London calling. This is London calling." There was a brief pause and then… "Ash before oak. We are in for a soak. This is London calling."

The announcement ended as abruptly as it had started; leaving only the faint sound of distant static buzzing in Julia's ears. She removed her headphones, turned off the radio and wrote down the message: "Ash before oak. We're in for a soak."

For several minutes she sat perfectly still, staring at the message on the page in front of her. She knew exactly what it meant. She didn't need a code book to decipher it. Anyway, she knew that you wouldn't find it in any code book, even if such a book existed. No; she had learnt the meaning of this saying by heart some six weeks previously, at a secret training camp near Cambridge. Along with scores of others from all over the occupied areas; mostly young women, she had been smuggled through the German lines and spent a week being trained in the finer arts of the clandestine radio operator; including coding. This particular code was the very last thing that they had been taught. Linked to the code was a sequence of actions that needed to be triggered immediately after it was broadcast by London and received by the radio operators. None of the actions were written down, but they were firmly fixed in the minds of the operators.

Julia suddenly felt cold again. She tore the small sheet of paper from the pad and slipped it into her jacket pocket, extinguished the oil lamp, stood up and made her way towards the exit. Half way up the ladder, she stopped and listened for at least a minute. Nothing. On leaving the hideout, she headed straight for the main forest track that led back towards the village. It was as dark as ever in the woods and she had to walk carefully under the great beech trees, but once she was on the main track, her eyes had adjusted to the poor light and she was able to quicken her pace.

Julia slowed her pace as she approached the Clay's house, checking all the time that no one was following or watching her. Satisfied that she was alone, she knocked at the door. Mrs Clay answered, and seeing Julia, she quickly ushered her inside. She followed her to the kitchen where Henry was sitting at the table reading a newspaper.

"Look who's come to see us!"

"Julia!" exclaimed Henry as he stood to greet her, "How lovely to see you."

Mrs Clay offered to take her coat and Julia slipped it off, removing the note as she did so.

They all sat down and she slid the note across the table to Henry.

"What does it mean?"

"I received it over the radio about three quarters of an hour ago. It's from London. It's gone out to all radio operators this evening. It's the only broadcast to go out, because it's the most important broadcast they've ever sent out."

Henry read the message out loud. "Ash before oak. We're in for a soak."

"That's it," continued Julia, "Now throw it in the fire and I'll explain its meaning."

Henry stood with the note, opened the fire door of the kitchen range and threw it in.

"Right," he said, "I'm listening."

"You remember that a few of us spent a week up near Cambridge on that radio operators' course. We learned a lot there; not only about how to operate our radios, but also how to decipher codes and how to interpret certain messages. This one is not a code in itself. It's a message that we were taught to listen out for and to explain to our Resistance leaders what the meaning is behind the message. It means… it means that the British Army and the RAF are about to mount a major counter offensive across the entire front line, pushing the Germans back. It means that the Royal Navy will attack them in the ports and in the Channel. It's going to be huge. It'll be… it'll be the biggest thing we've seen since the occupation..."

Henry interrupted, "This is the best news we've had in a long time. Do we know when it will start?"

"We don't know yet, but it will be within days. They wouldn't give out this sort of sensitive information if it wasn't imminent. They'll almost certainly give out the precise day and time within days. The message that I have to give to you is to be ready. That's what we were all told, at the end of our training course; if ever we received that message, to immediately tell the local Resistance leaders to be ready."

"Don't you worry about that. We'll be ready alright. I'll get messages out to my men tonight. They'll be ready to move at a moment's notice."

He stopped talking for a while as a new thought crossed his mind. "Who else knows how to operate the radio?" he said.

"Charlie Stewart," replied Julia, "He came on the course with me and we take turns to monitor the radios with three or four others who we've trained up."

"Right," said Henry, "The first thing to do is to make sure they know what's going on. They all need to know that we've received this message and to stand by in case anything should happen to you. I don't want to be melodramatic; but if for some reason you weren't able to get to the radio; I mean, well…"

"Yes," said Julia, "I'd thought of that too. I'll go and speak to Charlie and the others next. That's if it's alright with you?"

"I think that'll be best," replied Henry, "I might be stating the obvious, but for God's sake be careful. Don't ever go together to the hideout. Just make sure that you all know what's going on and find a way of letting each other know that all's well every day at a set time. We can't afford a cock up at this stage; with no one listening to the radio."

"Don't worry," said Julia, "We'll sort out a system." "Good," replied Henry, "I'll make sure that Charlie is always close by in the village and not out with the rest of us on distant operations."

"Right," said Julia as she stood up to go, "I'd better get on with it then… I don't… don't… I really…"

Julia felt odd and suddenly the room started to spin. She felt sick and reached out for the back of the nearest chair as her legs started to give way. Henry was up in a flash and managed to grab her as she started to collapse. Mrs Clay joined him, and between them, they managed to get Julia back into a chair.

Mrs Clay held on to Julia and spoke gently. "Put your head down between your legs my love. You'll feel better then. I bet you haven't eaten properly today, have you?"

Julia did as she was told and stared at the floor as Henry fetched a glass of water.

After a couple of minutes, she started to feel better and gradually sat back upright.

Henry handed her the glass of water and she sipped the water slowly.

"That's better," she said, "I'm sorry about that. I don't know what came over me?"

"Get her one of those sweet biscuits that I've been saving," said Mrs Clay, pointing towards the pantry.

Henry fetched the biscuits as Mrs Clay pulled a chair in and sat close to Julia, putting a comforting arm around her as she did so.

"You are a poor old love," she said as Henry handed Julia a biscuit, "but you'll be as right as ninepence in a minute."

After a while, Julia said, "I'm feeling fine now. I'd better get on."

"You don't have to rush," replied Henry, "Are you sure you're alright?"

"Yes," said Julia as she stood again, "See, I've got my balance back now."

They walked together to the front door, and after saying their goodbyes, Julia turned back, leaned in, and whispered to Mrs Clay, "I'm three months pregnant. I'm carrying Joseph's baby."

Chapter 9

GONE TO GROUND

At just after ten o'clock on the evening of 15th November 1940, German soldiers kicked at the door of number 7, Rose Green.

The Browns both jumped up from the kitchen table and Jack grabbed his coat from the back of the chair and immediately ran out through the back door.

Janet ran towards the stairs as the front door finally gave way and flew open. She screamed and pushed herself against the wall of the hallway as two soldiers pushed their way past her, into the front room and the kitchen. Two more ran upstairs, bursting into the two small bedrooms.

Jack was long gone. He was down the garden path and over the back fence well before the sergeant opened the back door and peered out into the darkness.

"Where's your husband?" shouted the sergeant.

"I don't know!" sobbed Janet, "He went to the pub about an hour ago and hasn't come home yet."

The Sergeant stepped nearer to her, and leaned in closer,

so that his head was almost touching hers.

"We'll find him!" he whispered in her ear, and then abruptly, turned and marched back out through the front door. His men followed, leaving the broken front door swinging on its hinges.

Slowly, and desperately trying to control her emotions, Janet moved towards the door and pushed it shut, jamming a splintered piece of wood against it to hold it closed. She looked up the stairs to see her two children sitting next to each other on a step near the top. She smiled at them and waved for them to come down. Together they walked to the kitchen where they stood hugging each other. Janet stared out into the night through the window, tears running down her cheeks.

"Run Jack! Run!" she said under her breath.

Earlier in 1940, with the very real threat of Hitler's Operation Sealion invasion plans of Britain, Winston Churchill instructed the War Office to set up special Auxiliary Units to create an effective British Resistance force. These men and women were recruited from the existing Home Guard and given special training. Hideouts were dug and constructed all over the country, especially in coastal areas where it was most likely that invasion would come. Most of these hideouts were built on private land, away from public gaze, and were known only by the men of the special Auxiliary Units. They were well equipped; being issued with Thompson sub-machine guns before the regular army had them. Churchill's idea was that, should there be an invasion, these men would go to ground and harry the enemy wherever they could. It was never intended that the Auxiliary Units should face the invading forces head on; their numbers were too few to do that. Their value would be in causing the maximum amount of damage to the German supply lines, fuel depots and transport systems, including railway lines and bridges. Their hide-outs were essential; not only as a place to keep their stores, including food, but as a place of refuge between attacks. The life expectancy of the men in the Auxiliary Units was expected to be very short. They all knew that it wouldn't be long before their hiding places were discovered.

Jack Brown knew exactly where he was headed. It was easy to get out from the village in the dark, and within ten minutes, he was on its outskirts. At the end of Lye Lane, he stopped and leaned against a chestnut fence that ran along its edge. He was breathing heavily and sweating and it took some time for him to calm down. He stood in the pitch dark and listened to the sounds of the November evening. It was relatively warm and a gentle breeze rustled the few remaining leaves of the beech trees that stood on the other side of the lane. A dog barked a long way off in the distance, the breeze dropped momentarily, and there was total silence.

After another minute, Jack turned and made his way along the lane. About two hundred yards further along, he stopped and listened once more, then deciding that there was no one around, he stepped into the woods. He could hardly see where he was going, but he knew the rough pathway through the trees well enough and he made good progress. After fifteen minutes of hard walking, he came to a small grassy clearing, where a cock pheasant clattered out, squawking its alarm call as it flew up and away from a low branch where it had been roosting. For a split second, Jack jumped and his heart missed a beat. Throughout his forty years, living and working on the farms and in the woods around Watersham, he was regularly startled by pheasants and other game birds such as snipe and woodcock suddenly flying out from their hiding places. He had never got used to it; they made him jump every time. He stood still again, listening to the pheasant as it settled again deeper in the woods. Jack took several deep breaths and looked up between the great trees to the open black sky at the twinkling stars. He stared at them for a long time and then found himself thinking of his wife Janet and their kids. He hoped that they were alright and that the soldiers had left them alone. He hoped that he would be able to see them again soon, but he knew that would be too risky for a while. He thanked God that he hadn't said anything to Janet about the hide-out in the woods or the Auxiliary Unit to which he belonged. If she didn't know about it, she wouldn't have to try to lie if things turned nasty. He was sure that none of the other men in the Unit would have said anything to their families or friends either; even their friends in the Home Guard never knew what the Auxiliaries got up to.

He moved forward again. Walking wasn't so easy now, as the land began to rise as it ran into the South Downs. The woods here had been thinned some years before, leaving more space between the trees. The light from a half-moon, though weak, was strong enough to filter through the branches, so that Jack could see a little more clearly the way ahead. He walked on for a further ten minutes, purposefully changing direction and zigzagging between the trees, so as not to follow or leave a clear path. He knew that he was close to his destination as in the dim light, he could see the ancient earth bank boundary ahead. On reaching the entrance to the hideout he stood still and listened for a while and after satisfying himself that there was no one else around, he reached through the branches that camouflaged the doorway and gently lifted the wooden hatch. With it only a few inches open, a faint glow of orange light escaped from the opening and Jack, in shock, immediately dropped the lid. Inside the hideout, Julia froze, as she heard the hatch drop. She soon recovered her senses, removed her headset, turned off the radio and turned the wick right down on the oil lamp until its flame extinguished and the room was in complete darkness. She felt for the desk drawer, located the revolver that she knew was there, lifted it and released the safety catch.

Jack hurried around to the other side of the earth bank, wondering all the time who might be inside. He also wondered which way it would be best to run if someone suddenly emerged from the main entrance, especially as he wasn't armed. In thinking that, he remembered that there was an emergency exit from the hideout, that came out further along the earth bank. Jack retreated back into the woods, far enough away to give himself a head start in case there was trouble, but still close enough so that he could observe.

Julia felt her way along the cold walls until she came to the tunnel that led to the emergency exit. She knew that it was there; they all did. The few people that knew about the hideout, had all familiarised themselves with its layout. They had all practised in the dark escaping from the emergency exit, for just such an occasion as this; but no one ever thought that they would have to do it. She knelt down, and with the revolver firmly in her grip, but with the safety catch back on, she worked her way on her hands and knees along the tunnel. She was frightened. She realised that she was in a dreadful position. If the enemy was outside, she wouldn't stand a chance, but she was fully committed now and to turn back would be even more dangerous. On reaching the exit, she pushed back some of the brush wood that had been purposefully piled up to hide the opening, and listened. Nothing. No voices. No footsteps. She pushed more of the branches and twigs away and slowly poked her head out. Still nothing. She eased herself fully out and crouched by the exit looking all around, and then, risking everything, on her hands and knees, made her way to the base of the nearest beech tree, swung around behind it and peered back towards the hideout. All was still.

Jack watched all of this, half in amazement and half in fear. It was too dark to make out who it was, but he felt more confident now that it was one of his colleagues. But he couldn't be sure. Jack and Julia were only about twenty five yards apart. They both stayed motionless for several minutes, until Julia decided to risk standing up. After another minute, she stepped out from behind the tree, looking all around and with the revolver pointed straight ahead and the safety catch off. She took very slow steps back towards the hideout and every now and then she stopped, listened and checked all around for movement. As she moved closer to the hideout, it suddenly dawned on Jack who this mysterious figure was. He nearly called out her name straight away, but remembering that she was holding a revolver, he thought better of it. Instead, he ducked back behind the trunk of the great beech tree and quietly stood up. Once he was sure that he was completely out of Julia's line of fire behind the tree, he called her name. "Julia!"

Julia jumped, nearly pulled the trigger of her revolver and dropped to the ground.

"Who's that?" she called back, aiming the gun in the general direction of where she thought that the voice had come from.

"It's Jack," he said, "If you'll put the gun down, I'll show myself."

"Come out you idiot!" she replied, "What the hell are you doing out here at this time of night? You frightened me half to death."

Jack stepped out from his hiding place, but realised immediately that Julia was still pointing the revolver straight at him. He stopped and put his arms out.

"Julia," he said, "Could you put the gun away please?" "Yes; I'm sorry," she replied, "I forgot."

She lowered the revolver and pushed the safety catch back on. Jack walked up to her and threw his arms around her.

"Bloody hell," he said, "That was all a bit scary." "Scary is hardly the word," replied Julia, "I thought I'd had it. Why are you here?"

"I might ask you the same question," said Jack.

"You know very well why I'm here," she replied, "I have to make radio contact with HQ at set times. You know; to let them know what's happening in our sector and to take and pass on orders."

"Yes, I know all that," said Jack, "I just didn't expect anyone to be here."

"So why are you here?" repeated Julia.

"I'm on the run," replied Jack, "Soldiers came to our house about an hour ago. I got out the back door by the skin of my teeth and made my way up here. I thought that I'd stay here tonight and then decide what to do in the morning. I daren't go back home, or to a friends' house."

"What about your wife and children?" said Julia. "Are they safe?"

Jack looked at the ground. "I don't know. I hope to God they're alright."

"Don't worry Jack. I'll check on them first thing in the morning and get a message to you to let you know that they're okay."

They walked back to the main entrance to the hideout and Julia handed the revolver to Jack.

"Put this back in the drawer, will you? I'm sure you won't need it." said Julia, "There's matches for the lamp in the drawer and please don't touch the radio. It's a bugger to tune in if others mess about with it. I think that you know where everything else is: water, food, blankets and the rest. I need to get home. Have a good night and I'll get word to you in the morning."

"Yes, thanks Julia. Keep your wits about you on your way home."

Julia patted Jack on his arm and set off back through the woods. He watched her walk away until her outline merged with the trees and she disappeared into the night. He lifted the hatch and stepped down into the hideout, closing the hatch tightly behind him. The room smelt of paraffin and it was pitch black. From memory he felt his way to the desk, opened the drawer, placed the revolver carefully in it and found the matches. He felt across the desk top, found the oil lamp and struck a match. As the orange light of the lamp came to life, he looked around the room. It was going to be a long night.

Jack slept fitfully; tossing and turning in the dark of the hideout. Coping with the cold wasn't too bad, because he had plenty of blankets, but the rough wooden slatted bed was hard and the air was damp and stale. After hours of disturbed sleep, he couldn't stand it any longer, and stood with one of the blankets draped over his shoulders. He felt his way to the ladder, carefully climbed the first few steps, stopped and listened, and hearing nothing unusual, he slowly opened the hatchway. It was still very dark outside, but nowhere near as dark as the inside of the hideout. He took several deep breaths of fresh cold air and climbed out onto the earth bank, walked away from the hideout, and was pleased to be able to stretch his legs. Feeling slightly better, he took out his pocket watch and held it up near to his face, tilting it slightly to catch what little light there was. 04:45.

"Jesus," he muttered to himself, "It's still the middle of the bloody night!"

He pulled up his jacket collar, pulled the blanket tighter around his shoulders and walked amongst the beech trees. He stopped every now and then and listened. During his early training with the other hand-picked Auxiliaries, as well as all the weapons training, they had been taught something about survival techniques. Jack knew how important it was to listen. He, along with most of his friends had grown up in the small villages and on the farms in this area. They knew every sound that had its place in the woods, the fields, on the Downs and all through the countryside. If there was any noise out of place, they would be alert to it immediately. For twenty minutes or so he walked under the trees, thinking about his wife and children, and wondering how they would manage without him. He had already accepted that it would be too dangerous to go back and he was thinking of how he might be able to get them out and away to the north. He knew that was the direction that he would have to go in the morning. As soon as he got news from Julia, he would be off. Checking around once more, he made his way back to the hideout.

At 07:50, Julia knocked on the hatchway, stepped back and waited. It was lighter now; a breeze was gathering strength and dark clouds moved threateningly across the early morning sky. Jack, holding the revolver with its safety catch off, slid the hatch back.

"It's me again," called Julia quietly.

Jack pushed the catch back with his right thumb, tucked the revolver into his jacket pocket and stepped out into the fresh air.

"Morning Julia," he said as he walked up to her. "What's the news?"

"Don't worry," she said, "Janet and the children are fine. The soldiers haven't been back. I got to see her about an hour ago. I told her that I had seen you and that you were okay."

"Thanks Julia," replied Jack, "I've been worried sick... hardly slept a wink all night... I'll have to get them out as soon as I can."

"Yes, but you need to think of yourself first," said Julia.

"I know," replied Jack, "I'm going to see if I can get through to our forces on the other side first. Then I'll find a safe place for us and come back for Janet and the children. Can you get a message to her for me? Tell her I'm alright and tell her to pack some personal things, but only essential things, and be ready to leave at a moment's notice. I don't know exactly when I'll be back, but it'll be soon. Tell her to be ready and tell her I love her."

"I'll tell Janet all that," replied Julia. "Are you ready to go now?"

Jack pulled the revolver out from his coat and handed it to Julia.

"Put this back for me, will you?" he said.

"Of course. And here, I've brought some sweet tea for you." she said as she handed a bottle to him.

"Ah, good. That'll keep me going for a while."

They stood and looked at each other for a moment and then Jack put his arms around Julia, hugged her, pulled away and then said, "Right; I'm off. Stay safe Julia."

"You too." she said.

Julia watched him until his outline was lost against the dark trees. The wind whistled through the tops of the beech trees and Julia looked up at the scudding clouds. Looking around to check that there was on-one watching; she quickly made her way back into the hideout and carefully laid the revolver back in its place. A minute later, she was back outside. The first drops of rain were just beginning to fall as she set off back to the village.

Jack made good headway for nearly two hours, not seeing anyone, keeping to the deer and badger tracks that ran through the beech and larch woods that covered this part of the South Downs. In most places, the pathways ran in straight lines, and every now and then they crossed, so he had to decide which one to choose. Having lived all his life in the area, he had an instinctive sense of direction, rarely deviating from the best route north. He had already skirted the villages of Eartham and Upwaltham and was following a steep path adjacent to the Duncton Hill road, when he heard the unmistakable sound of trucks. He stopped, listened and then edged forwards through the trees until he was close enough to the road to see what was going on. A few empty

German troop trucks were moving slowly up the hill and heading south. Queuing down the hill and heading north was a long column of German army vehicles: troop trucks pulling artillery pieces, light tanks and a number of staff cars and motorbikes. Jack moved slightly closer, taking cover behind a holly tree. He watched for some time as the column of vehicles moved unhurriedly down the hill, and then stooping low, he made his way back deeper into the relative safety of the woods. He kept up a steady pace travelling east for a while and then turned north again to skirt around Petworth.

As he walked, he wondered about the German vehicles and troops that he had just seen. They must be moving up to the front line to get ready for another push against our forces. Jack knew from recent intelligence reports that the British Army was dug in along an east-west line that ran near to Guildford. That was where he was headed.

Jack cut across the parkland to the north of the town, staying under the cover of the oak woods that ran along the side of the Guildford Road. Every now and then, staying well under cover, he moved closer to the road, to see what was going on. There were German Army vehicles everywhere. He stopped for a rest and looked at his watch. It was two o'clock already. There was at least 20 miles to go and he knew that he wouldn't be able to cover the remaining distance before dark; not that he knew exactly where he would find British troops. He had long finished the tea that Julia had given him and he was now hungry and very thirsty. He would have to risk asking a local for some food, before finding a suitable barn where he could sleep for the night. He was dog tired now and wondered how much longer to keep going. He decided it would be best to stop well before dark.

At just before five, he came across a lane that led away from the main road. Walking parallel to it, he came to a meadow being grazed by a large flock of South Downs sheep. The sheep looked up at him as he stepped over the fence into their field. He kept close to the tall hazel hedge that separated the field from the lane, as the sheep started to gather behind him. By the time he reached the corner of the field, climbed back over the fence, and made it back under cover of an over-mature hazel coppice, most of the sheep had gathered in a tight group near to where he had left the field, staring after him. Looking back at the flock, he was cross with himself for his mistake. He realised that anyone who saw the way that the sheep had suddenly crossed the field, would know that someone was on the move.

"I hope no one was watching," he muttered to himself.

Five minutes later he came across a small farmhouse, set back fifty yards from the lane, with a number of ramshackle outbuildings to one side. The whole place had an uncared for look about it. The chestnut rail fence running around the property was rotten and broken in several places, the garden was overgrown and the dark green paint was peeling from the woodwork of the house. Jack hesitated for a while, but then headed down the pathway to the front door and knocked. He leaned in closer to the door and listened and hearing no response; he knocked again. He was about to turn away to see if there was anyone out by the outbuildings, when he heard movement. The door opened very slowly to reveal a very elderly woman leaning on a walking stick.

"Yes?" she said in a surprisingly strong voice. "What do you want?"

"Sorry to bother you madam. I wondered if you would mind if I took shelter in one of your outbuildings tonight? I've been walking for most of the day."

The old woman edged slightly further forward and looked beyond Jack, towards the lane.

"Anybody else with you?" she said, still looking around. "Where have you come from?"

"No. I'm on my own. I've come from Watersham."

"Watersham you say? Watersham near Arundel? That's a

mighty long way to walk. Why are you walking all this way? Are you in trouble young man?"

For a few seconds, Jack wondered how to reply, but trusting his instincts, he decided to tell the truth and hope for the best.

"It's a long story. I'm on the run from the Germans." "Guessed you might be," said the woman as she took a couple of small steps back. "I expect you could do with a cup of tea. You'd better come in."

Jack couldn't believe his luck.

"That's very good of you!" he said. "Are you sure you don't mind?"

"I won't ask again. Now; are you coming in or not?"

Jack stepped into the hallway, closed the door behind him, and followed her down the passageway to the kitchen. The room had a strong odour of wood smoke mixed with the unmistakable scent of warm dogs and a very pleasant smell of slow cooking. Sitting in a winged chair to one side of the jet-black kitchen range was an elderly man and next to him, in a wide basket, was a very old sheep dog who looked up at Jack through cloudy eyes as it wagged its tail.

"Look what I found on the doorstep George," said the old woman.

"Who is it?" replied her husband without looking at Jack. "I'm not entirely sure." she said. "Did you say what your name was young man?"

"It's Jack." he said, "Jack Brown. I live in Watersham with my family."

"Well Jack Brown," replied the old woman, "You'd best sit down and tell us all about it. I'm Rose Clarke and this is my husband George. Pull yourself up a chair and I'll make some tea. You'll need to speak up as George can't hear so well these days. Don't mind our dog Jim; he's harmless. Pretty much completely blind now and his hearing isn't too good either."

Jack pulled out one of the chairs from next to the kitchen table and positioned it near to George, facing the warm range. He noticed as he did so, a big brown kettle gently steaming away, and next to it, a large black lidded pot, also steaming, from which the mouth-watering smells of cooking were emanating. He guessed that it was some sort of game stew.

"Well, as I say," started Jack, "I had to get out from Watersham a bit quick yesterday when German soldiers came to our house."

"You don't need to tell us why they're after you," said Rose as she reached for the kettle, "I think we can guess that bit and it's probably best if you don't tell us."

Rose poured steaming water into a teapot on the kitchen table and put the kettle back on the range, this time, placing it on a back plate.

Jack carried on, "So, I got away as fast as I could when they came knocking and spent last night in the woods. I've spent all day today making my way here. I've kept away from the roads as much as possible as there's been lots of German vehicles on the move today. Have you seen any activity around here?"

"No. Not down this lane," replied Rose, "but we know there's been a lot going on today. Old Arthur Spriggs, the local gamekeeper, told us this afternoon when he dropped in."

Rose poured the tea and passed the cups and saucers across to Jack and George. Jack blew on the steaming tea and took a sip. It was too hot to drink.

"Please could I have a glass of water too?"

"Of course, of course."

Rose fetched a glass of water and Jack gulped it down. "Another?" she said.

"Yes please."

Rose refilled the glass and she watched Jack as he drank the water more slowly this time.

George shifted in his chair. "So, you're from Watersham

you say."

Jack took a sip of tea. "Yes, I've lived there all my life. Do you know it?"

"Yes, I know it very well. I used to go down there fairly regular; sometimes twice a month. A lot of the cattle and sheep farmers around here used to buy straw from the cereal farmers down your way. See, the land up here's not good enough to grow cereals. We always have to buy in straw for our animals."

For the next thirty minutes, they drank tea and exchanged news and gossip. Jack was careful not to say too much more about his own circumstances. He realised, that without thinking, he had already said enough. After all, although Rose and George seemed genuine enough, you could never tell these days where a careless word might lead.

George occasionally had something more to say, but for the most part, he just smiled and sipped his tea. Every few minutes, Rose lifted the lid on the simmering pot, and gave the contents a stir. Jack's stomach rumbled as the aroma from the cooking filled the room. Rose prepared cabbage, carrots and potatoes and placed them in various sized pots on the range. Twenty minutes later, Rose laid the table, and shortly after, they sat down to eat. The game stew was a mixture of venison, pheasant and rabbit.

"Wow, this is good! It reminds me of my mum's cooking when we were kids."

"You can't beat a bit of country grub," mumbled George.

When they had finished, Rose said. "I'm afraid there's no pudding."

"Don't worry about that!" replied Jack, "That stew was more than enough for me. You've been very kind. I really appreciate your hospitality."

"So," said Rose, "you'll need a bed for the night."

"Oh no. Please. I don't want to put you out anymore. I'd be more than happy to sleep in one of your barns."

"Well that would be silly wouldn't it, given that there's a perfectly good bed going spare upstairs. It's our son's old room."

"You're too kind," said Jack, "Where's your son now?"

There was a sudden and prolonged silence and Jack instantly knew what the answer was going to be.

George eventually spoke quietly and slowly. "He was lost at Dunkirk."

"Yes," said Rose, "He was one of the unlucky ones. He never made it off the beach." Rose walked over to George and put her hand on his shoulder. "He was a Captain you know. Captain Peter Clarke, Royal Sussex Regiment. That's him there." she said, pointing to a large framed photo that hung on the wall.

"They say he was trying to help a group of his men get into a rowing boat, to get to one of the ships, when they were all hit by a bomb dropped by a Stuka bomber. I don't suppose he knew much about it. I don't think he suffered."

George, with tears forming in his eyes, looked up at his wife and patted her hand. Jim looked up at them both and uttered a soft whimper. There was silence for a moment as Rose made her way across to the kitchen sink.

"I'm so sorry," said Jack. "I'm sorry for your loss. We've lost too many good people already and I wonder how many more we will lose before this is all over?"

"I saw it all the first time around," said George, "Those bloody trenches... bloody machine guns..."

Rose walked quickly back to where George sat and placed an arm around him.

"There, there," she said softly, "Don't you fret now my love. It's alright. I'm here."

Jack watched them for a while and then stood up and walked over to have a closer look at the photo of Captain Peter Clarke, looking very smart in his soldier's uniform.

"A fine-looking man," he said.

"Yes," replied Rose, "He was a good son, a good soldier and a good Dad. Our daughter-in-law and their two boys live over at Midhurst. We see them quite often. They're both the spitting image of their Dad."

"I'm so pleased you've got the grandchildren," said Jack as he walked back to his chair. "They must be a great comfort to you."

"They are. They certainly are," replied Rose.

For the next hour or two, Rose and Jack talked about farming and how things had changed since the outbreak of war. George joined in briefly every now and then, but mostly he was concerned with keeping an eye on the fire, feeding it with a fresh log every now and then, and constantly stroking and reassuring Jim.

Just before ten o'clock, Jack looked up at the kitchen clock. "Well, if you don't mind, I'd like to get off to bed. I've just about run out of steam."

Rose stood. "Follow me. I'll point you in the right direction. You'll need a candle."

She collected a candle from the sideboard, placed it into a holder and lit it. They walked down the corridor. "There's a toilet and wash basin in here," she said, pointing to a door off to one side. "Your bedroom is the one to the left at the top of the stairs."

Rose handed the candle to Jack. "Goodnight." he said, "And thanks again for supper and your kindness."

"It's been no trouble to us." replied Rose. "Goodnight." Jack found his way to the bedroom, removed his outer clothes, slid under the covers and was fast asleep within two minutes.

At 6:00 o'clock the next morning, Jack awoke and lay completely still for some time, listening to distant sounds coming from the fields and woods nearby. Pigeons were cooing somewhere close to the house and a pair of blackbirds were calling to each other further away. About twenty minutes went by as he listened and half dozed in his comfortable bed, not wanting to stir, until he heard the unmistakable sounds of footsteps on the stairs. Mr and Mrs Clarke were making their way downstairs for breakfast. Jack got out from his warm bed and instantly felt the coldness of the bedroom. He pulled back the curtains, and quickly got dressed in the semi-darkness.

"Good morning," he said, as he walked into the kitchen.

George was already riddling the fire and Rose was filling the kettle with fresh water from a large white enamel jug.

"Good morning to you," they said in unison, "Sleep well?"

"Like a log," replied Jack.

"Good," said Rose. "Fancy some breakfast?"

Chapter 10

THE FRONT LINE

Jack enjoyed his fried breakfast with Mr & Mrs Clarke. It reminded him of his childhood growing up with his family in the cottage next to the farm where his dad worked. The breakfast itself, the soft warmth of the kitchen, the steam blowing from the spout of the black kettle on the kitchen range and the taste of strong, sweet, milky tea; it was exactly as it used to be. As he drained his cup he wondered if this way of life was coming to an end. Regardless of the outcome of the war, he was fairly sure that nothing was ever going to be the same again.

Old Jim stirred in his basket by the range and George turned and spoke softly to him.

"That's alright old fella… We're all here. There's a good boy… Nothing to worry about..."

"You're a great comfort to him," said Jack.

"And him to us," replied George. "I don't know what we'll do when the time comes, and he – and he – you know…" His voice trailed off as he leaned down to give Jim a gentle stroke behind his ears. Rose walked over and stood behind his chair. As he straightened himself up again, she patted him on his shoulders, leaned down and kissed him on his head.

Jack looked on and smiled.

For several minutes they were all silent and then Jack spoke. "Well," he said, "It's been good to meet you and thanks for looking after me so well. You've really spoilt me, but I need to get moving again. I need to be on my way."

"Yes, of course," replied Rose, "You've things to do. We mustn't be holding you up any longer."

"Oh, believe me," said Jack as he stood and pushed his chair back, "I'd rather stay here with you; but as you say – there's things to be done."

Jack helped George and Rose clear the breakfast things from the table, unhooked his coat and bag from behind the kitchen door, bent down and stroked old Jim, and made his way to the front door. They said their goodbyes quickly and Jack turned and called back to them as he set off. "Thanks again. I'll come back to see you again when this is all over." George and Rose stood and waved and watched until Jack had disappeared into the greens and the browns of the woods.

Jack felt content. He had slept and eaten well and been in the company of good people. Now he needed to focus again on the job in hand. The closer that he got to Guildford, the closer he would get to the front line and the more likely it was that he would run into the enemy. He didn't know these woods, but they were familiar enough. They were typical of most woods in this part of the world; predominantly mature beech and oak trees, but with a sprinkling of ash and every now and then a small stand of hazel. As in the woods at home, occasionally there was a solitary old yew tree; a survivor through the centuries.

He felt comfortable and safe here. He trusted his senses.

There were no sounds of vehicles on the move, so he was fairly certain there was no road nearby. No smell of wood smoke. In fact, there were no signs of human activity at all, only the sight, sounds and smells of the countryside.

Jack walked on for several miles with not much change to his surroundings; but, as the land fell away slightly, the soil on the pathway changed to a lighter colour, looking more like sand. A little further on, the tree cover changed significantly. The heavy beech woods gave way, first to ash and then to more open heathland, with widely spaced silver birch and gorse bushes. Jack stopped walking for a while, taking in his new surroundings. He wasn't used to this sort of countryside and he felt suddenly uncomfortable and uncertain. He squatted down on the pathway for a while, and then, having thought things through, crouching, he made his way back to the relative safety of the woods. He stopped and looked back out across the heathland ahead, wondering what to do. After a while, he moved off to his right, skirting the heathland and staying well under the cover of the trees.

An hour later, he had reached the other side of the heath, where the land rose up again, and there was a large over mature stand of hazel trees. Jack followed a deer track that led deep into the plantation, always taking care to keep broadly to a northerly direction. On reaching the far side, he came across a small meadow where half a dozen beef cattle were grazing. The nearest, lifted its head to acknowledge him, and then, deciding that he did not pose a threat, immediately returned to grazing. The other cattle didn't seem to have noticed him. He stood watching for a while and studying the farmstead on the far side of the meadow. He could see two middle-aged men mucking out some pens on the side of the main barn. Jack ducked back under full cover and moved back into the hazel plantation, walking slowly towards the farmstead. When he was level with the farm buildings, he moved in as close as he dared and watched and listened. He could hear the two men talking as they worked, but he wasn't close enough to hear what they were saying. He backed into the plantation again and walked further along until he could clearly see beyond the barn. There appeared to be no one else around and about fifty yards further along, he could see a pair of farm cottages. Some of the windows were open and he could see smoke rising gently from both chimneys. He guessed that the men's wives were busy about their work inside. He continued to watch for some time and then worked his way back to have another look at what they were doing. He was fairly sure that there was no one else about and decided to show himself. He had only made a few paces into the open, when the bark of a dog alerted the men that someone was approaching. The collie ducked under the fence and made its way cautiously towards him, as if it was approaching a stray sheep. The gaze of both men followed the dog to see Jack advancing towards them. Jack waved at the men as the collie stopped two paces from him. They leaned on their forks, looking directly at him.

"He won't bite! Where did you come from then?" called out one of the men.

"Is it alright if I come over?"

The dog lay down, his head tilted to one side, looking straight up into Jack's eyes.

"Come on then," said the other man.

As he started forward again, he bent down to stroke the dog, but it backed away and watched him as he walked towards the fence, pushing the barbed wire down and stepping over. The dog followed him closely and ducked back under the fence and ran around to sit between the two men.

Jack held his hand out to the first man. "My name's Jack."

Harry Matthews wiped his hand on his corduroy trousers and shook Jack's hand.

"I'm Harry. Where are you from then?"

Before Jack could answer, the other man stepped forward

and offered his hand to Jack. "We're brothers. I'm Arthur."

"I need to get to Guildford," said Jack, "I'm headed for the front line. How much further is it?"

"You're on the right track alright," replied Harry, "Keep going straight on," he said, pointing towards the north, "And you'll run straight into it. That's if you can get that far."

"It's that difficult is it?"

"Yes," said Harry, "About one mile further on there's German troops everywhere, and all the way up to Guildford." Arthur tugged at Harry's sleeve. "We ought to go inside," he said.

"Yes," replied Harry, looking around. "He's right. Come on. Let's go into the barn."

Harry and Arthur leaned their forks against the brick sided barn, opened one of the great wooden doors, and made their way through. Jack and the dog followed on. Arthur pulled the door to. It was almost dark inside, but rays of light broke through the cracks in the timbers of the doors and through some of the brick air vents half way up the tall sides of the barn.

"We have to be careful," said Arthur, "You never know who's watching."

"I know," replied Jack immediately, "That's why I'm on the run. That's why I'm here. They nearly caught me in Watersham two days ago. I need to get through to our lot on the other side."

"Right," said Harry, "But it won't be easy. I reckon it's fifty-fifty whether anyone gets through or not. They're watching every road and every little track. A lot of men won't risk it you know."

As Harry finished speaking, the dog turned and walked quickly towards the doors, gently grumbling as he went.

"What is it Jim?" said Arthur as he turned to follow the dog. He stopped by the doors and peered through a crack in the timber to see what had alerted the dog.

"It's alright," he said. "It's just Alice, my wife. It looks like she's dropped a bucket by the back door."

The three men chatted about what they knew was going on in their respective areas and how the locals were coping. "How often do you come across the Germans?" asked Jack.

"Down here on the farm?" replied Harry as he looked for confirmation from his brother, "Not very often; just the occasional patrol. It's completely different about a mile away on the main road that leads to the village. The road and the local villages are crawling with them. I'm told that, as you get closer to Guildford, it's even worse. There are thousands of them camped in the woods. Tanks, heavy artillery and everything…"

"So how close are our troops?"

"We don't rightly know. Probably on an east-west line near Guildford I expect. From what we hear, the Germans control most of Kent and Sussex and parts of Surrey. I don't think that they're into Hampshire to the west, nor further north than Guildford this way."

"That's pretty much what we think. So what's my best plan then?"

Harry leaned down to stroke the dog, who was leaning against his legs, looked across at his brother, and then straight at Jack.

"Well, it's far too dangerous to even think about crossing over during the day time, but at night you'd have a better chance. Mind you, you'll need help finding the best pathways."

"Yes," said Arthur, "You won't find your way in the middle of the night through the woods. You'll need us to show you the way."

"Would you do that though? I mean, show me the way during the night?"

Harry and Arthur looked at each other and then turned and smiled at Jack.

"Course we will," they said in unison.

"Well that's, that's just… Would tonight be too soon?"
"There's no point in waiting." replied Arthur.

"Right. Tonight, it is then," said Jack.

"I'll tell you what." said Harry, "Give us a hand with a few odd jobs around the farm this afternoon and then we'll all have some supper, have a bit of a rest and then we'll plan to set off just after midnight."

"Sounds good to me," replied Jack, "What do we need to do first?"

"Let's get the trailer loaded up with straw," said Arthur, "We need to change the bedding in the pig sties tomorrow."

The three men soon had the trailer loaded and moved on to other routine jobs around the farm. After checking that all the chickens were in their coops and that doors were firmly locked, Arthur stopped, pulled out his pocket watch and nodded.

"That's enough for today. It's just coming up to five o'clock."

The men and the dog walked slowly back towards the farm cottages.

On reaching the first cottage, Arthur and Harry loosened their boot laces and kicked them off. Jack followed suit, they all removed their caps and went inside.

Alice and Margaret were busy working at the kitchen table and both stood as the men entered.

"Let me introduce you to our better halves," smiled Arthur, "This is my wife Alice and this is Harry's wife Margaret. Say hello to Jack ladies."

"Pleased to meet you." they both said.

"I'm very pleased to meet you too," replied Jack, "Excuse me if I don't shake your hands. I'm a bit mucky from the farm work."

Alice and Margaret sat back down again and continued with their work.

"What's for supper tonight then ladies?" asked Arthur.

"Rabbit pie," replied Alice.

"You've struck lucky Jack!" said Harry, "They make a lovely rabbit pie."

The men went off to the scullery to wash their hands. "Let's go in the other room," suggested Arthur, "and I'll light the fire. You go on in and I'll fetch some kindling." Once the fire was well under way, the men chatted about everyday matters. The weather and the difficulties that the brothers had in getting in the last of the harvest when it rained every day for three weeks. They talked about how life used to be. They talked about boys who they'd gone to school with and grown up with, some of whom had joined the regular army at the beginning of the war and some who'd crossed over since. As the Germans had tightened up controls in the area, hardly anything had been heard from any of the men during the last few months.

"It's the not knowing," said Arthur as he put a couple of larger pieces of wood on the fire, "There's half the households around here that don't know whether their sons are alive or dead. It's very hard on the families. I think it's worse for the mothers."

"It's the same in Watersham," said Jack. "And on top of everything else, you don't know what's going to happen next. You're not sure who to trust and the Germans seem to be everywhere. We've lost some good people – too many."

The men sat quietly again, staring into the fire. After a while, Arthur spoke again.

"We need to talk about our plans for tonight. There's a few things we ought to get straight before we set off; you know… in case things go wrong."

"Right," replied Jack, "I realise this is very dangerous. Not just for me, but for you and your families as well. You don't have to help me you know. I'm quite prepared to go it alone if I have to... and I…"

"No, no," interrupted Harry, "That's all settled. We're

going to help you get across. We want to. We need to. We have to do something to help turn the tide."

"That's right," added Arthur, "Let's talk about what we're going to do tonight. Let's talk about getting you across to the other side."

"After supper," continued Arthur, "we'll all get an early night. At just after midnight, we'll set off through the woods and skirt around the village. It should take us about an hour to get to Forest Road. That's the road that runs east west, about a mile to the north of the village. Assuming that we don't run into any patrols before then, that'll be our first hurdle. We hear that's where they have a lot of heavy armour parked up. Tanks, field guns and everything, as well as troop trucks. The soldiers are camped all around apparently; in the fields, down both sides of the road. Getting through there is going to be tricky, but I've got a few ideas."

Jack sat forward. "Will you be armed?"

"Definitely not!" replied Arthur sharply, "That would be a big mistake. The only things that we will be carrying will be back packs with dead rabbits and snare wires in them. That way if we get stopped, they will see that we're just a few locals doing a bit of poaching in the middle of the night. They'll probably take the rabbits off of us; but hopefully, that'll be the worst that'll happen. We've got a few rabbits that we caught yesterday evening, hanging up in the lean-to, out the back. We'll take them with us."

"That's a great idea," replied Jack, "I've done a bit of poaching myself over the years. In fact, as a boy, me and my mates used to spend hours out on the Downs catching rabbits. There used to be millions of 'em. There were so many, that they kept hundreds of acres of grass nibbled and mown down as good as the grass on a cricket wicket."

"Yes," said Harry, "There's still loads around here. We catch a lot. It's good meat. I expect the Germans catch plenty too."

"Anyway," interrupted Arthur, "that's part of the plan. Before we go to bed tonight, we'll put the rabbits and snares in our packs."

"How do you reckon we'll get through the German lines then?" said Jack.

"There's a bridge at one point. It's where a stream goes under the road. I don't remember what it's called. We used to go there sometimes with our cousins. Do you remember Harry? We used to catch tadpoles there."

"I certainly do," replied Harry, "We used to spend many a happy hour there. I can even remember what the curved brickwork under the arch of the bridge looked like."

"And if we get stopped. What if they don't like our story about the poaching?"

"We'll have to play that by ear," replied Arthur. "Just stick to the story about the poaching though, and if we have to make a run for it, it'll be best to run sooner rather than later. Don't wait until they've got us in the back of a truck. It'll be too late then. If we have to run, it'll be best if we split up. It'll be a lot more difficult for them trying to catch us if we split up; especially in the woods in the dark. There's a good chance we'd make it back here."

"I think you're right," said Jack, "But let's say we get safely through under the bridge. What happens next?"

"That's when it gets more difficult," replied Arthur, "We don't know much about the German positions beyond the main road. In fact, we don't even know where the British front line is. We'll just have to follow our noses."

The room fell quiet again as each man thought through what tomorrow might bring. Eventually, the silence was broken by Margaret, who appeared in the doorway.

"Supper's up," she said, "Anybody hungry?"

The three men stood and followed Margaret back out to the kitchen, glad to be interrupted from their thoughts.

During supper, talk returned to everyday things. Most

of the farming topics were discussed at length; including: the lambing season during the exceptionally cold spring and the difficulties of the late harvest, caused by the late August rains. Jack was able to add to the farming stories from his knowledge of many of his friends' farms in Watersham.

Towards the end of their meal, as they were enjoying apple pie and custard, it was Harry who changed the subject. "We'll be out during the early hours tonight." he said, "We need to help Jack find his way. Me and Arthur should be back well before breakfast though."

Alice and Margaret looked across at Jack and Alice spoke first.

"We'll be thinking of you tomorrow," she said, "I'm sure that Arthur and Harry will keep you safe. They're good men and I know they'll do the right thing."

"I'm sure they will," replied Jack, "And I wish that..." Alice interrupted him before he could finish his sentence.

"Is there anyone... is there anyone that... you know – that we should let know if... that is, if... if, you know. If something should happen?"

There was silence around the table for a while and then Jack spoke again.

"Yes, thank you, that's a good idea. Have you got paper and pencil? I'll write down my address for you. I've got a wife and kids at home. My wife's name is Janet and we've got a boy called John and a girl called Sarah. Janet knows where I'm headed and I know she'll be worried sick."

Arthur suddenly stood up. "Listen," he said, looking straight at Alice and Margaret. "Don't write anything down. Harry and I will start doing the washing up whilst Jack gives you his address and anything else that he wants to tell you. It's better if you memorise it and that Harry and I don't hear.

What we don't know, we won't have to try and lie about, if the worst comes to the worst."

Arthur and Jack collected up the pudding dishes and moved to the other side of the kitchen. Jack leaned towards Alice and Margaret, and in a low voice, gave them the necessary details about his family and address in Watersham. He repeated it twice.

"That's fine," said Alice, "We'll make sure that your wife gets a message from us in a few days' time. We'll find an excuse to go down that way."

With so many hands, the washing up and drying was completed in no time and Arthur spoke again. "I know it's early," he said, "but I think it would be a good idea if us men were to put our heads down for a few hours. It could be a long night. Jack; there's a bed made up for you in the spare room."

Jack said his goodbyes to Alice and Margaret, thanked them for their kindness and wished them every happiness. Alice and Margaret wished Jack the best of luck for tomorrow and made him promise to come back to see them with his wife and kids "when this is all over." Arthur showed Jack towards the spare room and Margaret walked outside and said goodnight to Harry and Alice, as they made their way the few steps back home to their cottage next door.

Just before midnight, Arthur gently pushed opened the door to the spare room and called Jack's name. Jack, who had slept in most of his clothes, sat straight up, jumped out of bed and grabbed his shirt from the end of the bed.

"Morning," whispered Jack, as they made their way downstairs. The only light in the kitchen came from the moonlight that shone in through the small window above the sink. The light was just good enough for the two men to find their coats, hats and boots. They picked up the backpacks as they stepped outside and stooped for a while to do up their boot laces. As they finished, Harry stepped out from the front door of his cottage.

"Morning Harry," Arthur whispered, "Ready to go?"

"Ready when you are," Harry replied.

The air was clear and fresh outside and with a very bright, nearly full moon, it was easy to see where they were going. In single file, with Arthur leading, they set off north, towards the woods. Arthur and Harry knew the pathways through the local woods like the backs of their hands, and for the first mile or so, it was easy going along the fairly dry, wide paths between the, oak, ash and beech trees that populated the mixed woodland. Every few hundred yards, Arthur slowed his pace, raised a hand and stopped. The three men stood completely still, listening. All was quiet, apart from the occasional sounds of leaves rustling in the tops of the trees, stirred by the light breeze that ran above the woods. There were animal noises too. Tawny owls hooted in the distance, and every now and then, some unseen creature would make a sudden noise as it scuttled hurriedly away through fallen leaves. After walking for nearly an hour, they came across the first signs of the village. There was the unmistakable smell of wood smoke in the air. The men stopped again.

"Right," Arthur whispered, "This is where things might start to get a bit more difficult. We'll move out a bit wider now to make sure that we don't get too close to the village. This way."

The woods were much denser here, with skinny ash saplings growing in great thickets in the gaps between mature oak trees, and the pathway was much narrower. Even in the poor light, it was clear to see that this path was far less trodden than those that they had walked along earlier. Tendrils from nearby bramble clumps lay across the path, tearing at the men's trousers as they made their way, far more slowly now, around the village. Eventually, the path widened out, and they found themselves standing in a clearing between a group of ancient yew trees. There was a distinctive and very strong smell of fox scent in the air. No doubt, over many centuries, the yew trees had acted as a useful boundary marker for the foxes.

Harry caught hold of Jack's arm and leaned closer so that he could speak quietly.

"We used to come here as kids," he said, "I remember it smelled of foxes then. We used to play round here for hours. Cowboys and Indians. That sort of thing. Often up to ten or more of us. Must have been about thirty years ago now. Seems like yesterday."

"It was the same for us at Watersham," whispered Jack, "We used to play in the woods and across the fields all day. A whole gang of us. We didn't have a care in the world then. It's all a lot different now. Nobody lets their kids go off on their own now, do they?"

Harry shook his head and kicked at some leaves as Arthur stepped in closer to speak.

"Come on," he said, "let's keep going."

Harry and Jack followed Arthur in single file as he led them away from the yew trees and off down another narrow pathway. After only a few minutes walking, Arthur stopped suddenly and crouched down. Harry and Jack instantly followed suit.

"There's a light up ahead," whispered Arthur, "I know it isn't from the village as we're too far out, so, it could be one of the German camp-sites. We'd better turn back and look for another way round. The bridge that we need to get to isn't far away from here."

The men stood, turned around, and Jack led them back to the yew trees.

"Let's try this way," said Arthur, veering off down another path.

The new path was slightly wider and the going easier.

Ahead, the night sky looked brighter and it was soon clear that they were coming to the edge of the woods. Arthur called a halt and the three men crouched close together again.

"Look," he said, "That's the road up ahead. We'd better move up very carefully before we try to cross. I've no ideawhat's there."

The men, half doubled, walked slowly forward. As the light improved, they could clearly make out the dark outline of parked vehicles. About twenty yards from the edge of the road; the men stopped and crouched back down again.

"Look there – tanks!" whispered Jack, "And look, there's some lights off to the left."

"Have you seen any movement?" said Arthur.

"No," replied Jack, "I think we need to move in a bit closer. Even if there's no men here; they might be camped on the other side of the road."

The three men spread out and moved up a further dozen paces before crouching down again. They could see the dark outlines of the tanks and other vehicles more clearly now. Very slowly, the men moved forward again until they were only a few paces from the edge of the road. Keeping low, they moved around, looking through the gaps between the tanks, trying to make out what might be on the other side of the road. After a while, Arthur stood up, double checked each way, and walked briskly across the road between two of the tanks. He peered out into the darkness of the woods on the other side and looked up and down the grass verge. There were no lights to be seen nearby, nor any signs of tents or soldiers. He turned back and waved Harry and Jack across. Soon they were back under cover of the trees on the other side. It was more difficult to see now, but they soon found a path and followed it deeper into the woods. After a few minutes walking, Arthur brought them to a halt again.

"Right," he said, "We've managed to cross the road without using the bridge, but we need to find the stream that runs under it. We need to follow it north from here. If we can't find it, we'll get hopelessly lost. If we walk parallel to the road, I reckon we'll run straight into it in less than half a mile. Come on. Let's find it."

As the men walked in an easterly direction, keeping the road on their right side, the lights that they had seen earlier became brighter as they moved closer to one of the camps of the German soldiers. Arthur called a halt again.

"I'll bet that camp is right by the bridge," whispered Arthur, "We must be very close to the stream now."

As the men stood to move again, a torch light flashed on through the trees and they immediately ducked back down. Peering through some brambles, they watched as a soldier shone his torch at one of the larger trees, put his torch down on the ground, unbuttoned his flies and peed against the tree. After what seemed like an age, he picked up his torch and walked slowly back towards the camp. They waited for some time, before moving on again. A few minutes later, they reached a gully with the stream flowing in a southerly direction. Arthur stepped down into it and the others followed closely behind. The men turned sharp left and followed the stream heading north.

It was easy going, walking on the sandy path that ran along the side of the stream that meandered through the woods, and they made good progress for over an hour without stopping. Jack wondered how long it would be before they came across civilisation again; a road, a farm or perhaps even another village. Suddenly, Arthur raised an arm and Harry and Jack ducked down behind him and they all peered ahead into the semi-darkness further up-stream.

"Looks like another bridge to me," whispered Jack.

"I think you're right," replied Harry.

They continued to stare at whatever it was for some time before Arthur said, "Okay. There doesn't appear to be any movement so, let's take a closer look."

Three minutes later, they were standing on a narrow

lane that ran across the top of the red brick bridge. They stood quietly, looking all around and listening. They neither saw nor heard anything; only the gurgling of the stream as it ran under the bridge.

"Onward," said Arthur. A mile further on, the men stopped again as they spotted dim lights through the trees up ahead.

"Let's move away from the stream," said Harry, "We'd be better off under cover of the trees. We can be seen too easily down here."

"You're right," replied Arthur, "Follow me."

Thirty paces further on, Arthur waved at them to stop again and they all dropped to the ground as quickly and quietly as they could, making themselves as small as possible, as torch lights shone towards their position.

"Bugger!" Whispered Arthur, "We've walked straight into a bloody German patrol!"

The three men laid as still as they could as they heard men coming towards them. Jack guessed that the soldiers were less than ten yards away when they stopped moving and the beams of light fell directly on them. There was complete silence for a moment and then a very English voice called out. "Right. Stop right where you are and don't move!"

The three men breathed great sighs of relief as they realised that the soldiers were British.

"Right," said Sergeant Bennett, as he walked purposefully over to where the three men were lying, "Now. I need you all to stand very slowly and put your hands up. Do you understand me?"

"Yes," Harry replied as they all started to stand. "We're English!"

"Keep your hands up! What brings you blokes out here in the middle of the night?"

As the Sergeant spoke, one of the other soldiers moved in closer with a torch and checked to see if the men were carrying weapons.

"We came to find you!" Arthur replied, as he pointed with his upheld thumb towards Jack.

"We've brought Jack here to join you."

"That's right," said Jack, "I've come up from Watersham to join you. These chaps have helped me to get here."

"What's in your bags?" asked the Sergeant.

"Only snares and rabbits," replied Harry, "We don't have any weapons."

"Right," said the Sergeant, waving the soldier back to check the bags. "Keep your hands up while we just check what you're carrying. You first," he said, pointing at Arthur. Their bags were quickly checked.

"Yes Sarge," the soldier said as he dropped the last bag on the ground,

"Nothing but snares and rabbits."

"Good," replied the Sergeant, "Now pick up your bags and follow me. Let's get you lot debriefed."

Two of the soldiers led the way; the three men, Sergeant Bennett and the rest of the patrol followed on.

In a clearing in the woods they were taken to a large tent that had a lantern glowing above a table covered in files and papers with two soldiers sitting behind. They both stood as they saw Sergeant Bennett before them.

"Get these three registered as quickly as possible," said the Sergeant, "I need to get them debriefed straight away, so be as quick as you can."

"Right away Sarge," replied one of the soldiers.

"Over here please!" he said to the men, pointing to another table and chairs behind him.

"Corporal," said the Sergeant, "Leave one of your men with me and you can take the others back out on patrol with you."

"Will do," replied the Corporal, indicating to one of his men to stay with the Sergeant. "Bates!" called out Sergeant

Bennett to the soldier left behind, "Nip over to the mess and get us five mugs of tea, will you? One sugar in each. There's a good man."

"Certainly Sarge."

By the time Bates returned with the tea, Arthur, Harry and Jack had finished registration and were seated with Sergeant Bennett around another table nearer to the centre of the tent. A larger lantern, hanging from a central pole, gave out a strange orange glow, casting long shadows all around. Bates set the tray of mugs down on the table.

"Help yourselves gentlemen," said Sergeant Bennett, "You too Bates."

Arthur and Harry explained who they were, where they lived, how they had met Jack and what they were doing risking their lives getting through enemy lines during the middle of the night. Jack then took over and explained how he had been working with the Resistance in Watersham and how he had had to leave so suddenly.

For the first time, the Sergeant interrupted and addressed Jack directly.

"So, your family is still in Watersham?"

"I'm afraid so," replied Jack, looking at the floor.

At this point, an officer arrived at the table. Sergeant Bennett stood and saluted and the others stood too.

"Major Foster," he said, "It's good to see you. These are the gentlemen that you will have heard of."

"Good morning Sergeant and good morning gentlemen. Please carry on with your tea whilst I have a word with the Sergeant here."

Major Foster and Sergeant Bennett walked away and stood talking for a few minutes on the far side of the tent. When they returned, Major Foster sat down and spoke directly to Jack. "I'll make sure that we get a message through to your wife to let her know that you're safe. And after you've had something to eat, Sergeant Bennett will introduce you to one of our special units. They're made up of chaps like you. Men who have managed to get through enemy lines to join us."

"Thank you Major. I've been worried sick about my wife and kids since I left Watersham."

The Major then turned to Arthur and Harry and thanked them for their efforts in getting Jack safely through the enemy lines.

"After breakfast, we'll get some men to escort you back through the woods; but not quite the way that you came. We know a couple of safer ways back."

Major Foster then stood and reached across the table to shake their hands. "Right," he said, "I must be off. I'll leave you in the safe hands of Sergeant Bennett. Good luck to you all."

Sergeant Bennett and Major Foster saluted each other and the Major walked away.

"Breakfast it is then!" said the Sergeant, pointing towards the exit, "The canteen is that way."

After breakfast, Sergeant Bennett left the men for a few minutes and returned with three soldiers.

"These guys will get you safely back through the enemy lines," he said, "I suggest that you set off immediately, as it will start to get light in about an hour."

Arthur and Harry stood and hugged Jack.

"Once this is all over, I promise to come back to the farm to see you all," he said, "I'll bring the family. Thanks again for all your help and I hope that you have a safe trip back."

Arthur and Harry shook hands with Sergeant Bennett, said their goodbyes, and left with the three soldiers. As the first of the morning light appeared, they crossed back through the enemy lines, thanked the soldiers for helping them, and headed for home.

Meanwhile, Sergeant Bennett had taken Jack to another

part of the camp to where the special units were billeted. It was still early; all the tents were closed and the only sign of life was a soldier on guard duty.

Sergeant Bennett spoke to the guard, "I don't suppose the Captain is about yet?"

"No," replied the guard, "I should think it'll be another half an hour or so before anyone's up and about. They were all out on patrol until late last night."

"Thanks," replied the Sergeant, "We'll have a walk around the camp whilst we're waiting."

They walked off and the sergeant pointed out to Jack anything that he thought would be of interest. The campsite was far bigger than Jack had first thought, with tents spread out through the woods and army vehicles of every description parked up in small groups amongst the trees. Nearly an hour had passed by the time that they returned to the tents of the special unit. The light was improving by the minute and a number of men were now on the move. The captain was talking to another sergeant by one of the tents.

Sergeant Bennett and Jack stopped a little way off from the captain and waited.

"Good morning captain," said Sergeant Bennet as he saluted.

"Good morning to you too," replied the Captain, returning the salute, "What can I do for you this early in the morning?" "I've got a new recruit for you sir." replied the Sergeant, "Name of Jack Brown. He got through the lines during the night."

"Excellent. Has he been debriefed?"

"Yes sir," replied the Sergeant, "Registration's all done and he's met Major Foster."

"Good," he said, offering a hand to Jack, "I'm Captain Blake. Good to have you on board."

They shook hands and Captain Blake suggested that they should carry on their conversation in the canteen. Sergeant

Bennett explained that they'd already had breakfast, but was sure that another cup of tea would be welcome. Whilst Captain Blake ate, Jack told him as much as he could about life under German occupation in Watersham, the Resistance and how he had had to make a run for it.

"Well," said the Captain, as he wiped his plate clean with a large slice of white bread, "You're more than welcome here. There's several men like you in my special unit. I'll introduce you to them in a minute."

They walked back to the tents, which had now been opened up with their flaps tied back to air. Soldiers were checking guy ropes, shaking out blankets and generally tidying the place up. Sergeant Roberts stepped out to greet them and Captain Blake spoke to him.

"All ship shape Sergeant?"

"Yes, Sir," replied Sergeant Roberts, "Everything is in order."

"Jack Brown is joining us," the Captain said, waving his hand towards Jack, "Tuck him under your wing Sergeant and show him the ropes. I'm sure he'll tell you all about himself later; but in the meantime, get him across to the stores and get him kitted out properly and allocate him space in a tent. He's used to handling guns, so, issue him with a Thompson. Okay?"

"Yes Sir!" replied Sergeant Roberts, "I'll do that straight away."

Sergeant Bennet spoke as they turned to go, "I'll see you later Jack " he said, "I need to get back to my other duties."

"Thanks " replied Jack as he set off with Sergeant Roberts, "Thanks for all your help this morning…"

Jack settled in very quickly with the specials; most of them had similar backgrounds to him and many had found their way to the unit as he had. After only three days of familiarising himself with the camp, he found himself on night patrol with Sergeant Roberts and five other soldiers. For much of the night they patrolled the same woods that he, Arthur and Harry had walked through earlier in the week. At four in the morning, they came across a German patrol. Sergeant Roberts, walking up front, spotted them first and immediately dropped to his knees. The men behind him did the same.

"Germans," whispered Sergeant Roberts to Jack who was crouched immediately behind him.

They waited, hoping that they would go the other way, but they didn't; the German patrol of about ten men headed straight for their position.

"Get ready," he whispered again to Jack, "If they come any closer, we'll have to fire."

Jack whispered to the soldier behind him and the message was passed down the line. Twenty seconds later, Sergeant Roberts raised himself slightly and fired a volley of shots at the German patrol. Jack followed suit and they both threw themselves to the ground and rolled over several times to their right, towards the base of a large oak tree. Fire was returned immediately and bullets zinged over their heads. The other men in their patrol managed to get a few shots away and then dived for cover, all of them lying as flat on the ground as they could. Pigeons clattered out from the branches above them. Suddenly, everything went quiet and then shouts could be heard coming from the other side. Clearly, the German patrol was trying to pull back. Sergeant Roberts and Jack crawled the last few yards to the tree and they both pulled themselves up behind its great trunk. Very slowly, the Sergeant eased himself around its trunk so that he could look forward; Jack did the same on the other side. The sergeant couldn't make out any movement ahead, but fired a short burst in the rough direction of where he had last seen them. A split second later, Jack also fired a short burst in the same direction. Again, they were answered by return fire almost immediately – but this time from further away.

"They're definitely pulling back " whispered Jack to Sergeant Roberts.

"Yes. I think so," he replied, "Just wait a minute and we'll have a look."

The other men in the patrol got to their knees and peered out into the dark woods ahead of them. There was certainly nothing moving directly in front of them, but it was impossible to see much beyond about thirty yards. Even then, with so many trees dotted around and thick undergrowth in places, they were fully aware that any number of Germans could be hiding out there.

"Is everyone alright?" called out Sergeant Roberts.

"Yes. I think so." replied Private Frank Stacey.

"Good," said the Sergeant, "Now; very carefully, spread out, stay low and let's just check the ground in front of us. I'm fairly sure we hit one or two in that first exchange."

The men spread out and slowly edged forward; keeping as low as they could.

"Here's one!" called out Frank, "I think he's dead."

"Okay," replied Sergeant Roberts, "Stay where you are. I'll come over. The rest of you, keep searching."

Sergeant Roberts soon joined Frank and checked the soldier for signs of life.

"You're right Frank. He's definitely dead. Pick up his rifle. We'll take that. They'll come and get his body later when it's daylight."

Frank picked up the rifle as Jack called out from the front.

"There's nothing here!" he said.

"Right. Come on then," called out the sergeant, "Let's get out of here before they come back with reinforcements."

No one spoke as they walked back and in less than an hour they were back to the camp.

"Everyone, stay right here for a debrief," said Sergeant Roberts, "Frank. Get that German rifle over to the stores. Make sure it's safe and get it labelled with the name of our unit and today's date. With the right ammunition, we can make use of it."

Frank Stacey set off with the rifle and the Sergeant turned to speak to Jack.

"Jack. You know where to find Major Foster or one of his men, don't you?"

"Yes," replied Jack, "Do you want me to fetch him Sarge?"

"Yes," replied Sergeant Roberts, "We'll need to report what happened."

Jack headed off to find the Major as Captain Blake arrived to speak to Sergeant Roberts. As Jack returned with Major Foster, Frank arrived back from the stores.

"Let's go over to the Ops Room in the main tent," said Major Foster, "You can stand your men down Sergeant."

The patrol was pleased to be stood down and the men went to the canteen for an early breakfast. Major Foster, Captain Blake and Sergeant Roberts headed for the Ops Room.

"Right," said Major Foster, "Tell me all about it. Sounds like you had a close shave Sergeant."

"Yes," replied Sergeant Roberts, "Far too close for comfort."

Following a thorough debriefing, Major Foster set off to discuss the incident with his fellow senior officers whilst Captain Blake and Sergeant Roberts walked over to the canteen and joined the others. They queued for a while to get their breakfasts and then took their trays and sat at an empty table.

"I reckon we'll be doubling up on patrols from tonight," said Captain Blake.

"Yes," replied Sergeant Roberts, "We were lucky last night. It's all getting a bit tense out there. Something's got to give soon. When do you think we'll get the order for the big push?"

"I've no idea," said Captain Blake, "But it'll have to be soon. We can't sit around here forever."

Chapter 11

FROM THE SKY

It was late morning at the end of November 1940, as Julia and her friend Sylvie were walking through Watersham, that they became aware of the distant sound of an airplane. They stopped and looked up. It was cold, but the sky was crystal clear and they both raised their hands to shield their eyes from the glare of the sun. The plane was too high to work out whether it was one of ours or one of theirs, and after a few seconds, they both looked away and continued walking, arm in arm along the pavement. After a few more steps, Julia pulled on Sylvie's arm and they stopped walking.

"That's strange," said Julia, "I thought I saw something just now. There was something different about that plane."

They both looked back up at the sky, again shielding their eyes.

"There!" shouted Julia, "There! Look! There's something else in the sky."

By now, the plane had moved further away and appeared as just a dot in the distance; but in the open sky, beneath the path where it had flown, the sun's rays were catching something else; something falling from the sky, like confetti. The two women stood transfixed for some time; just staring at this strange spectacle, not being able to understand what they were watching or what it meant.

"Leaflets!" shouted Sylvie, "They're leaflets." Sylvie put her hand over her mouth immediately after calling out, realising too late that she had spoken out loud. They both looked around, but as far as they could tell, no one else had looked up.

Sylvie pulled on Julia's arm. "Come on," she said in a low voice, "Let's go and see what we can find."

The two women walked steadily on until they reached the footpath that cut diagonally across a meadow that lead to Chapel Bottom. They both looked up occasionally as they walked, keeping the falling leaflets in sight. The gentle breeze was carrying the leaflets away from the village, and as they reached the end of the path that lead to the chapel, the first of the leaflets dropped into the woods on the far side of the field. They hurried on, and on reaching the woods, Sylvie picked up a leaflet that had managed to find its way through the canopy of the trees to the pathway and read it out aloud:

NOTICE FROM HIS MAJESTY'S GOVERNMENT
28th NOVEMBER 1940
FEAR NOT. HELP IS AT HAND. STAND BY.
RELIEF IS ON ITS WAY.
BRITISH FORCES ARE MUSTERING AND WILL
PUSH THE ENEMY BACK FROM WHENCE IT CAME.

"Bloody hell!" screamed Julia, "I can't believe it! After all this time. Bloody hell…"

"Too true!" replied Sylvie, "Too bloody true…" The two women hugged each other.

"Come on," sniffed Julia, "Let's get a grip. Let's see if

we can find anymore and get them back to the village."

The two women scrabbled around in the woods for half an hour, but could only find a few more. They realised that most of the leaflets had become trapped in the branches of the trees above them.

Julia folded in half the few leaflets that she had, opened her coat, lifted her cardigan and pushed them down the front of her skirt. Sylvie did the same and they started to walk back towards the village.

"I'm not quite sure what we're going to do with these leaflets when we get back though," said Julia.

On reaching the village, they stopped and stood chatting for a while.

"Listen," said Julia, "I know what we'll do. You drop your leaflets off at the Vicarage and I'll take mine to Commander Clay's house. I'll catch up with you later. Okay?"

Sylvie nodded and they both set off down the street. At the first junction, Sylvie turned off, waved and headed for the Vicarage. Five minutes later, she knocked on the front door, and the Vicar opened it.

"Sylvie. How lovely to see you. Come on in."

Sylvie didn't hesitate and stepped straight into the hallway. Reverend Timothy Streeter closed the door and ushered Sylvie into his study. Sylvie pulled the leaflets out from under her cardigan and held them out for the vicar to see.

"Julia and I picked these up half an hour ago – they were dropped by a plane. We saw them fall. Julia's taking hers to Commander Clay."

The Vicar read one of the leaflets and a wide smile spread itself across his face.

"This is wonderful news. Well done for spotting them.

Did you see anyone else picking them up?"

"No. I don't think that anyone saw the plane or what was dropped from it. It was very high up. Then, all the leaflets drifted away from the village and landed in the woods. We didn't see anyone else. Mind you, they might have dropped more elsewhere."

"Yes, of course," replied the Vicar. "They probably did."

"What will you do with them?" said Sylvie.

"I'm not sure yet. But we need to let as many people know as possible. I'll nip round to the Clay's shortly and we'll decide what to do."

"Good," replied Sylvie as she started to move back to the hallway, "I'll leave you to it then and be on my way."

"Thanks again," said the vicar as he saw Sylvie to the door. Ten minutes later, he was sitting in the kitchen at the Clay's house.

"Julia obviously got the leaflets to you okay," he said, looking at them on the table. "Sylvie brought a similar lot to me."

"I wonder who else has picked them up?" replied Commander Clay, pointing at the single leaflet on the table in front of him. "They must have dropped thousands in the area. They won't just have dropped them over Watersham! The Germans are bound to have copies by now."

"Almost certainly," answered the vicar, "But the question is: what are we going to do with this lot?"

"I've been thinking about that," said Commander Clay, as he pushed his chair back and stood looking down at the pile of leaflets, "I think that the best thing to do is to get them all down to the Post Office. Olive will see to it that they get dotted around the village with the morning post. By mid-morning, the whole village will have got the message."

"That's a good idea," replied the Vicar, "Shall I take both lots, or do you think it's best to keep them separate?"

"No Tim, that's fine. If you're happy to, you take both lots down to Olive this evening. There's no point keeping them separate now."

The Vicar, picked up the leaflets, undid three of his shirt buttons, slipped the leaflets in against his vest and did the buttons up again.

"I'll be on my way then," Tim said to the Commander as he did up his jacket and started towards the door.

"Well done Tim," replied the Commander, patting him on the back as they made their way to the front door. "You stay safe now, won't you?"

"Of course, I will Henry, my old friend – and you stay safe too."

The Vicar nodded or said hello to a number of villagers on his way back to the Vicarage and some distance away, further down the street, he saw a German staff car parked, but otherwise, saw nothing to be concerned about. Returning to the Vicarage, he went straight to the scullery that adjoined the back of the kitchen and pulled out a grubby hessian bag from one of the cupboards. He tipped the contents out over the stone floor. Potatoes rolled across the floor and crumbs of dried soil fell around.

"What on earth are you doing?" called out Mrs Streeter, as she looked on from the scullery doorway.

"Don't worry," replied Tim, "I just need this bag for something."

As he spoke, he stood, undid his shirt, pulled out the leaflets and pushed them into the bottom of the dusty bag, which he immediately dropped back to the stone floor.

"I won't be long," he said, as he gently pushed passed his wife, "I'll be right back."

On reaching his office, he lifted the hinged seat on his office chair and picked up the other batch of leaflets and made his way back to the scullery. Mrs Streeter had already taken down the dustpan and brush from one of the shelves in the scullery and was standing ready.

"That's the lot," he said as he pushed the last of the leaflets into the bag. "Now for the spuds."

One by one, he retrieved all of the potatoes and refilled

the bag. As he pulled the drawstring to close and tie off the bag, Mrs Streeter bent down and swept the soil and dust from the floor.

"So. What's all this about then?" She said as she straightened.

"Leaflets," replied Tim. "There's one in my office for you to see. Come on, I'll show you."

Tim carried the bag and placed it down by the front door. "I need to deliver that to the Post Office later on," he said as they walked into the office.

"Here," he said, pulling out the folded leaflet from his desk diary and handing it to her, "Read it."

"My God," she said, "That's marvelous news! Where did you get the leaflets from? I mean – there's so many of them."

Tim explained to her as much of the story as he knew and added that he would need to pop out later on to get the potato sack to the Post Office.

Mrs Streeter carefully refolded the leaflet and slipped it back into the desk diary.

"My word," she said as they made their way back to the kitchen, "It really is great news; of course, it is, but it... it's, you know... it's all a bit frightening, isn't it?"

"Yes," Tim replied as he reached over and slid the kettle onto the hot plate on the kitchen range. "It could all get very nasty now."

Later that evening, after supper, the Vicar carried the bag of potatoes down to the Post Office and knocked on the door. As he waited on the doorstep, he looked up and down the High Street. About fifty yards away, at the junction with South Street, a troop truck was parked. Standing by the tailgate, three German soldiers stood smoking and chatting. He knew that they would be watching him. Trying to look as calm as possible, he put the bag of potatoes down on the pavement and knocked on the door again. He made a point of not looking back at the soldiers; although he desperately wanted to know if they were still watching him. After what felt like an age, he heard bolts being pulled back and the Post Office door opened.

"Tim!" said Olive as she stood to one side, "Come on in! I didn't expect to see you this evening. What brings you here?"

"Evening Olive," he said as he stepped inside. "I brought you some potatoes from our allotment. We thought that you could probably do with some as you don't have a vegetable garden or allotment yourself."

Olive re-bolted the door and led the way to her kitchen. "Well, that's very thoughtful of you, and the potatoes are most welcome," she said, "but what did you really come here for?"

Tim explained what had happened during the day and that there were a lot of leaflets in the bottom of the potato bag that needed delivering in the morning. They quickly agreed that Olive would make sure that the leaflets were distributed with the post the next morning, and within five minutes, the Vicar was back outside. It was almost completely dark and the soft glow of the street light attached high up on the gable end of the post office wall picked out the fine drizzle that was just beginning to fall. Tim looked up and down the street as he pulled up the collar on his overcoat. The troop truck was still there but the soldiers had gone. There was no one else about. Head down, he walked quickly back towards the Vicarage.

Early the next morning, many households in Watersham received an unexpected leaflet with their post.

Chapter 12

THE TIDE TURNS

On the 5th December, at the same time as all British officers on the front line, Major Foster received the order that he had expected for many days. At precisely 07:00 hours the following morning, the RAF would bomb and strafe the German front line, artillery would open up at the same time and cease firing at 07:55. The entire British Army would then advance towards the enemy at 08:00. As soon as he had digested the order, along with the finer details of the tasks and objectives set out for the units for which he had direct responsibility, he sent out runners to call his commanders in for an immediate meeting. Twenty minutes later, Major Foster stood on an upturned wooden beer crate and addressed the senior officers gathered in the operations tent.

He explained very clearly to his men what would be expected of each unit during the following morning and talked in some detail about timings, objectives and rendezvous points. He also spoke about communications, frequencies, call signs and codes that only their units would be using. He spoke further of fallback positions in case of strong resistance and at what point reserves were likely to be committed. As he finished speaking, very unusually for these sorts of serious briefings, spontaneous applause broke out amongst the men. There were no questions, and the gathering broke up quickly, as each man was eager to get back to their individual units and to share the information with their men. For the rest of the day, men busied themselves with cleaning weapons, checking ammunition and packing essentials into their day packs, ready for the following morning. They also packed other personal belongings and kit from their tents into boxes with their names written in large capitals on them. Each man hoped that they would be safely reunited again with their boxes and tents later the next day, by which time they were convinced that they would have pushed the enemy well back towards the coast.

Major Foster spent the rest of the day pouring over ordnance survey plans of the local area with his officers and sergeants. He sat at a wooden trestle table in the centre of the operations tent with maps and aerial photographs spread out and overlapping each other. Until late in the evening; officers, radio operators and the heads of various engineering, artillery and ordnance supply teams came and went. At 10:00 hours; Captain Blake looked around, and seeing that there was no one else at the table with the Major, pulled at Sergeant Roberts arm and nodded in the direction of where the Major was sitting, still studying the maps and photos in front of him. The two men walked slowly over to him.

"Might be a good idea if we called it a day, Sir," said Captain Blake, "We've an early start in the morning."

Major Foster looked up at the Captain Blake and Sergeant Roberts, but said nothing.

"Yes," chipped in Sergeant Roberts, "I think that everyone will need a good night's sleep, Sir."

The Captain and Sergeant glanced at each other,

wondering if they'd overstepped the mark.

Major Foster held his arm out in the poor light and looked at his wrist watch.

"Good grief!" he said, "I didn't realise it was so late. It's gone 10 o'clock. Absolutely, yes of course... time to get our heads down."

Captain Blake and Sergeant Roberts stepped forward and helped the Major tidy up the maps, aerial photos and other papers.

"Right," said Major Foster as he tucked the last of the papers into a huge map case, "Let's be off and thanks for your help today gentlemen. We've quite a day ahead of us tomorrow."

Major Foster walked off, with Captain Blake and Sergeant Roberts following towards their tents. As the major reached his, he stopped, turned and held out his hand.

"Good luck tomorrow boys," he said as he shook their hands, "See you bright and early."

At 05:00 hours the next morning, the entire camp was up and about preparing for the day. Although so many men were on the move, there was very little chat, as most were deep in thought about what might lie ahead. Even in the canteens, where thousands queued for their breakfasts, it was unusually quiet. At precisely 7:00am, RAF bombers could be clearly heard overhead and at the same time the artillery bombardment began. The noise was deafening and the soldiers could hear individual shells whistling overhead and bombs exploding in the distance. By 7:30am all the men were lined up in their specific units and the order was passed down the line to move forwards further into the woods. RAF fighters could now be heard flying very low, and seconds later, the unmistakable, intermittent rat-tat-tat of machine gun fire could be heard in the early morning air, as the German lines were being strafed.

Major Foster looked at his watch constantly after 7:45am, as did every officer all along the front line. As promised, at exactly 7:55am the bombing ceased and the field guns fell silent. At 8:00am the entire British front line moved forwards; mostly through woodland and good cover, but in some places, through open fields. They knew exactly where the German lines were, and because of intelligence reports from the likes of Jack Brown and others who had come through them earlier, as well as reports coming back from daily patrols and aerial photographs taken by the RAF, they knew where the weak and the strong points were. Major Foster's men, totaling some 500, were headed for what they believed to be a weak link, a camp sitting between two areas where heavy artillery, tanks and other vehicles were known to be parked up.

It was still quite dark in the woods. The early morning light was weak, and although there were few leaves left on the trees, what light there was seemed reluctant to penetrate through to the forest floor. The troops walked steadily forward. As yet, no incoming fire had been heard. No doubt German soldiers were still taking cover and looking to the skies, but the British soldiers knew that it would only be a matter of time before the Germans pulled themselves together and looked to defend themselves from a ground attack. Sergeant Roberts, walking up front, was one of the first to spot movement ahead.

"Germans," he whispered to the corporal nearest to him, pointing with his Thompson machine gun to the right, "Over there."

The leading line slowed its pace, all eyes fixed firmly on the area where movement had been spotted. The soldiers knew that they had an advantage in their position, as with the light being so poor, it was far easier to look out from the woods than to look in.

When the first British soldier was within forty yards of the camp, a German soldier stood shouting and pointing into the woods. Sergeant Roberts and the group around him didn't wait for orders, but fired from the hip as they quickened their pace and then ran forward to take up better positions behind some of the larger trees. Others ran to take cover as best they could as incoming fire ripped around them. German soldiers could be seen bent double and running away from their camp area towards the trees on the other side. Many were hit and fell to the ground as they tried to escape. Cries of "Move up! Move up!" were shouted out along the British front line as the officers were determined to push home their advantage. The sounds of engines coming to life could be heard off to the left and right. As expected, some of the German drivers had managed to get to their tanks. As the first one drove out from its parking place and swung into view, several bazooka shells hit it at the same time and one of the tracks became detached and the tank ran off out of control through the field of tents. Thirty seconds later the beleaguered tank was hit by a second volley of shells and ground to a halt. The hatch was thrown open and three men scrambled out. They were hit by a hail of bullets before they could reach the ground. Other vehicles were on the move, but the bulk of the British soldiers were now even closer and the vehicles were being riddled with machine gun, rifle and bazooka fire. Mortar teams had now taken up a forward position and were launching their shells at the German soldiers who had fallen back to the distant trees. Incoming fire was now heavier, as the defenders were starting to get themselves organised with the British taking some heavy casualties.

The situation was similar along much of the front line and the enemy was being pushed back; but where the countryside was more open, success had been limited. A few miles to the east, the Germans were not only holding the line, but they were inflicting heavy losses on the British Army that was now bogged down in grassy fields with little cover. Many cattle and sheep had already been killed in the constant shooting from both sides and those that remained ran terrified in all directions, eventually crashing through the wire fences that held them in their fields. Many British soldiers now took advantage of the stricken animals, crawling through the grass and taking cover behind their bodies.

Chapter 13

THE AUXILIARIES

For days and nights after Julia had received the radio message for the Resistance to stand by; she, Charlie Stewart, Don Steel, Bethany Andrews and several hastily trained reserves, had taken it in turns to man the radio continuously in shifts. After each shift, taking great care never to take exactly the same route back to the village, they would report back to Commander Clay. For eight consecutive days each shift change brought the same message, there was nothing to report. One early evening, as Charlie was finishing his shift, the radio suddenly sprang to life. He jumped, pulled the headphones up from around his neck, and pushed the earpieces firmly to his head and turned the volume up on the radio.

"London calling. This is London calling. London calling. Stand by."

Charlie sat leaning forward, his hands pressing at his earphones as his heart pounded. He stared at the dull orange glow of the radio dial. He could hear the gentle crackling sound of radio static, but there was nothing else. He sat waiting for what felt like an eternity as the minutes ticked by. He pulled his pocket watch from his waistcoat and held it out towards the tilly lamp that hissed comfortingly at the other end of the desk.

"Five past six," he muttered to himself as he looked towards the ladder that led up to the hatch. It was past shift change time, but he knew that he couldn't move away from the radio.

Outside, in the dark, Julia stood under the trees looking towards the hide-out. She had already checked her watch several times and was becoming concerned that Charlie had not put out the usual signal to show that all was well and that it was safe to enter. It was difficult to see in the gloomy light, but she was sure that the branch near to the entrance had not been turned outward. All four of the radio operators would, without fail, just as their shift was due to finish, reach up from the ladder to the hatch, lift it enough to get a hand to the branch and turn it outwards. For eight consecutive days and four shift changes each day, that's exactly what had happened without fail. Inside the foul-smelling underground chamber, Charlie was fully aware that he had not been able to move the branch. He couldn't. He dared not risk moving away from the radio in case the vital message came through. Julia looked around in all directions and listened. She was sure that she hadn't been followed and that there was no one else nearby. She decided she would have to act. Slowly and as quietly as she could, she circled the hide-out, making sure always to keep well back and under cover of the beech trees. She circled again, this time moving in closer. There was nothing. No sound or signs of anything untoward. On the third circuit she moved in close to where she knew the emergency exit to be. For a minute she squatted motionless by the exit. Now that she was so close, she caught the unmistakable and unpleasant whiff of burnt paraffin fumes coming from the exit. She leaned in closer, gently pulled away some small branches, stuck her head into the narrow tunnel, and as loudly as she dared, called out.

"Charlie! Charlie? Are you there?"

Charlie jumped, swiveled round to face the other end of the chamber, and called back.

"Julia! It's alright – come in! I'm sorry I couldn't set the branch as usual. Get in here quick!"

Julia sank back on her haunches and breathed several sighs of relief.

Thank God for that, she thought as she made her way back to the main entrance, taking care to replace the branches over the emergency exit before she did so.

Charlie turned his head as he heard Julia lift the main hatch and step on to the ladder.

A minute later she was standing next to him.

"What's up mate?" she said. "I was really worried out there."

"Yes. I know. I'm sorry. I didn't dare leave the radio to move the branch. There's a message about to come through. I had a stand-by come through just before six."

"Nothing since?"

"No. Nothing since." He half turned to look up at Julia, "Do you want to take over now?"

"No. You stay as you are for the moment. It's your call. But if there's nothing in the next fifteen minutes or so, I'll take over so that you can let the Commander know what's happening. If we leave it later than that, they'll start to worry."

"Right. That makes sense."

She patted Charlie on the shoulder and moved a few paces away. The poor light in the room was the usual subdued orange and the mixture of damp and fumes from the oil lamp smelt awful. She looked forward to the day that they wouldn't have to do this anymore, but she knew in her heart that life would probably get a lot harder before it got better again.

Charlie continued to stare at the glowing radio dial and just as he was about to say to Julia that it was time for her to take over, there was a sudden crackling noise as the radio came back to life.

"London calling. This is London calling. London calling. Stand by."

Charlie jumped again and waved at Julia. She stepped back in close and quickly lifted the spare single earpiece to her ear.

This time, there was not just static, but the distinct sound of pips on the airwaves.

"Stand by," the voice called again; and then, pip … pip … pip … pip … "To all units. Repeat. All units. Stand by." pip … pip … pip … pip …

Charlie and Julia held their breath.

"Here is the news from London. Stand by. Here is the news from London."

They glanced at each other and then returned to stare at the radio.

"Ash before oak, we're in for a soak. Oak before ash we're in for a splash. There's no time like the present. There's no time like the present."

There were three more pips broadcast and then the radio fell silent.

"Bloody hell!" shouted Julia as she dropped the earpiece back on the table, "That's it! That's the message we've been waiting for! You need to get that message to the Commander without delay. Here; give me the headphones and you get going."

Charlie handed them to her.

"Good luck," she said as she pulled the headphones on, "And be careful…"

"Don't you worry," he replied, already turning to make his way to the ladder. "There's no way they'll stop me from getting this message through!!"

Two minutes later, Charlie was out into the cool, fresh night air, making his way back towards Watersham. He breathed deeply and shook his coat as he walked, desperately trying to rid himself of the stale fumes. He felt excited as he got closer to Watersham and on spotting the first dim light coming from one of the outlying cottages; he stopped and listened for a while.

"All quiet on the western front," he muttered to himself. Five minutes later he stood at the end of the street where Commander Clay lived. Hiding by the cover of an overgrown box hedge, he waited and watched for a long time. A man emerged from one of the houses nearby and cycled off down the road. A front door nearer to him opened and he heard a woman say "Go on then. Get on with you. It's too cold standing here with the door open." A moment later, a very overweight tabby cat stepped slowly out from the front path of the house and ambled across the road into the neighbouring garden. There was no other movement.

At a few minutes past seven Charlie knocked gently on Commander Clay's door, all the time looking around to make sure that no one was watching. Mrs Clay opened it.

"Come in Charlie."

"Is the Commander here?"

"Yes, he's here. Come on through. He's in the kitchen."

The two men shook hands and before Commander Clay could say anything; Charlie excitedly blurted out, "I've come straight from the hideout... Julia's just taken over... We've just received an urgent message from London... The one we've been waiting for!"

"Sit down," Henry replied, "You're shaking. Now take your time. What's the message?"

"Well," said Charlie, once they were seated around the kitchen table. "None of us have heard anything from the radio for ages, and then at six this evening, just as Julia was due to start her shift, the radio came to life and we got this message: Ash before oak, we're in for a soak. Oak before ash, we're in for a splash."

Charlie looked straight at the Commander who nodded his head to show that he understood.

"And then a moment later, " continued Charlie as he wiped his mouth with the back of his hand, we received the next part of the message, "There's no time like the present. There's no time like the present."

Commander Clay pushed his chair back, stood up and put both hands up to his face.

"My God. This is it… that's the message we've been waiting for… it'll be all hands to the pump now, by God it will!"

Charlie and Mrs Clay stood too; waiting for Henry to speak again. He paced around the kitchen, his head in his hands, looking at the floor, deep in thought.

"Right," he said, "Charlie. Well done. I need you to get back to your radio operators and tell them to keep up the good work. Tell them that it's essential that radio contact with London is monitored at all times and that you have back-up arrangements in place in case the hide-out is discovered. Make sure that the radios in the other three hideouts are fully functioning at all times, in case you suddenly need to switch bases."

"I'll get the message out to all the radio operators and I'll check the other hide-outs first thing tomorrow."

"And another thing," said the commander as he placed his hand on Charlie's shoulder, "Please ask Julia to call in here when she's finished her shift."

"Will do," replied Charlie as he turned to go, "I'll pop back to my place first, to let the wife know that she might not see much of me for a while, and then I'll get the messages out to Julia and the others. I'll check out the other hideouts myself."

"Good man!" said Henry, as they walked back to the

front door, "Look after yourself, won't you?"

"And you too." replied Charlie as he stepped back outside, "Let's hope we all get through this."

As soon as Charlie had left the Clay's house, Henry sat down again with Margaret.

"You know what this means, don't you?" Henry said, as they held hands across the kitchen table, "I'm going to be running around all over the place for a little while, and I won't always be able to get home or get a message to you. I expect that you knew that it would come to this one day, didn't you?"

Margaret squeezed Henry's hands. "I know what you and the others have to do and I wish that you didn't have to go, but I understand. I just want you to promise that you'll look after yourself and that you'll come home safe when it's all over. That's all I want…"

Margaret looked down at the tabletop as the tears started to form in her eyes.

"… and you do your best to look after all those men… all those men… they've all got families you know… we've already lost too many… too many good people… I don't think that the village can take much more… everybody's so frightened …"

Henry smiled at Margaret. "Don't you worry my love. You know that I'll do my best… what's right."

They stayed holding hands for a minute and then Henry said, "Come with me a minute. I need to show you something in my workshop."

Margaret stood, wiped her eyes and followed him to the workshop.

"If the worst should happen," he said, "if they should ever come for you, to take you away for questioning – you need to know about this."

Henry pulled open a drawer beneath the main work bench. It was full of small tools and spare parts and at the back was an old biscuit tin.

"Look," he said, as he reached in and lifted out the tin.

Margaret watched as Henry opened the tin and unwrapped a revolver from its green cotton cover. She took half a step back and put a hand up to her mouth.

"As I say. If the worst comes to the worst. You'll know what to do. It's loaded with six bullets. You just have to slip the safety catch off. There's spare ammunition in the tin. Whatever happens, don't let them take you away for questioning Margaret. If they know that I'm the Commander and you're my wife... well... I don't want to think about it. You mustn't let them take you. You understand that don't you Margaret?"

Margaret watched as Henry wrapped the revolver back up, placed it into the tin, pushed the lid back on and shut the drawer.

"I'll know what to do," she said.

They embraced and stood holding each other tight in the middle of the workshop.

Half an hour later, Commander Henry Clay arrived at the Post Office, where Olive greeted him and waved him through to the back room.

"I need your help again Olive."

"Always glad to oblige. What can we do for you this time?"

"I need to get a message out to all my men without delay. If I give you seven names, and we can get the message to them, they will spread the word from there. I expect all the postmen have already gone out on their rounds, haven't they?"

"Yes, they went out ages ago, but George is still here. He's on some of the bigger parcels today and won't be going out for a while yet. Shall I call him in?"

"Perfect. Yes, please do."

George Marsh and Henry greeted each other warmly.

They had both lived in Watersham all their lives and attended the village primary school, although Henry was a lot older than George. Recently, George had helped Henry many times when he needed to get messages out to his men and they had total trust in each other.

"More messages to be delivered?" said George.

"Yes, and possibly the most important message you'll ever deliver."

George stepped in slightly closer to Henry and lowered his voice. "How many names?"

"Seven," replied Henry, "And I know that you know them all and where they live."

"Right. Have you written them down for me or do you just want to tell me who they are so that I can remember them?"

"I think it's safest if I just tell you."

Henry then turned to Olive. "Olive, if you don't mind, it'll be best if you don't hear the names. If you don't know them, you don't have to pretend that you don't know... if you know what I mean. That is, if you-know-who comes asking."

Olive knew exactly what Henry meant and stepped out from the back office, leaving the two men alone.

Henry told George the names of the seven men who he was to get the message to, and George repeated the names back to Henry three times to be sure that they were correct.

"So, what's the message?" asked George.

"Just say," replied Henry, "it's football practice at six o'clock tonight."

"It's football practice at six o'clock tonight," repeated George.

"Yes. That's it. They'll all know exactly what that means."

Twenty minutes later, George set off on his rounds.

After a quick wash and brush-up and change of clothes; Charlie Andrews sat with his wife, Peggy, in their front room. It was mid-morning; they were alone in the house as their children were at school.

"I might be away a lot more over the next few days," he said.

"Not again," replied Peggy, "Why's it always you?"

"It's not just me. There's lots of us in the Resistance. You know that. We're all doing our best. We're all trying to do the best for everyone in the village… for the whole country I suppose."

"So, what do I tell the kids this time? I mean, they already wonder what you're doing, being away night after night. I wonder myself sometimes."

"Don't be daft Peggy. You know I can't tell you what I'm doing or where I am at any time. It's better that you don't know. It's safer for you that way."

"I know you're in some odd places at night. Your clothes stink of paraffin fumes and God knows what else. If the Germans ever stop you, they'll wonder the same as me. They'll wonder what you've been up to."

"Yes, you're right, it's a problem, but we can't really do anything about the smell, there's just not enough ventilation where we are. If anyone ever mentions it, just tell them it's because I'm always working on smelly engines down at the garage."

"Look Charlie, I know you're doing what's best for us and I know you always will. It's just… you know… just such a worry all the time. The not knowing I mean."

"I know that too, and I wish I could tell you more, and I wish it wasn't like this, but it is, and we've just got to keep going. One of these days soon it'll all be over and we can get back to normal family life again."

"God, I hope so. I don't think that any of us can go on much longer like this."

Charlie stood and held out his hand and Peggy stood too. He folded his arms around her and she rested her head on his shoulder. They stood holding each other tight for a long time and then Charlie gently let go and she looked up at him. "You need to get going. I know you've a lot to do today."

"You're right. I need to be off."

Charlie walked down the hall, lifted his spare coat and hat from the hanger and slipped them on. As he opened the front door, he turned to Peggy and kissed her.

"Look after yourself. Kiss the kids for me and tell them I'll be back just as soon as I can. I love you."

"I love you too Charlie. We all do. Stay safe Charlie. For God's sake… stay safe."

They kissed once more and then he set off through the village. He had already thought long and hard about which route he would take to check on all of the local hideouts; but first, he knew that he needed to get back to see Julia to let her know that he was safe and that the messages were going out. On foot, he took a circuitous route this time; leaving the village westwards towards Eastergate and then turning north towards Fontwell. After crossing the main road, he followed a footpath that led him into Slindon Woods and eventually to the South Downs. He knew these woods well. He had walked here with his family and dogs many times. It was one of their favourite places; with the giant beeches and scattered ancient yew trees running along each side of a broad and grassy gallop.

Here he knew that it was highly unlikely that he would run into German soldiers and for the first time for many hours he felt that he could relax for a while. In fact, the only people that he saw was an elderly couple walking a pair of red setters. Charlie touched the peak of his cap as he wished them a good morning and they returned the greeting as the dogs bounded up and down the pathway. Two minutes later, he turned and looked back, they had disappeared from view and he was all alone again. A little further on he stopped, checked all around and then stepped off the main foot path between a stand of coppiced hazel trees. Three hundred yards further on, he came to a halt and listened. All was quiet and he walked on. The further he walked, the narrower the path became and the more he had to push springy branches to one side to allow him to pass. He was deep into the woods now and he knew that only foresters, deer and men like him ever came this way. Ten minutes later he reached a huge oak tree that stood alone in the middle of the coppice; no doubt spared decade after decade by the woodsmen. He knew exactly where he was and that the hideout was only a little further on. He stopped for a moment, enjoying the space under the branches of the great tree. He looked up and noticed a pair of red squirrels looking back at him from their lofty position on one of the higher branches.

"Well I'll be…" Charlie muttered to himself, "I haven't seen any of you fellas for many a year."

He watched them for a while, until they decided that enough was enough, and they skipped away and behind the great trunk of the oak. He looked at his pocket watch and saw that it was a quarter to ten. He knew that the shift change would take place soon and was keen to make sure that he was there when it happened. He walked on.

In the clearing, just back from the bank where the hideout was, Bethany Andrews stood waiting. She had arrived some five or six minutes before and had kept well under cover whilst every now and then looking towards where the branches covered the entrance to the hideout, waiting for the signal that all was well. She looked at her watch for at least the tenth time since arriving: it was five to six. Off to her left, she heard the unmistakable sound of a dry twig snapping and she instinctively ducked down behind the beech tree next to which she had been standing. From her crouched position, she peered out through the woods and straight away was sure that she saw something or someone move. She looked again across at the branches that covered the entrance to the hide-out, just in time to see the main branch being twisted and laid to point in the other direction. A deep shiver ran through her body and she suddenly felt very scared. She crouched even lower to the ground and muttered under her breath, "Bugger..."

Charlie knew that the crack of the twig would have alerted anyone who was nearby to his presence, and he too had ducked down. He checked his watch again and knew that the shift change was imminent, and that, according to the rota, it was Bethany who was due to take over from Julia. He needed to be sure that no one else was around before showing himself. As quietly as he could, and keeping low, he edged closer to the clearing. When he was within twenty yards of the hideout, he made a call such as a crow might make. Bethany breathed a sigh of relief as she heard the call. She was sure it was Charlie. She'd heard him make the same call many times before. She waited, knowing that if it was Charlie, he would repeat the call very soon, but this time with three calls. Half a minute later, three more calls came from the woods. Bethany stepped out from behind the tree and, spotting her, Charlie stood and walked over to meet her.

"Jesus Christ you scared me!" she said as they shook hands.

"Sorry Beth. I didn't mean to. I knew I'd make you jump; however, I did it because I knew that you weren't expecting to meet anyone else."

"Exactly. So why are you here? You were on last evening's shift, weren't you?"

"Yes, I was, but lots has happened today and I need to update you. Let's get inside and I'll tell you all about it. Is Julia in there? When we were at the Watersham hideout last night, she told me that she'd be doing an extra shift at this one."

"I'm assuming it's Julia in there," replied Bethany.

Julia was very surprised to see two people joining her in the hideout, but was pleased to see that it was Charlie and Beth.

"You made it down and back then," she said, looking at Charlie, as she shook hands with them both.

"Yes. All's well. I told Commander Clay all about the messages that we received last night and he's already started the ball rolling."

"Thank God for that," replied Julia, "The radio's been silent since then, so I've nothing further to report."

"What was the message then?" asked Beth.

"Sorry, Beth. Yes. We need to explain what's going on, don't we?"

For the next five minutes they explained what had happened earlier; exactly what the message was and what it meant. Charlie also added about his meeting with the commander and what he was doing for the rest of the day.

"Thank goodness!" said Beth, "I suppose that means that everything is likely to get a bit lively from now on, doesn't it?"

"I'm sure it will," replied Julia, "And we will all have to be doubly careful from now on. These hideouts will probably get used a lot more in the coming days and the more that they get used, the more they're likely to be discovered by the Germans, so we're on the front line too now."

Charlie motioned to Julia that they both ought to get going.

"Right," she said, "I hope you have a peaceful shift, Beth. See you tomorrow."

Charlie patted Beth on the shoulder and said, "Sorry again for frightening you earlier. I'll see you again soon."

"That's alright. Just don't do it again."

Beth watched as they climbed out from the hideout. As soon as they were gone, she carried out the normal routine checks: the paraffin level in the tilly lamp, the loaded revolver in the drawer, the message book and the general stores on the shelves behind her. Everything appeared in order. She checked that the radio was set on the correct frequency, took a couple of sips of water from her water bottle and sat down. She opened the second drawer in the desk and took out the book that she had been reading for the last few shifts: A Tale of Two Cities.

Outside, Charlie gave Julia the message that she needed to check in with the Commander on her way home and then set off to check out the other hideouts. Julia headed off in the other direction. It took her over an hour to get back to the outskirts of Watersham, and as she started down Green Lane, she spotted two German soldiers with rifles slung over their shoulders, standing in the road ahead of her and looking her way. It was too late to change direction as it would have been too obvious that she was trying to avoid them. She kept walking. A few yards from the soldiers, one of the men raised his hand and said in a very strong German accent "Stop!" Since the occupation, Julia had been stopped many times by German soldiers and she knew the drill, but usually it was in the middle of the village, with others around. This didn't feel the same. She was on her own, she was on the edge of the village and there was no one else around. Suddenly she felt very nervous.

"Papers!" said the same man as he held out his hand. The other soldier stepped away from them both and slipped his rifle from his shoulder, holding it pointed at the ground.

Julia said nothing and reached for the papers that she knew were in her inside coat pocket. From the corner of her eye she noticed the other soldier raise his rifle and point it straight at her. She knew exactly what was going through his mind and she very slowly withdrew her hand from the inside of her coat to show that she was only holding her papers.

Again, carefully and purposefully, she handed the papers

to the soldier's outstretched hand. She breathed slightly easier as she saw the other soldier lower his rifle. The first soldier held the papers close to his face, looked at them from different angles and then said something in German to his mate. It was clear, that because of the poor light, he couldn't see the papers very well.

"Come!" he said, as he waved his hand at Julia and then pointed down the street towards a street lamp.

Julia walked slowly between the two soldiers towards the street lamp where they stopped and the soldier looked again at Julia's papers.

"Name?" demanded the soldier as he held out the papers towards the light.

"Julia," she replied as calmly as she could, "Julia Adams."

The soldier could see that her photograph was a good likeness and decided not to bother with the other questions about her address and date of birth. He stepped closer to her and handed the papers back, but he didn't step back. Julia sensed instantly that there was a problem. She looked straight into his eyes and tried to stay calm. The soldier then walked around her, staying close, and looked her up and down. He then returned to face her. Julia knew exactly what the problem was and waited for the next question. She knew that he had smelt the odour coming from her clothes. The scent of the foul-smelling oil lamps. Everyone complained about it.

In good English he spoke again. "Where from? What smell?"

"From the farm," she replied, turning slightly and indicating with her hand the rough direction from where she had come.

"Farm smell?" questioned the soldier.

Julia noticed that the other soldier had raised his rifle again.

"Yes," said Julia without hesitating, "We use oil lamps

on the farm in the winter. When we milk the cows." she mimed lighting an oil lamp and milking a cow as she spoke. "They give off a terrible smell… the oil lamps, I mean… not the cows." she realised that she was starting to babble now and that her explanation was getting too complicated. "I'm sorry about the smell. It's awful isn't it?"

The soldier looked her up and down again and held out his hand for a second time.

"Papers," he said.

Julia took out her papers again and handed them to him. She could feel her heart rate going up and she was beginning to feel very worried.

He looked at her papers again for some time and then took a small note pad and pencil from his coat pocket and wrote down her details.

Looking straight at Julia, he handed the papers back to her and said, "Julia Adams go now."

The soldier stepped back and she slipped the papers back into her pocket, she muttered "Thank you." and walked off, nodding at the other soldier as she did so. The two men watched as she walked away. She walked as steadily and normally as she possibly could, desperately trying not to show how frightened she really was. Once she was a good distance away, she started taking in great gulps of fresh air. She felt that she hadn't breathed at all for the last ten minutes.

Julia knew that she needed to call in on Commander Clay, but knowing what had just happened, she was worried. She made her way straight home. She would visit the Commander later in the day.

Charlie Stewart made it to the next hideout without incident. It was two miles further north in Madehurst. By the time that he got there it was dark. On arrival, as usual, he stopped a good distance back from the hideout, under cover, watching and listening. After about five minutes, he was sure that there was no one around and that it was safe to enter. Once inside, he went through his normal routine; systematically checking that everything was in order. His main concern was always the radio batteries and he always carried out a quick test to check that they were fully charged. He was pleased to see that they were fine, as he hated having to take newly charged accumulators to the hide-outs and to take the empty ones back to the village. It was such a high risk. If the Germans caught you with those, it was as bad as being caught with a gun. You'd be done for.

Within ten minutes he had finished checking everything and was on his way to the next hideout at Houghton. He crossed the bridge and made his way along the north side of the railway line with the chalk cliffs towering above him. Where the old railway yard ran out, a rough footpath cut through the brambles for about one hundred yards until it reached the bottom of the chalk cliff. A single heavy wooden door, half covered in ivy and old mans' beard, shuttered the long disused entrance to the back of the ancient lime kilns cut into the main chalk pit further in. Charlie bent down to look closely at the large iron bolt that secured the door in its place. Hooked through the eye hole of the bolt was a twisted piece of honeysuckle twine that he had left in place following his last visit some ten days before. He satisfied himself that the bolt hadn't been touched since then and removed the twine, slid the bolt back and opened the door. After closing the door behind him, it was pitch black in the tunnel and he edged forward very cautiously, feeling for the chalk walls as he walked. After about twenty paces he came to a side door. He felt for the bolt, slid it back and entered the small chamber that was the Houghton hideout, bolted the door behind him and felt his way to the desk and located the oil lamp. Finding matches in the drawer, he was surprised when the first match struck well and burst into life.

Many a time on previous occasions he had been frustrated by damp matches refusing to light. Once the oil lamp was lit, the chalky white surface of the cave reflected the light back and forth in all directions. Charlie squinted as his eyes adjusted from total darkness to the new glaring bright light. He looked around. Everything seemed to be in its place and he looked up at the dark hole in the middle of the rough ceiling where an air vent had been bored right up through to the top of the hill. It now acted as a very useful chimney, carrying the fumes from the oil lamp away to the scrubland above. He checked everything thoroughly and then, as usual, he made his way further down the tunnel towards the emergency exit that led into the back of the old lime kilns. As he reached it, he heard voices coming from the other side. He bent down and put an ear hard to the door and listened. There were a lot of noises coming from the kiln and clearly there was a great deal of activity going on, including a lot of shouted instructions – all in German. He checked the bolt. It was pushed hard home and, just like the main door, the piece of twine that he had left in position on his last visit was still in place. Charlie breathed a sigh of relief and looked around the edge of the door to see if there was a gap to look through. There was no keyhole, but next to where the bolt was fitted, there was a small piece of damaged door frame with a splinter of wood missing. He bent down again and peered through. Instantly he could see that the old kiln chamber was well lit by artificial lights and he could now hear a generator running in the distance. Soldiers were busy carrying and stacking wooden and steel boxes onto pallets. Charlie could just about make out some of the letters and numbers on the boxes nearest to him, and although the writing was in German, he knew exactly what the boxes contained: ammunition, grenades and explosives.

As quickly and quietly as he could, Charlie made his way back, put out the oil lamp and felt his way back to the main door. He closed it very carefully and placed a fresh piece of twine in the eye of the bolt. As he made his way back along the path towards the road that led to North Stoke, he was already thinking of a plan to sabotage the great stock of munitions that he had just seen. It would mean losing the hideout, but it would be worth it.

Charlie arrived at the North Stoke hide-out about an hour later. He walked in the fields that ran parallel to the road and slowed as a small herd of cows spotted him and started to bellow, but they soon lost interest in him as he climbed over a five barred gate to the next field.

North Stoke was a very small hamlet made up mainly of a farm and farmhouse, a few farm workers cottages and a church. The fields all around were part of the flood plain that bordered the River Arun and were made up of permanent grassland. The chalkland to the east rose sharply as part of the South Downs. About a quarter of a mile from the hamlet, there was a large area of dense scrub running up against a steep grass covered embankment. Stone Age Man had quarried for flint here some three thousand years ago and caves had been cut into the hill, following the flint seams deep into the chalk. Charlie pushed through the undergrowth that was threatening to overwhelm the pathway until he reached one of the caves. About ten paces in there was a bolted door with a large rusty sign fixed to it. Some of the letters had lost much of their red paint, but it was still clear what they said: DANGER - KEEP OUT, and to add emphasis, a picture of a skull and crossed bones had been added to the metal plate. Charlie felt for the bolt on the door and immediately found the hazel stick that he had pushed behind the hasp on his last visit. He yanked it out, pulled the bolt back, stood still for a while, listening, and feeling sure that there was no one around, he opened the door and stepped inside, pulling it back shut behind him. Taking small steps and keeping his hand touching the wall on his right side, he walked for about twenty yards through the darkness. He knew from many earlier visits that the tunnel went on for a further one hundred yards and eventually opened up into a large cavern, but where he was now was another opening in the side wall. He felt his way along the wall on his right until he came to the desk that he knew was there. He opened one of the desk drawers and found the box of matches. The heads fell off of the first two that he struck, but the third flared to life. The chalky room sprang into life immediately, throwing his shadow to the bare wall behind him. The oil lamp lit easily and he adjusted its wick until a steady bright light filled the room. Charlie always felt more nervous in this hide-out, as he knew that there was no emergency exit. He knew that if he or any of the Auxiliaries were ever caught here, they'd be done for. He worked quickly checking that everything was in order.

Two hours later he was back in Watersham reporting to Commander Clay that everything was in order. Whilst they drank tea in Henry's kitchen, Charlie told Henry as much as he could about the munitions dump that he had seen at Houghton and he drew a rough plan of the site.

"We have to destroy that dump as soon as we can," said Henry, stabbing a finger at Charlie's sketch. "I think it needs to be tonight."

"Right," replied Charlie, "What do you want me to do. Shall I start getting a small team organised?"

"No," said the Commander. "You get yourself home and get some rest. You've done more than enough for one day. Meet me and the others in the woods behind The Spur pub at 22:00 hours tomorrow evening. I'll organise the men and the kit that we'll need."

"If you say so boss," replied Charlie, "I'll get off then and see you tomorrow."

The two men stood, shook hands and Henry showed Charlie to the front door.

Henry sat back down at the kitchen table and poured himself another cup of tea. He turned the piece of paper over that had Charlie's sketch on it; and in pencil, wrote a list of explosives, detonators and wires that they would need to collect from the stores. At the bottom of the list he wrote five names: Henry, Charlie, Bert, Alan and Alex.

After finishing his tea, Henry made his way into the front room, where his wife, Margaret, was sitting reading a book. "Margaret," he said, "I need you to run an errand for me. Could you pop down to the Stubbs' place and pass on a message for Bert?"

"Straight away?" Margaret queried.

"Yes please, my love. It's urgent, as usual. If you could go straight away, that would be very helpful."

Margaret closed her book, stood and followed Henry back to the kitchen.

As they stood in the kitchen, Henry ran through the key points that Margaret needed to relay to Bert. At what time and where they were to meet, who else he was to contact and exactly what Bert needed to fetch from the stores. Henry went through everything twice and Margaret repeated his instructions back to him, so that they were both absolutely clear that there was no misunderstanding. Henry helped Margaret on with her coat and opened the front door for her. "I won't be long." she said. Henry watched as she walked down the front path and set off down the road.

The following evening, the five men met in the woods behind The Spur pub, just to the north east of Slindon. It was a dry evening, a gentle breeze was blowing and there was heavy cloud moving slowly from west to east. Every now and then; a half moon could be seen between the gaps in the clouds. Bert and Alan had already checked over thoroughly what they had taken from the stores, but with all five men now together, they went back over exactly what they had brought with them.

As soon as the equipment check was finished, Henry explained where they would be headed and what they were going to do.

"What we don't know at the moment," he said, "is how many guards they have there during the night. If there are only one or two, we'll see if we can take them out and go in through the front, but if there are a lot, we'll have to go in through the back way. If it has to be the back way, it'll be more difficult, as the guards will still be out the front."

Each man picked up one of the back packs full of munitions and they helped each other hitch them over their shoulders. Henry and Charlie carried Thompson machine guns and the others each carried their Lee Enfield rifles; Henry also had his revolver holstered on his belt.

"Right," said Henry when he could see that everyone was ready, "Let's push on."

Henry led the men along a narrow path through the woods that ran uphill and parallel to the main road. On reaching the top of the climb at Whiteway's, the men crossed the Arundel Road and started downhill towards Houghton Village, walking along the edge of the fields and keeping tight against the hedge that ran along the side of the road. As the first of the houses came into sight, Henry continued to follow the edge of the field that took them away from the road and down to the bank of the River Arun.

Henry stopped and spoke to his men. "Now then, we'll walk single file in the field until we reach the bridge. Whatever you do, don't walk up on the bank, you'll stand out like a sore thumb."

The grassy meadow was wet under foot and in places there was standing water. On the other side of the bank, two swans sat sleeping; both parties totally oblivious of the other. Half way to the bridge the men came across a small herd of black beef cattle laying down on a dryer patch of the meadow. The men skirted around them, each steer watching their every move, but not showing any sign of concern and making no sounds of alarm. Alex, being the last man in the column, looked back at the cattle once he was well clear of them, and to his surprise, he could see that they had already given up any interest in them, as they were all looking in the other direction. A few minutes later they reached Houghton Bridge.

Henry stopped and waited until they were all standing together. They all stood quietly for some time as they listened and looked around. There was no traffic, no sounds of voices or dogs barking, no noise coming from the railway station; only the gentle sound of a light breeze running through the branches of the willow trees and reed beds by the river. The water itself made soft gurgling noises as the ebbing tide rubbed against the ancient stone pillars that supported the bridge.

"This could be tricky," whispered Henry, "I don't think that the Germans have guards on the bridge, but I can't be sure. We'll just have to watch for a while and see if there's anyone about. Let's all spread out and watch."

Henry stayed where he was, Alex and Bert crossed over the road and Alan and Charlie moved further out into the field to get a better view across the far side of the bridge. They all crouched down and watched for about ten minutes, until in the distance, coming up the line from the south, was the unmistakable sound of a train. As the noise became louder, Henry waved to his men to move and he stepped up from the corner of the bridge and walked smartly across, all the time staying close to the wall on one side, with the safety catch off on his Thompson machine gun and his finger pressed firmly against the trigger guard. His men followed on; two behind him about ten paces apart and two on the other side of the road. As the train rattled over the railway bridge ahead of them, the men all cleared Houghton Bridge and took up positions on the far side. As the train moved away, Henry and his men ran under the railway bridge and turned in towards the entrance to the railway station; Henry, Alex and Bert taking cover behind the hedge that sheltered the path that led to the chalk pits, and Charlie and Alan ducking behind a wooden fence that ran up towards the station. For a few minutes they all kept still; fairly certain that, until now, they had avoided detection. Once certain that there was no one else around, Henry waved Charlie and Alan across to join them behind the hedge.

"Right," said Henry, "Alex and Charlie. I need you to make your way down the path and have a good look at what you can see around the front of the chalk pits. We need to know how many soldiers the Germans have there."

Without hesitating, Alex and Charlie set off down the path. On reaching the small gate at the end of the footpath, they stopped and peered through the gaps in its slats. It was difficult to see very far as it was so dark there, but they could make out some lights near to the main entrance to the chalk kilns and there were a number of vehicles parked neatly off to one side. It was difficult to make out much more; certainly, there was no obvious movement, but it was impossible to tell how many German soldiers were there. They would have to get closer.

"You stay here," whispered Alex, "and I'll work my way around to the other side so that I can get a better view."

"Ok," replied Charlie, "But, for goodness sake be careful. If you get spotted, all hell is likely to break out."

Alex tapped Charlie on his arm and smiled as he slowly opened the gate. "Don't worry. I'll be careful. I'll be back before you know it."

Crouching down, Alex worked his way along the edge of a low brick wall that ran down the side of the main yard. Reaching the end of the wall, Alex realised that he couldn't go any further without the risk of being seen by anyone looking out from the main doors in front of the chalk pits. He turned, and still keeping low, doubled back towards Charlie. Charlie watched as Alex crossed in front of him and headed towards the closed main gates off to their left. It was even darker by the gates and Alex quickly crossed over to the other side and disappeared into the shadows. There were a number of smaller outbuildings here, and Alex slowly worked his way around them, all the time keeping an eye towards the lit areas near to the large wooden doors at the front of the chalk pit. Soon, he found himself crouching behind a low wooden fence in front of an administration building. From here, he had an excellent view of the front of the huge main doors in front of the chalk kilns. He stayed perfectly still and watched. He could see two German soldiers talking, off to the right of the main doors, but otherwise, he couldn't see signs of any others. As he watched; the main central doors parted slightly, light spilled out onto the yard, followed by three more soldiers. One of the soldiers walked over to the parked vehicles and the other four stood in the yard, lighting cigarettes and smoking as they talked. Just as Alex was thinking of making a move back towards Charlie, three more soldiers emerged through the doorway and joined the main group, as the other soldier walked back towards them from where the vehicles were parked.

That's seven already, and I've no way of knowing how many more there might be behind the doors, thought Alex.

He watched for another minute or two as the soldiers milled around. Off to the right, a small door opened suddenly and three more men appeared; but this time, they didn't look like soldiers; dressed in overalls, they looked more like engineers, mechanics or workmen of some sort.

Alex had seen enough. Keeping low, he worked his way back towards the main gates. Making sure that he kept in the shadows, he crossed back to where Charlie was waiting.

"Well," asked Charlie, "What do you think?"

"I think," replied Alex slowly, "that there's no way we can attack from the front. There's too many of them. I saw seven soldiers and three workmen in the yard. Judging by the number of parked vehicles, there's probably a lot more men inside."

"Let's get back and tell the Commander then," said Charlie as he turned to go.

The two men made their way back to the railway station car park where the Commander and the others were waiting. It didn't take long for Alex to give his report.

"Right," said the Commander, "There's no choice. We'll have to go in through the back way. Follow me."

Henry led the way along the far side of the railway yard, keeping well away from the station itself. The others followed on in single file, six or seven paces apart. At the far end of the yard they found the path that led through the brambles.

On reaching the doorway that Charlie had used the previous day, Henry waited for Charlie to come forward.

"Check it," whispered Henry.

Charlie bent down to look closely again at the large iron bolt that secured the door in its place. He quickly checked that the piece of twine was still in place, removed it, and gave the thumbs up sign to Henry. Alan stepped forward and carefully opened the door. Henry waited for a moment, and then satisfied that all was clear, he moved forward, feeling his way along the tunnel, and the others followed. On reaching the side door that led to the hideout, he slid back the bolt and opened it. Charlie walked into the chamber, found the box of matches and lit the lamp. The new light filled the small chamber and escaped into the tunnel outside, throwing dark shadows of the men onto the off-white walls.

Charlie moved forward to the door that led to the chalk kilns and bent down to look through the crack in the wood.

He watched for a while and then straightened himself up and whispered back to Henry. "There's only a dim light showing in the distance and there doesn't seem to be any activity out there."

"Right," said Henry, "Pull that bolt back as quietly as you can and open the door so that the dog can see the rabbit."

Charlie eased the bolt back and gingerly opened the door. The hinges creaked slightly, but not enough for the sound to carry very far. Henry stared into the gloom. As Charlie had said, the light at the end of the cavern was a long way off and very dim, but there was just enough light to show the outline of box after box of munitions.

"Here we are then," whispered Henry, "Let's get on with our work."

Alex walked towards the light that hung from the ceiling at the far end of the cavern. He knew that that was where the door was that led to the kilns and the large doors at the front where the soldiers were. At the doorway, he stopped and studied the door. It was closed, but there was no bolt or any sort of lock visible on his side. He looked around, and seeing a broken wooden ammunition box, he up ended the box, pushed it under the large iron door handle and jammed it in as tightly as he could.

That should hold them up for a while! He thought to himself.

Alan Benton was in charge of laying the explosives, and although each man had clear instructions as to what to do, Alan checked everything. He double checked where and how the explosives were attached, and most importantly, that the wires were all connected properly. It was important that everything was done precisely, as all the wires were to be connected to just one timer that would be set for a ten-minute delay, short enough time to reduce the risk of the explosives being discovered and long enough for the men to get away.

The men worked quickly and quietly for about twenty minutes, and as each one completed his task, he dropped back and waited by the door. Henry was the last to unroll his wires back to where Alan was waiting.

"Are you okay?" asked Henry to Alan.

"Yes. I'm alright here. You get off out with the others and I'll finish the wiring and set the timer."

"Good man," whispered Henry, "We'll see you in a minute."

Henry and his men retraced their steps back to the edge of the railway yard, each man pleased to be back in the fresh air.

Alan soon had all the wires connected as he wanted them. He carefully took an accumulator battery from his back pack, placed it on the ground and linked its wires to the junction box that connected all the wires together. Lastly, he connected up the timer, wound it and set it for exactly ten minutes.

As Alan stood to leave, he looked back at the great stacks of munition crates and boxes and thought to himself: I hope never to see you lot again.

As soon as Alan joined the others on the edge of the railway yard, Henry set off towards the railway line. They crossed it about two hundred yards to the south east of Amberley Station, dropped down onto the road and headed towards North Stoke.

They walked as quickly as they could. About three quarters of a mile from the Station, the men stopped in their tracks as a massive explosion ripped through the night air. They all turned to look back as a great plume of smoke shot up into the dark sky and the sounds of secondary explosions echoed around the valley.

Cock pheasants, woken by the sudden din, called out in alarm. Pigeons, crows and rooks took to the night air and wheeled around in confusion in the artificial light. Ducks, geese and swans, resting on the river bank, took to the water and hurried downstream, away from the cacophony of noise and light. Cows stood from their slumbers in the meadows and stared towards the exploding chalk cliffs, sheep panicked and flocked to the far side of their fields and horses bolted.

"Good job," said Commander Henry Clay as he waved his fist in the air.

"That should slow them down a bit." replied Alex.

The men turned on their heels and hurried off again down the dark road.

Back at the chalk pits, three of the German soldiers picked themselves up from where they had been thrown across the yard, and scrambled out through the gates. Behind them, a fierce fire raged, small explosions continued to crackle, acrid smoke filled the air, the vehicles in the yard and all the outlying buildings were on fire. None of the other soldiers or workmen had survived. The three soldiers who had managed to get away sat under the railway bridge watching the scene in disbelief. As they watched, a great slab of the chalk face slipped and fell into the inferno sending up more smoke and chalk dust into the night sky. Unseen by anyone, the little hideaway collapsed under the falling cliff, all evidence of the Resistance ever being there, buried under a thousand tons of chalk.

Now more than a mile away, having left the road and joined a rough path that ran behind a hedge parallel to it, Henry and his men passed by North Stoke unseen. The farmers, farm workers and the families who lived in North Stoke were all wide awake and looking out from their bedroom windows towards Houghton. The adults were shocked and worried and talked quietly amongst themselves, careful not to let their children hear the fear in their voices. What would this mean now? What might the repercussions be?

They all knew that the German army was using the old chalk quarry as some sort of munitions dump. It had been impossible not to notice the comings and goings of military trucks full of goods moving in and out over the last few months.

Ten minutes later, Henry and his men stopped to catch their breath near to the hideout to the south of North Stoke.

"Right," said Henry, "Charlie. You need to get a message away to headquarters. We need to let them know that the munitions dump at Houghton has been destroyed. Can you get to it?"

"Straight away Commander," replied Charlie as he handed his rifle and kit bag to Alex and pushed his way into the surrounding scrub. Without further instruction, Alan handed his weapon and kit to Bert, pulled out his torch and set off after Charlie. The three remaining men waited nervously, looking back down the track. There were still sounds of muffled explosions coming from the direction of the chalk pits and there was an orange glow in the sky. Even at this distance, there was the unmistakable and unpleasant smell of detonated explosives in the air.

Disturbed by Charlie and Alan pushing through the undergrowth, a cock pheasant suddenly flew out from its roosting place on a spindly branch of an ash tree. Charlie and Alan stopped dead in their tracks and Henry, Alex and Bert jumped as the low flying bird nearly clipped their heads as it clattered away into the darkness. Charlie and Alan took deep breaths and carried on towards the door that led to the hideaway. On reaching it, Charlie checked that the twig that he had left poking through the bolt hasp had not been disturbed. Within seconds, they had the door open and they walked slowly through the tunnel, feeling their way. Once they were a good distance inside, Alan switched on his torch and the scene suddenly came to life. Their shadows loomed larger than life all around them as they walked on more quickly now that they could see where they were going. On reaching the radio, Charlie pulled out the chair and sat down. Alan shone his torch at the oil lamp and Charlie found the matches in the drawer, lifted the glass from the lamp and lit the wick.

"Right," said Charlie as he pulled the earphones onto his head, "Let's get this message away."

Alan looked on as Charlie threw a switch, twiddled some knobs and brought the radio to life. A gentle buzzing and humming noise emitted from the radio and Charlie noticed tiny bubbles rising behind the glass sided accumulator batteries that sat on the desk wired to the radio.

There was a clicking noise and Charlie began to speak. "NS calling. NS calling. NS calling HQ. NS calling HQ."

There was no immediate response and Charlie sat staring at the chalk wall in front of the desk. Alan stood absolutely still holding on to the back of Charlie's chair. A minute passed by and Charlie tried again. "NS calling. NS calling. NS calling HQ. NS calling HQ."

This time, within seconds, the buzzing and humming noises changed pitch and a voice crackled into Charlie's headphones.

"This is HQ London calling. HQ London calling NS. What is the message from NS?"

Alan couldn't hear what was being said but he knew that contact had been made and he leaned in closer to Charlie. Charlie cleared his throat and spoke again.

"NS calling HQ. This is NS calling HQ. Message begins. I repeat. Message begins. The storage cupboard is empty. Repeat. The storage cupboard is empty. Over.

There was a slight delay as static crackling noises came back over the airwaves and then someone spoke again.

"This is HQ London calling NS. HQ calling NS. Message received and understood. Repeat. Message received and understood. The storage cupboard is empty. Repeat. The storage cupboard is empty. Over and out."

The tone of the crackling static noises changed again and gradually fell away until there was just a slight hum coming from the radio.

Charlie flicked off the main switch, removed his headphones and turned to look at Alan.

"It's done," he said, "They've got the message."

Alan patted Charlie on his shoulder and turned the torch back on as Charlie stood, reached forward and turned the wick down on the lamp. They watched the flame die and made their way back to the exit.

Outside, the three men were beginning to get anxious. They all knew that the whole area would soon be crawling with German soldiers and that they would be sure to check down this road. As they paced up and down, they heard noises coming from the scrub as Charlie and Alan re-emerged and joined them on the track.

"Everything alright?" whispered Commander Henry to Charlie.

"All done," replied Charlie, "They've got the message okay."

"Great job," said Henry, "Let's get going. We need to get as far away from here as quickly as possible."

Chapter 14

THE RECKONING

At 10:00 hours the following morning, Captain Weber SS arrived at Watersham Barracks with two trucks loaded with his own soldiers. Two of his Lieutenants accompanied him as he marched straight into Captain Muller's office and stood in front of his desk. Captain Muller looked up as they approached and then slowly stood as he recognised Weber. The men saluted each other and Weber handed him an envelope.

"You have new orders Captain," said Captain Weber, smiling.

"Really? That's a bit of a surprise… a bit sudden."

Still standing, he opened the envelope and read the short message inside.

"I have orders to return to Berlin immediately..." said Captain Muller, his voice shaking slightly as he stared at Weber in disbelief. "And you are to take over my command!"

"That's correct," replied Weber coldly, "I will introduce myself to everyone here and leave you to clear your desk and pack your things. My driver will take you to the airfield as soon as you're ready. I believe that a plane will leave Ford for Berlin at precisely 12:00 hours. I hope that you have a pleasant flight Captain Muller."

The two men saluted each other again and Weber set off through to the back offices with his Lieutenants. Captain Muller stood staring at his new orders for another minute before slowly making his way to his private quarters. At 11:00 hours, after saying goodbye to a few of his closest colleagues, he placed his cases in the boot of the waiting staff car, and they set off for the airfield. Throughout the short journey to the airfield, he wondered what might be awaiting him when he got back to Berlin, and more than once, he thought about what life might be like on the Eastern Front.

Captain Weber wasted no time in stamping his authority on his staff at Watersham. By mid-afternoon he had visited every office and made it clear that he was going to bring discipline and control to everyone under his immediate command and to the wider community in this part of England. At 17:00 hours, Officers and Sergeants arrived at the Watersham barracks for a briefing. Most of the men had only just heard that their commanding officer had been replaced and had no knowledge of Captain Weber SS, but a few of the older soldiers knew him by reputation.

"Weber!" called out one of the Sergeants, to no one in particular, as he approached the barracks. "My God... Weber! I don't believe it. He's a bloody bastard!"

A few of the other soldiers made similar comments as word spread as to who their new commander was. By the time the men reached the barracks, just about everyone knew of his reputation, and they filed into the meeting hall very quietly and in unusually good order.

Captain Weber stood on the wooden stage to address them.

"Good evening gentlemen. You probably know who I

am already; but, for the avoidance of doubt, for the more slow-witted amongst you, my name is Captain Weber SS. My predecessor, Captain Muller, is on his way back to Berlin and I have been sent here to replace him and to instill some discipline back into this unit, and at the same time, to bring some control and order to the local population."

He paused and then walked slowly along the front of the stage, head down and hands clasped behind his back. On reaching the centre of the stage again, he stopped, turned to face his audience and continued.

"Guerrillas are operating with impunity in these towns, villages and in the countryside. They attack and harry us every day. Only a few days ago they killed eight of our soldiers and destroyed a key arsenal at Houghton. It has to stop… It will stop!"

The room was absolutely silent. The fifty men present knew that there was more to come. Weber, still with his arms behind his back, marched up and down the stage once more, looking at the floor. He stopped and addressed them again.

"Our job… your job, is to show these people who's boss. If we don't show them who's boss, they'll continue to run circles around us. Once we have regained control, we can look to our main objective, that is to push on and to claim the rest of England for our Fuhrer and the motherland!

"So, as from this moment on, you are to be firm with the locals. You will not stand for any nonsense and you will punish them if they do not cooperate fully with any instruction that you give."

The room remained silent as Weber stood, leaning slightly forward and staring at the men gathered before him. He was not a big man, and in the opinion of most who saw him, he didn't have the appearance of a leader; but, on the stage, and with that stance and his ability as an orator, he certainly exuded power.

"Well," he shouted, "Do I make myself clear?"

There was uncertainty amongst the soldiers; and then, hesitatingly at first, a few started to applaud, and soon, they all applauded loudly, only ceasing once Captain Weber had left the stage and marched off with his Lieutenants to his office.

The next day, again accompanied by his two Lieutenants and a Sergeant, he marched with twelve of his soldiers, straight into the centre of Watersham. The soldiers stood at ease on the edge of the village square as Weber and the Lieutenants watched the villagers going about their business. No one spoke to them. After about twenty minutes, the Captain walked slowly over to Sergeant Lange and spoke quietly to him.

"In your own time Sergeant, make your way over to the corner there, and at random, select one person... any adult, and bring them over here."

"Certainly Captain," Sergeant Lange walked nonchalantly to the corner of the square and waited. After a short time, he stepped out in front of an elderly woman – Mrs Rosemary Arnold. She was carrying a shopping basket and was on her way to buy bread.

"This way," commanded the Sergeant in a moderately forceful voice as he motioned towards the square. Rosemary looked around, and then reluctantly, walked towards Lieutenant Huber who was waving her towards him.

"Wait there," said Huber, pointing to a spot on the paving, in front of the heavy wood panelled fence that bordered one side of the square. She placed her basket on the ground and looked around.

Captain Weber spoke to Sergeant Lange again, "Five more."

Lange made his way back to the corner, and this time, without delay, returned with two sisters: Jenny and Mary. Jenny was twenty-four years old, married just before the outbreak of war to Ted Brown, a carpenter. Mary Foster, her sister, was two years younger and not yet married. She still lived at home with her parents. They had come out shopping together this morning as they usually did once a week. Shopping got more difficult with each week that went by as most food was being rationed and nearly everything else was in short supply. They were both slim and good looking, both with their long blond hair tied back. On reaching the far side of the square, Lieutenant Huber pointed to a spot a few paces away from where Rosemary stood.

"There," he said.

Rosemary nodded at the young women as all the soldiers looked Jenny and Mary up and down. Jenny whispered to Rosemary "What's going on?"

"No idea," Rosemary whispered back, "I expect they're going to give us another one of their lectures about something or other."

Sergeant Lange walked quickly towards them again, nudging Bob Marsh the green grocer ahead of him. "Stand there." said Huber, pointing to a spot one pace to the right of the women.

Bob looked around at the women, and recognising them all, he touched the peak of his cap and gave them a half smile. He looked over at the German soldiers standing in line down one side of the square, and towards the villagers who were starting to gather in larger numbers now, wondering what this was all about.

Sergeant Lange returned again. This time with two men. Bert Strange, a motor mechanic who worked at the village garage and Sid Duncan, a bus driver from the neighbouring village. Lieutenant Huber walked slowly behind them, moving them slightly further apart and making sure that they were all standing in a straight line, with the wooden fencing behind them. As he worked his way along, the soldiers spread themselves out evenly so that they were positioned exactly opposite the six villagers.

Captain Weber stood at the corner of the square on

an upturned crate. "Right," he shouted, "I want you all to remember today," he paused for a long time. There was total silence in the square, with only the sound of a crying baby in the distance.

"Last week, your fellow villagers killed eight of my soldiers at Houghton," he paused again. "It has to stop! And this is why!" he nodded at Lieutenant Huber.

"Sergeant!" cried Huber.

"Rifles!" shouted Captain Weber... "Take aim... Fire!!"

All six villagers dropped as one to the ground, each with two bullets through their chests, the trajectory of the bullets only stopped by the solid fence behind them.

The noise from the twelve shots, in such a small square, was ear splitting and the sounds echoed and reverberated around the buildings for several seconds after.

The watching villagers stood silent, stunned, many with hands over their mouths; most too shocked and frightened to move. Some further back, turned and hurried away as quickly as they could.

The soldiers stood absolutely still, staring at the dead bodies before them.

Blood trickled across the paving stones, pooling in small red puddles.

Captain Weber walked purposely over to the prostrate bodies, his Lugar already drawn. One by one, he looked down at the still bodies, and satisfying himself that they were all dead, he re-holstered his pistol, gave orders to his men, who turned and set off back towards their barracks.

As the last of the German soldiers left the square, some of the villagers walked over to where the six had fallen, whilst others went in search of covers for the bodies. Jack Turner, the butcher, emerged from his shop carrying a large hessian bag full of sawdust and immediately went about the business of spreading it over the paving to soak up the blood. As some laid sheets gently over the bodies, more and more villagers gathered around and stood, still stunned and in disbelief at the horror that just happened before them. The only sounds to be heard were of men and women weeping.

Chapter 15

PRESSING HOME

Unbeknown to Major Foster and his men, at the same time as they were advancing through the Sussex countryside, six villagers lay dead in the market square at Watersham.

At midday, the British forces continued to advance strongly along the entire front as the Germans were pushed back. Even in areas where the German army had held the line and resisted well, they eventually had to give way and fall back, or risk being over-run on their flanks and isolated. Jack had fought well alongside Major Foster, Captain Blake and Sergeants Roberts and Bennett and their men. By mid-afternoon they were exhausted and the advance slowed. By late afternoon Major Foster called a halt, the sounds of gun fire diminished, and they watched as the retreating Germans fell back even further. During the evening the men set up camp under cover in an oak wood. Before darkness fell, in case of a counter attack, Captain Blake checked with the men dug-in in their forward defensive positions.

He walked quietly amongst them praising them for what they had achieved so far, and warning them to be watchful and to be ready in case there was a counter attack. He also encouraged them to make sure that they got something to eat and drink, and to take it in turns to get some sleep. "There'll be more of the same tomorrow boys." he said, "You can be sure of that!"

Jack joined some of his mates to get water boiling on the carry stoves that they had brought with them. They were all gasping for a cup of tea, even though they knew that they would have to use powdered milk, which they all hated. Ten minutes later, all the men were holding out their tin mugs to be filled with steaming tea. There was absolute quiet in the camp. Further back, the walking wounded were being treated in makeshift hospital tents that had sprung up as soon as the advance had halted. Trucks were carrying away the more seriously wounded and the dead; both British and German.

Sitting together, with their backs to a great ash tree and dipping hard biscuits into their tea, Sergeant Bennett and Jack Brown started to talk.

"Thank God for tea!" said Jack in a low, slightly trembling voice, his hands still shaking from the effort and strains of the day.

"Yes," replied Sergeant Bennett as he took another of his biscuit rations from the bag. "It's most welcome." he hesitated for a while and looked directly at Jack, "We don't want too many days like that do we…? I mean… talk about blood and guts and all that…"

"No. I don't want to have to do that every day. I mean it's… I mean… Christ… I think you'd go mad…" Jack looked back through the woods. The light was beginning to fade, small flickers of flames showed from the camping stoves dotted throughout the woods and men moved slowly between the trees.

Jack's thoughts were running back over the day's events,

and suddenly, he turned back to face the Sergeant and blurted out, "How many men do you think we lost today?"

Jack's sudden outburst made Sergeant Bennett jump and tea spilt from his cup onto his trousers. "Blimey! Steady Jack. We won't know how many until this is all over… I mean… how can we?... It's impossible to tell at the moment… perhaps one in ten? Mind you; there'll be a lot of wounded as well."

"Sorry Sarge," replied Jack, "I'm a bit worn out after all that… I'm a bit jumpy."

"That's alright mate. Don't worry about it. We all feel like that. You'll feel better once you've had a chance to rest for a while and catch your breath."

Jack smiled and nodded. He knew that Sergeant Bennett was right. He drank the last of his tea, put the cup down, folded his arms, closed his eyes and leaned his head back against the trunk of the tree behind him. Instantly, his thoughts took him back to Janet and the kids, and his home in Watersham. Were they safe? He had no way of knowing and he knew that they would be worried sick about him. He wondered if his messages had reached them from the Clarkes or the Matthews. He thought about others in the village too; his mum and dad, other members of his family; Commander Clay, Alex and Julia, and his mates in the Resistance. How were they all? He wished that he was still with them and that they would all be together again soon. His mind went back to the events of the day and his thoughts started to mix with dreams until he was asleep. He slept fitfully until four o'clock the next morning, when he was woken by Sergeant Bennett, tugging at his arm.

"What… what is it?" said Jack, startled.

"Wake up Jack. We need to move forward and relieve some of the blokes dug in up front. Come on. Pick up your kit and let's get going."

Jack rubbed his eyes, stretched and looked over at Sergeant Bennett. He could hardly see him in the darkness.

"What time is it?"

"It's about four o'clock. Come on. We need to move."

Jack jumped up, collected up his belongings and stuffed them into his back pack, picked up his rifle and followed the sergeant and five or six others towards the edge of the woods where groups of men were dug in or laying behind fallen trees.

The soldiers were glad to be relieved and quickly collected up their belongings and made their way back into the woods. Sergeant Bennett soon had his men spread out, and Jack and the others, laying on their stomachs, stared out into the gloom looking for signs of movement ahead of them. It was difficult to concentrate and to keep their eyes open. They all fought with the natural instinct to go straight back to sleep. Every time a soldier's head started to drop, a prod in the ribs would come from the man next to them. At half passed seven, the first of the morning light appeared in the sky to the east. It was cool, but not too cold, no sign of rain and the air was still. As it lightened further, it was clear that there were no clouds in the sky.

Jack turned to the man lying next to him and whispered "It looks like it's going to be a sunny day!"

"Maybe for some," replied the soldier.

Half an hour later, everything in the camp had been packed up and the soldiers readied themselves to move forward again. Scouts had been out before daybreak to check on the positions of the enemy, and as reports had come in, it soon became clear that they had retreated further back than expected.

All was quiet as Major Foster and his men moved out. They walked purposefully but cautiously for more than a mile with no sign of the enemy, when a single shot rang out and Sergeant Roberts fell to the ground. Everyone ducked for cover. Jack crawled over to the Sergeant, and on reaching him, he could see straight away that he had been hit in his side. He was laying on his back, his eyes were closed and his breathing was shallow. Jack knelt by him and unbuttoned the Sergeant's jacket as quickly as he could. His shirt was already soaked in blood and Jack struggled to get the bloody buttons undone. Pulling up his vest, he could see blood seeping out from the hole where the bullet had entered, and more running out from the hole where it had exited further round the Sergeant's side. Jack took out his pocket knife, cut a strip of the bloodied vest away, screwed it up and pushed it into the wound at the front. As he repeated the exercise and stemmed the flow of blood from the exit hole, Jack hoped and prayed that none of Sergeant Roberts internal organs had been damaged. He pulled his water bottle from his pack and poured water over the bloodied areas. The blood was only trickling across Sergeant Roberts white skin now, and as Jack washed some of the blood from his hands, a medic knelt down beside him.

"Well done mate," he said as he gave the Sergeant a quick look over, "You've done a good job there. I'll take over now, shall I?"

Jack watched as the medic opened his first aid bag and found a syringe.

"Pull the top of his shirt and jacket back, will you?"

Jack quickly moved around near to Sergeant Roberts head, leaned over, grabbed hold of the collars of his shirt and jacket and pulled them back as far as he could. Jack watched, as without hesitation, the medic stuck the needle straight into the fleshy part of the Sergeants' arm.

As the medic pulled bandages from his bag, another shot rang out, and further to Jack's left, a soldier cried out.

Jack looked over to Captain Blake who was waving his men forward, but at the same time, indicating that they should keep low. Jack picked up his kit and rifle, and walking half doubled, made his way over to join his unit who were taking cover behind a group of ash trees.

"There's a sniper out there somewhere." said Captain Blake. "I think he's over there to our right. Probably up one of those trees." He pointed in the general direction of a clump of pine trees about one hundred yards away. The Captain called out to Sergeant Bennett. "Bring up our snipers Sergeant."

Sergeant Bennett, moved quickly back to where the main group of soldiers were.

"Quick," he called out, "Snipers follow me."

Three soldiers immediately stood and followed him back to the trees where Captain Blake and some of his men were peering out from behind the trunks of the trees to where they thought the sniper was hiding.

"About there," said the Captain, pointing towards the clump of trees, "Probably about half way up that tree second on the left."

The three snipers each positioned themselves behind a tree, leaned out with their rifles and looked through the telescopic sights. They could make out the branches of the tree well enough, but not the sniper. They knew that they would have to wait until he took another shot; which they were certain that he would.

Minutes ticked by, and then suddenly, another shot rang out from the distant trees. At the same time, the faintest flash of light sparked from half way up the tree that Captain Blake's snipers were watching. Within two seconds of the first shot ringing out, all three snipers returned fire to where the flash of light had appeared. Immediately, one of the branches of the tree bent and a man fell thirty feet to the ground.

"Good job," called out Captain Blake, "Now. Let's get on."

Major Foster moved to the front and waved his men forward. Everyone was wide awake now, fully expecting more trouble from snipers, but as they walked through some more open land, with just long grass, brambles and scrubby blackthorn, the dull and unmistakable sounds of mortars being fired ahead of them rang out. Everyone dived to the ground, and after five seconds, seven or eight shells exploded around them. Four fell short, but the others fell amongst the soldiers, instantly killing four men and badly wounding several others.

"Move left and right!" screamed Major Foster. "Take cover." shouted Captain Blake. The middle of the open patch was quickly left to the dead and those too badly wounded to get away. As most of the men reached cover, another salvo of mortars landed near to where the first lot had landed.

The Major and the Captain were now on opposite sides of the clearing and they waved to each other, indicating that both groups of men should make their way forwards. In the distance, to both left and right, the sounds of gun fire were getting louder. Clearly, more and more units were re-engaging with the enemy. More mortars were being fired from enemy positions, but they had miscalculated the direction, as although they had shortened the distance of their aim, the shells were falling harmlessly in the centre of the clearing, whereas both groups were moving forwards quickly to the sides. Captain Blake was the first to spot two of the German mortar men, who were fully focused looking forwards and on reloading the next mortar. The Captain ducked down and pointed ahead. Jack and Sergeant Bennett also ducked down and looked out to where the Captain was pointing. Sergeant Bennett nodded at Jack and whispered, "Ready?" Jack nodded back, slowly stood up, took aim and fired. Within a second, Sergeant Bennett also fired, and both German soldiers dropped to the ground. Other British soldiers moved swiftly into position from both sides and quickly overran the rest of the German mortar team.

Major Foster looked at the hazel coppice woods ahead of them and called Captain Blake and Sergeant Bennett over. "This could be tricky." he said, as he waved his revolver in the general direction of the hazel coppice. "Make sure that the men are spread right out and keep in a line as we make our way through here."

Orders were quickly issued, the men spread out and started to make their way through the dense growth of the hazel trees, constantly looking left and right to make sure that they were holding the line. Fifty yards in, a machine gun opened up ahead of them, the spraying bullets sending splinters of hazel branches flying in all directions. Everyone dropped to the ground. The sound of the machine gun was deafening, relentless and terrifying. Two men to the right of Jack lay motionless and a third was on all fours and crying out in pain. Jack crawled towards him, and as he reached him, the man slowly fell to one side and rolled onto his back. The soldier was dead, his mouth half open and eyes wide staring up through the branches of the hazel trees. Jack patted the dead soldier on his shoulder, turned and crawled ahead towards the sound of the machine gun still spitting bullets through the branches of the trees all around. As soon as they could see that the machine gunner was lying behind a tree stump in a small clearing, one soldier after another opened fire on his position, and finally the dreadful chatter of the machine gun ceased. British soldiers, their pulses still racing, breathed great sighs of relief and looked around at their mates, listening to the welcome sounds of silence. Somewhere high in the sky and out of sight a buzzard cried out its cat like call.

Two or three scouts moved cautiously forward to check on the machine gunner. When they reached the position, they found not one but two German soldiers; one clearly dead and one badly wounded. "Medic!" called out one of the scouts.

Soldiers stood and started checking on the dead and helping with the wounded as radio operators busied themselves passing instructions from Major Foster and Captain Blake back to support units. Scouts made their way further forward through the hazel coppice to check for more enemy positions. On reaching the edge of the coppice, there was a wide clearing where other older hazel trees had recently been cleared; perhaps five acres or more. One of the scouts, Corporal John Cooper, knew exactly what he was looking at. His thoughts went straight back to a few years before war broke out, before he had joined the army and before his horrendous experiences in France and at Dunkirk in particular. He knew that he was one of the lucky ones to have made it this far without so much as a scratch. He scanned the open ground before him, not only looking for signs of the enemy, but noticing the way that the hazel trees had been cut, the bare stools that stood like mines; their cut stems pointing towards the sky like stubby sharpened pencils. The sight and smell of woodland was so familiar to him. As a boy and as a young man he had spent many winter months working with his dad, grandad and other family members; coppicing hazel woods just like those around him now. His right hand automatically tightened around the wooden stock of his rifle as he thought about the smooth handles of his favourite sharp axe and bill hook; the tools that he would rather be carrying today. He remembered the dry, sunny, frosty days when they would make great bonfires of the branch cuttings that were of no use for hurdle making, bean poles, thatcher's spurs or the one hundred and one other uses that hazel could be put to use. He thought about the sudden appearance of fox gloves and other wild flowers that always appeared during the following summers, after an area of woodland had been cleared. He thought about the secretive night jars that loved to nest on the ground between the hazel stools where the new flora grew. Many a June evening, just before dusk, he had sat under cover with his mum, dad and sister watching the night jars flying over the clearings like giant moths in the half light, flapping their wings that produced a striking sound, like the crack of a whip. As these thoughts ran through his head, a similar sound rang out as a bullet whistled past him and clattered through the branches behind him. He and the other scouts dropped to the ground. John held a hand to his chest. He could feel his heart pounding. "Shit." he said out loud and then closed his eyes for a few seconds and thought to himself: That was bloody close… too bloody close! If it's going to be like this all the way down to the coast, I'll be lucky to make it!

By the time the main group had worked its way around the clearing and reached the oak woods on the other side, the lone German sniper had retreated to a new position. Sergeant Bennett joined the scouts up front and they spread out, moving cautiously forwards. It was much easier walking through the oak woods. There was no undergrowth and the mature trees were well spaced out. Small numbers of crisp brown leaves floated down from above as a gentle breeze picked up to shake the last of summers' growth back to earth. Every five or six paces, the men stopped to look and listen. Visibility was good as the midday December light broke through the naked trees to the woodland floor. Sergeant Bennett found himself thinking about other days like this, in better times. On a sunny, dry and not too cold day like today, he would often be out with his two black Labrador dogs, double barreled 12 bore shot gun at the ready; hoping for a shot at a rabbit or pheasant for the pot. That all seemed like a life time ago now.

After walking for about fifteen minutes, Sergeant Bennett and the scouts halted and waited for the main group of soldiers to join them in the middle of the woods and then pressed slowly ahead again, spread apart by twenty or thirty yards. Five minutes later a shot suddenly rang out and the scout to Sergeant Bennett's right fell to the ground. The Sergeant ran half doubled from tree to tree and then dropped down to where the soldier lay. He could see straight away that there was nothing to be done. There was a large ragged hole in the middle of the soldier's forehead.

Major Foster and Captain Blake knew that the sniper would have moved off as soon as he had taken the last shot and that they would just have to keep edging forward until they got a chance to get at him. Captain Blake called Jack and a group of others over.

"Right," he said, "We need to deal with this sniper. What I need you to do, is to split up. Six of you go right out to our left flank and six to the right. Work your way out as wide as you can and then make your way back towards the centre. With a bit of luck, you'll find him. We'll keep edging forward with Sergeant Bennett and the scouts up front. Good luck!"

Jack and his group set off to the left and spread out as far as they could, but still within sight of the next man. They moved as quickly as they dared, as did the other group, not knowing what might be ahead of them. After only travelling a short distance forward, a further shot rang out to the right and another soldier fell to the ground. Jack and the men with him hesitated and then moved forward again. In the middle of the woods, Sergeant Bennett and his scouts also continued forward as the group on the right flank took cover and waited. In the far distance; both to the left and right, there was clearly more heavy fighting going on, as the sounds of shooting and mortar rounds exploding drifted in from both sides.

Jack was on the far end of his line of men and as he thought that they had probably advanced far enough, he quickened his pace to move ahead of the line and to start to move in towards the centre. As he did so, the man twenty paces to his right followed suit, as did the man next to him, and so on, until the whole line curved around in an arc. Jack was very conscious that he was probably the most advanced man, and most exposed, in the whole group and he walked more slowly now with his rifle held out in front and his finger close to its trigger. Bang! Another shot rang out and this time Jack was sure that he had seen where it had come from. He leaned against the trunk of the nearest tree and took aim at a spot by another tree about thirty yards further on. He waited, fairly certain that the sniper would want to move back again. A few seconds later; the sniper stepped out from behind the tree into full view. Jack held his breath, and keeping the sniper in his sights, gently squeezed the trigger. The sniper fell forward and onto his side and immediately tried to stand again. Jack fired again and the sniper dropped to the ground; completely still this time. Jack and the others ran over to him and turned him over. He was dead.

They waited until Sergeant Bennett and the scouts joined them.

"Well done chaps," said the Sergeant, "Perhaps we can get on now?"

It wasn't long before the entire company reached them and Major Foster gave instructions for everyone to spread out and go forward again. Jack moved off alongside Captain Blake; still thinking about the German soldier that he had just killed. Although he knew that he didn't have any choice in the matter, it wasn't a good feeling.

By mid-afternoon, they hadn't come across any more trouble and had made good progress, covering the ground at about two miles an hour. All the time, the radio operators were in constant contact with each other; checking their positions and making sure that none of the companies or units were getting too far ahead of each other. Down the main roads, lanes and forest tracks, tanks, heavy artillery and trucks followed the infantry close behind. At just before four o'clock, fighter aircraft appeared out of nowhere; RAF Spitfires and Hurricanes flew low over the tree tops and strafed German positions about two or three miles further to the south. Shortly afterwards, three Mosquitoes followed the same course, dropping their bombs along the German front line. Major Foster called a halt and the entire company, now down to about four hundred men, stopped, and most took advantage of the break and grabbed a quick drink.

"We'll just wait for a bit," said the Major to the men standing near to him. "I just want to be sure that the RAF aren't coming back for another run before we advance."

Five minutes later, with confirmation messages being relayed through the radio operators, Major Foster discussed their position with Captain Blake before giving the order to move forward again.

By half past four, messages were being received that the Germans had formed defensive positions no more than a mile ahead. Captain Blake checked his maps with Sergeant Bennett and then called out to the Major, "They must be dug in on the outskirts of Petworth."

"Right," replied the Major as he waved one of the radio operators over to him, "We'll move forward another half a mile and then wait for the heavy brigade to catch up with us." He turned to speak to the radio operator who was waiting for instructions. "Get on to your mates who are with the tanks and the artillery blokes. Find out where they are and how long it'll take them to reach us."

The operator stepped away from the Major and called his opposite numbers. A few minutes later he was back by the Major's side. "About ten to fifteen minutes," he said.

"Good," said the Major, "Pass the message down the line that the heavy brigade will be here in fifteen minutes.

Ten minutes later they heard the unmistakable sound of the first tanks approaching. Major Graham Standing, the tank commander, jumped down from the lead tank, walked over to Major Foster and they saluted and greeted each other. They were old friends who had both served for more than ten years in the regular army.

Chapter 16

HOME FRONT

On hearing the shots coming from the centre of the village, Commander Henry Clay and his wife ran into the back garden and stood looking at each other; wondering what on earth had happened. As there were no further sounds of shooting, they went back inside and Henry grabbed his coat from the rack in the hallway.

"I'll go and see what that was all about," he said to Margaret as he reached the front door, "Probably just some horse play… or something like that. I'll be right back."

They kissed and Henry opened the door. Hurrying down the path towards them was Charlie Stewart.

"What is it Charlie? What's all the shooting about?"

Charlie motioned to Henry that they should go into the house. "Inside…" he gasped.

"Unbelievable… bloody unbelievable…" said Charlie, still trying to get his breath back, "They've shot six people dead in the square… just picked them out at random… lined them up and shot them in cold blood… I couldn't believe it…

none of us could… it was terrible… just terrible!"

Margaret sat down at the kitchen table. "They've gone mad… they must have. Who did they shoot? Did you see who they were?"

"Definitely Bob Marsh and the sisters; Jenny Brown and Mary Foster. I couldn't say who the others were. I recognised them all, but I don't know their names."

"This is outrageous!" shouted Henry, "I suppose it's to teach us a lesson. An eye for an eye and a tooth for tooth and all that…" He leaned heavily on the back of Margaret's chair. "They won't get away with it… we can't let them… we mustn't give in to them… we mustn't!"

"But what can we do?" said Charlie, "If we resist further, they'll just line up more villagers and shoot them."

"Yes," replied Henry quietly, "That's the problem."

Charlie was about to speak again when there was a knock at the door. Margaret rose from her chair and went to answer it. Henry and Charlie listened to hear who it was.

"Julia, my love. Come on in."

"Hello Margaret. I've come as quickly as I could. Is Henry here?"

"Yes. Henry and Charlie are in the kitchen. Come on through."

Julia quickly greeted Charlie and then spoke directly to Commander Clay.

"Henry. It's started. They've advanced. They're already somewhere just north of Petworth. It's fantastic. They're on their way!"

"At last!" said Henry as he threw his arms around Julia.

When Captain Weber received the news that the British had broken through the German front line, he flew into a rage, telling Lieutenants Huber and Keller that it was sheer incompetence by weak German Officers that had allowed such a thing to happen. He made it clear to them that, if he had been in charge, nothing like this could have happened.

In fact, he was quite sure that under his command, they would have pushed forward by now and taken and secured London. Quite why they hadn't done that was beyond his comprehension. Captain Weber did not lack confidence in any way in his own ability to get things done. Immediately after his rant with Huber and Keller, he marched into his office and slammed the door behind him.

Lieutenants Huber and Keller called in the other Officers and Sergeants and explained the situation to them; finishing by telling them to get the men ready and to stand by. Half an hour later Captain Weber emerged from his office carrying a large map on which he had highlighted key roads that ran from Watersham and the immediate area north to the South Downs. He threw the map down on a table and shouted at the Officers around him.

"These positions that I have marked here," he said, pointing with his baton, "Are the key points that we will defend and hold!"

The Officers looked at the map and did their best to keep up as Captain Weber barked out who should take control of which place and how many men and what equipment and stores each officer should take with him.

"You have ten minutes to ready your men, one hour to load equipment and stores into trucks and we will all move out at exactly two o'clock. Sergeant Lange, you will remain here with six men to keep the barracks secure."

Officers and men went about their work as quickly as they could and at exactly two o'clock, trucks full of soldiers, stores and equipment headed out from the village. Captain Weber rode in his staff car with the driver, a secretary and a radio operator. In addition to trucks, there were soldiers on motorbikes, some with side cars with mounted machine guns and several utility vehicles pulling light artillery guns.

Concerned villagers watched as the columns made their way northwards. Within two hours all the troops were deployed at their allocated positions and Captain Weber drove from place to place checking that his officers had followed his instructions to the letter. At Houghton Bridge next to Amberley Station, he stopped to speak to Lieutenant Keller. "Here you must not only hold the bridge, but you must secure the railway station. Switch all the signal lights to red so that every train has to stop. Do not let any of them pass until they have been thoroughly searched. Do you understand?"

Lieutenant Keller saluted and said that he understood fully and headed off to deploy men onto the station and up and down the line to control the signals.

At Pulborough, Lieutenant Huber set a road block on the bridge that crossed the River Arun and positioned three artillery guns further back behind sand bags to the side of the main road. His men spread out each side of the main road and in the fields and on the river bank itself; all with clear views of the bridge and the road and houses on the north side.

Lieutenant Keller and his men blocked the road at the bottom of Duncton Hill and set up defensive positions in the hangar woods that overlooked the North side of Duncton village. The fourth unit was set up in the centre of the village of Graffham; some ten miles to the west of Duncton.

Captain Weber knew full well that these four positions in themselves could not halt an advancing army; however, he had already been in radio contact with his opposite numbers based further to the east and west and was confident that they would be setting up similar defensive positions in their areas. He also felt sure that if the main German forces to the north had to fall back to where his men were positioned, they could hold the line long enough for them to recover and counter attack.

Back in Watersham, things were happening very quickly. Most of Commander Clay's men were making their way to a meeting place in Binsted Woods; only a few hundred yards east of the Church, others were heading for the hideouts to the north. Since the start of the new offensive by the British forces, the radio messages had gone crazy. Julia and the other operators had been run off their feet; relaying messages between each other, back to HQ and out to the leaders of the Resistance. Henry had bided his time when news had reached him about the new offensive. He hadn't deployed his men immediately, but had put them on stand-by and was waiting for the best time to attack. He knew exactly what to do as he watched the Germans heading north out of the village. He knew that now the time was right. At five o'clock, as the last of the short day's light was beginning to fade, Henry and his men left Binsted Woods and headed towards the German Barracks just to the South of Watersham. He had already received messages that the Germans had only left a small group of soldiers behind to guard the barracks and he was fairly confident that Captain Weber and his men were by now a long way away and not likely to return for some time. Henry and his men approached the north side of the barracks with great care, making sure to stay under cover of the great lime trees that ran around the edge of the parkland estate where the Germans had built a high fence to enclose the old estate farm buildings that they now used as a barracks. A private road ran close to the elm trees and then turned at right angles to enter the centre of the northern fence through a large double gate. Just inside the main gate was a red and white painted barrier with a check point office off to one side. There was a light on in the office and, as Henry's men watched, they could see movement inside.

"Right," said Henry, "We'll go in through the other side." Twenty-four men worked their way around to the south side where, after watching for a while to be sure that no one was about, two men made short work of cutting through the wire stock fencing. One by one, the men ducked through the square hole in the fence and split into two groups; each heading down opposite sides of the buildings. Henry led one group and Alex the other. All the outbuildings at this end of the barracks were in complete darkness and it was clear that the few soldiers left as guards must be all together near the main entrance. As Alex was about to move up to the next building, he heard a noise and looked up to see a German soldier at the other end of the compound. He sent one of his men scuttling across the other side to let Henry know that a soldier was on the move and then he peered around the corner of the building again to see the soldier coming his way. He was walking very slowly, half way between the gable ends of the buildings and the fence, his rifle hitched over his shoulder. It was clear that he was carrying out a routine security check and that he would reach Alex and his men in about a minute or so. Alex realised that there was no point them all hiding and letting the soldier go on his way, as he was bound to find the broken fence and to raise the alarm. Alex leaned his rifle against the wall and pulled a long knife from its sheath on his belt and whispered to Alan Benton who was standing behind him.

"Cover me!"

As the young German soldier came level with the corner of the building; Alex rushed him, covering the few yards between then in a couple of seconds. Alex's left hand was across the soldier's mouth before he knew what had hit him and his right hand thrust the knife in, ripping through his heavy coat, up and under his ribs deep into his body. The soldier fell backwards and Alex fell hard with him, the knife digging in deeper under his weight. The soldier's body jerked and shuddered and then he was still. Alex sat up slowly and looking away he pulled the knife out, got to his feet and wiped the blood from the knife and slid it back in its sheath. He didn't look at the young soldier's face as he turned away; he didn't want to. As Alan and one of the other men dragged the body behind the building; Alex leaned against the wall and stared out into the darkness beyond the fence, his hands trembling. Alan walked slowly up to him, patted him on his shoulder and handed him his rifle.

Alex nodded and without looking Alan in the eye, they moved forward again.

They all realised that at some point in the next five minutes the soldier would be missed when he failed to return. They needed to get on with it.

Henry's group reached the main building first. Apart from the small office by the front gate, it was the only one with its lights on. He waited for Alex to appear from the other side and then following some well-rehearsed hand signals between them, they all ducked down below the windows as four of the men worked their way towards the front doors. Charlie Stewart and Alan Benton turned and faced the other way, their Thompson submachine guns pointing straight at the back of the gate office.

Henry waited for Alex to give him the thumbs up to show that they were ready and then slowly turned the handle on the front door and gently pushed it open. A soldier looked up from behind his desk as Henry opened fire. At the same time, Alex and the other men, smashed the front windows and sprayed the room with bullets. The door of the gate office flew open and a soldier peered around the corner to see what on earth was going on. Charlie and Alan both fired short bursts; great splinters flew out from the corner of the wooden office and the soldier fell head first onto the gravel pathway. The shooting behind them stopped; it was all over in a few seconds. Henry and the three others with him by the front door stood upright and stepped gingerly inside; each man with his gun pointing out front and with a finger on the trigger. One by one they checked the bodies lying on the floor. They were all dead; but, sitting on the floor and propped up in the far corner was Sergeant Lange, his arms hanging by his sides. He looked up as Henry edged towards him, his gun pointing straight at his chest.

"Mr Clay," mumbled Sergeant Lange, "It's you..." Henry placed his gun down on the nearest desk, knelt down by Lange's side, and looked him over. His right arm was in a mess where he had been hit several times and it also looked like he'd taken bullets through his shoulder. It was difficult to tell as there was a great deal of blood.

"Get this man on his feet and get him outside," called out Henry, "and call in the van."

Whilst waiting for the van to arrive, Sergeant Lange was carried outside of the perimeter fence and sat on a low brick wall, with Charlie and Alex propping him up on either side. Jim Barnes knelt before them, undid the buttons on Sergeant Lange's jacket and shirt inspected the bloody wounds to his shoulder. He opened his first aid kit, took out the heaviest bandages that he had and secured them as best he could to Lange's bloody shoulder. He then took out his knife, stepped over the wall and walked around behind the three men.

"Gently lift his arm," he said to Alex.

Alex lifted Lange's arm and Jim pushed his knife through the German's jacket and shirt, just under his armpit. Sergeant Lange groaned, not being quite sure of what was going on. Jim hopped back over the wall and pulled out a roll of cotton dressing from his bag, reached under Lange's armpit and pushed the end of the dressing through the slits that he had just cut. He then pulled the dressing through, around Lange's arm and back through the slit again and back to the font. He cut the dressing from the roll and tied the two ends together; pulling on them as hard as he could.

"You can let go of his arm now," he said to Alex, "and put your finger on this knot."

Alex did as Jim asked and Jim tied off another knot. Sergeant Lange groaned again and his head lolled to one side. "That should keep him together until we can get him seen to properly," said Jim as he packed away the first aid kit.

"Good job," replied Charlie, "Where's that bloody van? We can't hang around here all night."

Two minutes later, Bert Stubbs drove the van to the front

gates of the barracks and four men lifted Sergeant Lange into the back and laid him on the floor.

"What the hell am I supposed to do with him?" complained Bert.

"Take him straight to St Richards Hospital," replied Henry. "They'll sort him out. I think that Jim's stopped most of the bleeding, so I think he's got a fair chance of pulling through."

Jim muttered under his breath as he got back into his van "I never thought it would come to this… risking our lives to save a bloody Jerry…"

The van pulled away as Commander Clay ordered four of his men to go and fetch the body of the soldier who Alex had killed earlier.

"Lay him out with the others," said Henry, "We'll let the vicar know that they're here in the morning. He'll sort it out."

"Shall we clear all the papers out from the office and burn them?" asked Charlie, "It could properly mess them up with all their records destroyed."

"No. No. Definitely not," replied Henry, "Depending on how everything works out, those records could be very useful to us once all this is over. Let's see how things are going to-morrow. If there are no Germans in the village in the morning, I'll get others to take all the papers away and hide them."

Commander Henry Clay checked that everyone was present and ready to move out and then spoke to his men again. "Right. That was the easy bit. Now we need to move on and create some real damage. Let's go!"

With that, Henry led his men back across the fields, skirting around Watersham. They used the footpaths that had been used by locals for centuries, keeping parallel with the main road, heading north into the South Downs.

Chapter 17

WHITEWAYS

Commander Henry Clay and his men walked for two hours through the evening, reaching Whiteway's, a five-way main junction that split the London Road between Arundel and Pulborough. Waiting for them there were twelve more Resistance fighters, called out by Julia and her radio network.

"Good to see you Commander," said Don Steel as he stepped out to greet Henry.

"You too, Don. Any signs of enemy activity?"

"Not at the moment, but one of our men who lives out at South Stoke tells me that there's a German unit dug in around Houghton Bridge down in the valley. He thinks that it's the same lot that were based at Watersham."

"Yes, it probably is the same lot. They left the village earlier today. We'll send out some scouts in a minute to have a look at how many there are and how they've dug themselves in."

Henry asked Alex and Charlie to organise a scouting

party and to be ready to move out at first light. He then instructed the others to move back under better cover of the beech woods, off to one side of the junction.

"We'll be here for the rest of the night," said Henry, "So make yourselves as comfortable as you can. We'll be off again at first light."

Don spoke to Henry again, "What's the news from the front. Have you heard anymore?"

"Nothing much since first thing this morning. The last that we heard was that our boys were making good progress. The Germans have been pushed back quite a long way already; all along the line, from east to west. Some of our lot are just outside of Petworth."

"I guess that's why the German units have dug in at Houghton Bridge. We hear there's others up at Pulborough and Graffham, and some at the bottom of Duncton Hill. They must be expecting their mates to fall back a lot further yet."

"That's what we think," replied Henry, "and it's our job to make life as difficult for them as possible."

At seven o'clock the following morning, Alex and Charlie with two men each, set off through the woods that ran parallel to the road that lead down the hill to the bridge at Houghton, with Amberley Station immediately behind it and the castle and village a half a mile further on. Although there was light in the sky to the east, it was still very dark and they had to move carefully through the woods. The light improved as they broke out into the open fields beyond, where they split up; Alex with his two men, cutting across the main road and turning behind the first houses at Houghton, down to the banks of the River Arun, whilst Charlie and his men picked up a path that took them across more small fields behind the George and Dragon pub. Alex was careful to stay in the fields below the river bank so that their silhouettes did not stand out against the early morning sky. Keeping low, they moved across to the hedge that ran alongside St Nicholas' Church and entered the church yard through a kissing gate in the hedge. They peered out over the top of the hedge towards Houghton Bridge as the sound of a train reached them, coming towards Amberley Station from the north. They could see a red signal light twinkling in the distance, at which point the train slowed and stopped, about one hundred yards short of the station. They could hear voices coming from the direction of the train as the German troops searched it. Further over, Charlie and his men watched the same scene, peering out from behind an old hay barn. As the light improved further, both teams could make out the road block on Houghton Bridge where German soldiers were milling around. Further back they could see field guns defended by great piles of sand bags on the causeway that led up to the bridge, and either side, in the surrounding fields and on the river bank, more field guns and heavy machine gun positions. Alex did his best to count the soldiers that he could see from his vantage point and Charlie did the same from his. For about twenty minutes they observed the German defensive positions, and then, as the steam train started forward again, they turned and made their way back up the hill to Whiteway's. Charlie and his men were the first back and were almost finished debriefing the Commander when Alex and his men arrived.

"What kept you?" Charlie joked with Alex as he slapped him on his back.

"Charlie has given me the general layout of their positions and reckons that there's at least sixty men down there and well prepared. What did you see?" said Henry.

"Yes," replied Alex, "I think that Charlie's about right. Sixty to seventy men, well dug in; but we couldn't make out how many were up on the station or down the line a little way. Did Charlie tell you that they're stopping and searching the trains? I think that we had better assume that there's more at Amberley Station. The other thing is, that although they've got themselves well set up to defend the bridge, their heavy kit is all facing one way. As far as could make out, there's nothing facing this way."

"Good," replied Henry, "Let's hope you're right and that they don't get the opportunity to change things around before we get back to them."

Ten minutes later, as the sun peeped out briefly, low in the sky from behind broken clouds, Commander Henry Clay and his men set off through the woods towards their target. Two groups of seventeen men separated at the same spot as Alex and Henry had split up less than two hours before and headed down the hill to the flood plain.

In the hideout to the north of Watersham, Julia had been on duty most of the night, taking and sending coded messages from HQ to and from others sitting in similar hideouts across southern England. She was exhausted by the time she was relieved by Bethany Andrews. Knowing that there were no longer any German soldiers left in or around the village, they stood chatting outside for a while, swapping news. Julia was particularly pleased to be outside in the fresh air again. The cold-blooded murder of their good friends, Jenny Brown and Mary Foster, along with four other innocent villagers, was the main topic of conversation. After a few minutes, Julia said that she ought to be going. They hugged each other; Bethany noting the stench from Julia's coat.

"Phew… you stink," said Bethany mockingly.

"Don't you worry," replied Julia, "you'll be as bad in a few hours' time! Stay safe."

They waved at each other and Julia hurried off down the flint track back towards Watersham, but she wasn't heading straight home, she wanted to pay a visit to Janet Brown, Jack's wife. She was keen to let her know that British troops were moving south; getting ever closer to Watersham.

Janet opened the door and was pleased to see Julia

standing there smiling.

"Oh Julia. Come in. Come in. How are you?"

"Fine thanks. I thought I'd just pop in on my way by. Don't worry if you think I smell funny! I've been on duty half the night... Don't ask..."

"You do whiff a bit," replied Janet, taking Julia's coat and hanging it in the hall, "Cuppa tea?"

"Tea. Oh yes, please. I'd love a decent cup of tea."

Janet slid the kettle across the range onto the hot plate and motioned to Julia to sit down as she brought out cups, saucers, milk and sugar.

"How's it all going?" asked Julia.

"Not too bad," replied Janet, "But it would be a lot better if Jack was back here with me and the kids."

"Well," said Julia, "Look, I can't say too much, but I thought that you ought to know that things are happening. Things are happening very quickly by the sounds of it. There's been a big push by our lot, right along the whole front. We think that some of them have got as far as the outskirts of Petworth. That's probably the lot that Jack's with."

The kettle began to whistle and Janet lifted it with a padded kitchen glove and poured its steaming water into the tea pot. She brought the tea pot to the table and sat back down.

"Thanks, Julia. That's good news. I hope to God that Jack makes it back alright."

They spoke about the six murdered by the firing squad. It had shaken every villager. Most were still trying to come to terms with what had happened.

"I still can't believe it," said Janet, "That could have been any one of us. What on earth did they think they were doing? What sort of soldiers behave like that?"

"I know," replied Julia, "and you're right; it could have been any one of us. There's a new officer in charge. He only arrived the other day. It's his doing. It's his way of showing us who's in charge."

Janet put milk into the cups and poured the tea and Julia changed the subject.

"Let's drink to your Jack," she said, raising her cup.

Janet lifted her cup and chinked it against Julia's. "Here's to Jack." they said in unison.

"And what about you Julia? How are you coping with it all? It must be hard without Joseph. He was one in a million alright... one of the very best."

Julia put her cup down and looked away as tears formed in her eyes and started to trickle down her face. She found her hanky in her cardigan pocket and dabbed at her face.

"I'm sorry Julia. I'm so sorry... I didn't mean to upset you." Janet now began to cry too and she reached across the table and grabbed at Julia's hand and squeezed it.

The two women held hands for some time and eventually stopped crying. Julia blew her nose and took a deep breath as kitchen range, pulled the tea towel away that hung there and wiped her face with it.

"It's not your fault," said Julia, "You don't have to apologise. It's the bloody Germans fault, not ours. They're the cause of all this grief."

Chapter 18

PETWORTH & HOUGHTON BRIDGE

"Take cover," yelled Sergeant Roberts, "Stukas incoming!" Men ran in all directions heading for anything that might give them some cover as the scream of the Stuka bombers become ever louder. The noise was deafening. One after the other, running along the British front line hidden below them in the woods, the planes released their bombs at low level and climbed back up into the morning sky. A few soldiers fired after the planes as they pulled up and away, but to no avail. Sergeant Roberts counted six planes, the first of which dropped its bombs about thirty yards further away from him. Three men had been blown to pieces as the bomb landed right next to them; five others were hit by flying shrapnel, branches crashed down and great splinters of wood from the trees, stones and soil showered down on the men. The sound of explosions down the line was sickening.

"All clear!" shouted Sergeant Roberts as he stood and brushed himself down.

Jack got to his knees, his ears ringing, and leaning

against the trunk of a beech tree, he pulled himself up. There was blood trickling down the side of his face from where part of a shattered flint stone had cut his forehead and he had a stinging pain in his left arm. He looked at the sleeve of his jacket; a flap of ripped cloth hanging down from it. He slowly eased his jacket off, rolled up his blood-stained shirt and wiped his arm with his handkerchief. There was a large piece of flesh missing from his forearm. Sergeant Roberts walked over to him and looked at the wound.

"You'll live," he said, as he searched in his bag for bandages.

Major Foster and Captain Blake walked amongst their troops along the line.

"We need to move out," they said, "Move forward as soon as we can. Those Stukas will be back shortly. They're probably reloading at Ford as we speak; so, come on or they'll get us next time."

Men quickly gathered up their things and moved forwards, soon coming to the edge of the woods. Medics helped the wounded as best they could, lifting them into the back of trucks and driving back deeper into the woods as quickly as possible. The dead would have to remain where they lay for the moment. There wasn't time to deal with them now.

Major Foster sent scouts forward across the relatively open sandy heathland that lay ahead of them. Great clumps of gorse and broom, still with a few bright yellow flowers showing, gave some cover, with an occasional spindly silver birch tree poking up amongst them. Sergeant Bennett was one of the scouts. On reaching the far side of the heath, they could see Petworth Park, and in the distance, Petworth House and the town. Cattle were grazing in the park and all seemed quiet.

"The Germans must be in the town itself," said Sergeant Bennett to one of the other scouts crouched beside him, "Or they've already moved on further south."

Messages were relayed back to the main force, and

as quickly as they could, they all moved up to the edge of the Park. As the men awaited further orders, the sounds of approaching aircraft reached them. This time though, the bombs dropped by the screaming Stukas fell harmlessly in the woods, half a mile or more behind them.

Major Roberts gave out fresh orders; light tanks and Bren-gun carriers maneuvered to the front and soldiers spread out behind them; some heading straight through the middle of the Park, some to the east side of the Park Estate wall, near to the main road, and others to the west on the far side of the Park. Half way across, the unmistakable sound of mortar fire was heard coming from somewhere in the town, and a few seconds later seven or eight rounds landed fifty yards in front of the advancing forces. The central units immediately moved towards the limited cover of oak trees growing near to the boundary wall, but kept advancing. Two minutes later, another volley of mortars landed in the middle of the field; this time nearer to where some of the tanks had been before.

"They'll probably get it right next time." shouted Captain Blake, riding with one of the Universal Carriers, "Move back to the middle!" he shouted again; this time standing, holding tight to the back of his seat with one hand and waving his other arm to indicate that they should move back out.

"Accelerate!" he shouted at the driver, and as they moved back towards the centre of the park, they drove more quickly towards Petworth House and the rest of the unit followed; the men on foot now running. Sure enough, as the last man ran out from under the oak trees, more mortars landed, blowing great holes in the flint wall behind him.

As Captain Blake's Carrier approached Petworth House, a machine gun opened up from the side of the building, spraying bullets across the Park; several ricocheting off the front of Blake's vehicle. The driver swung the steering wheel to the left and stopped the carrier half behind a tree. The gunner lined up the bren gun and waited, his eyes peeled, watching a position to the side of the House. The moment that the German machine gun opened up again, the gunner returned a hail of bullets on the target and the machine gun stopped. All units moved forward again.

The tall wooden gates at the southern end of the Park were closed. One of the light Cruiser tanks trundled into them and they fell open with ease, flapping and banging against the sides of the tank as it pushed through. Three more Cruisers drove through the gates; then, the Universal Carriers, followed by the infantrymen. To the east, on the other side of Petworth House, they had made good progress and were ready to enter the town. The units working their way across the western side of the Park had also pushed well on and had reached the main gates that led onto the Midhurst road. Following a short exchange of messages between the three groups, and with few signs of the German forces, Major Foster instructed all units to push on through the town.

The first streets that they reached were completely empty. Towns people stayed in their houses, uncertain what to do. Their town had been occupied for six months and they had become used to being told what they could and couldn't do by the Germans. Less than an hour before, German troops had moved through their streets. They were frightened. What if the Germans counter attacked and came back?

As Captain Blake's Carrier pulled into the main square, the front door of the chemist shop opened. A man wearing a white coat and waving a union jack flag ran over to speak to the Captain.

"I'm the chemist," shouted David Price above the noise of the engines, "I'm also the Town Clerk. Thank God you're here. We've been waiting a long time."

"You're welcome," replied Captain Blake, "but where are the Germans? We thought they were all in the town."

"They were. Hundreds of them. They've been moving

out all day. The last few left only half an hour ago." "Where are they now then? How far have they gone?"

"We heard that some new German units had set up defensive positions at the bottom of Duncton Hill. I guess that's where they're headed; to join up with them."

"That makes sense," replied Captain Blake as Major Foster joined him in the square, "Thanks for your help."

Major Foster and Captain Blake discussed matters for a while and then agreed that they should move out from Petworth and join up with the rest of their forces to the south of the town at the Midhurst road junction.

"We need to be careful that we don't engage with them too soon," warned Captain Blake, "It'll be dark in about an hour."

Scouts were sent forward again, crossing the River Rother at Coultershaw Bridge and checking the small railway station a few hundred yards further on. The main road narrowed at Heath End and then opened up again on the approach to Duncton Village. Two scouts made their way back to report that all was clear to that point and Major Foster ordered all units to move up and prepare to take cover for the night.

Just before dark, as men made themselves as comfortable as they could and rations were brought out from the backs of the accompanying trucks, a lone Spitfire flew low along the north side of Duncton Hill.

Sergeant Roberts spoke to Jack, "That'll be a reconnaissance flight that will. I'll bet."

As darkness fell, a westerly breeze suddenly picked up and a light drizzle began to fall. Major Foster's men settled down for what was going to be an uncomfortable night.

Having slept badly, most of the men were up early; many of them walking around under cover of the trees, trying to warm up and dry out. It had stopped raining and the air was completely still. Several men had already started to heat up water, ready for an early morning cuppa.

On the north side of Duncton, looking out from the cover of a small copse, German scouts trained their binoculars on the woods at Heath End. They knew that the British had camped there overnight and they were trying to get some idea of how many they were and how well equipped they were. The mortar unit had already reported that they had seen some light tanks and Bren-gun carriers, but that was all. The Germans knew that they were short of intelligence. Staring out into the still very dark night wasn't helping. Apart from the occasional flicker of light, the German scouts couldn't make out anything worth reporting. Behind them, about one mile to the north, the retreating German units had met with Captain Weber and his soldiers from Watersham and they had spread out to take up further defensive positions on the side and at the bottom of Duncton Hill. They too were wet, cold and tired.

Earlier, on meeting for the first time, Captains Weber and Hoffmann had discussed at length what their best tactics would be in order to achieve their strategy of defending and holding their position. Captain Hoffmann suggested that it would be easier to defend a position at the top of Duncton Hill, but Captain Weber insisted that, as his men were already well dug in at the bottom of the hill, they should stay where they were and defend from there. He made it clear to Hoffmann that, in his opinion, the German line had broken far too easily and that they should have held on much better in the first place. Along with nearly everyone else who had ever met him; Captain Hoffmann took a dislike to Weber immediately, but eventually agreed that they would form a joint defensive position where they were.

Even at eight in the morning, the light was so bad that it was difficult to see very clearly in any direction. The German scouts sent messages back every twenty minutes or so stating that the British were not on the move. Major Foster was very unhappy about the weather conditions, especially the poor visibility.

"I'm not going to send the men out into that," he said to Captain Blake, pointing into the gloom. "I know that Jerry will have the same problem, but I'd rather the men could see what the hell it is that they're trying to do… what positions they're trying to overrun."

"I couldn't agree more," replied Captain Blake, "We can afford to wait for a bit. Why don't we tell the men to have another brew-up? They'll like that."

"Good idea. Send the message out and tell them we won't be moving for at least another hour."

The men were pleased to hear that they had more time and that for once they were not being rushed. Most were still cold and damp from the night before and welcomed the chance to move around and talk to their mates. Steam rose up from the boiling water on their field stoves, from hot tea in their enamel cups and from the slowly drying clothes on the soldiers' backs. Jack sat on an upturned wooden crate and looked out at the hundreds of men spread out under the branches of the surrounding trees. His arm throbbed and he continually flexed the fingers on his left hand to check that everything was still in working order. It seemed to be alright, and in an attempt to alleviate the pain, he slowly stretched out his arm and then gently dropped it back to his side again. As he looked around, he thought back to better days in his youth, when as a scout, he would go camping with the village scout troop. They would often get wet through too, but in those days, he couldn't remember that ever being a problem. The only time that he remembered the weather causing problems was when they all got caught in a freak snow blizzard before they'd had a chance to put up their tents. He thought back to how miserable he felt then; his fingers so cold that it was difficult pulling out the guide ropes and hammering in the tent pegs and then, with other boys in the tent, just lying there and shivering, until, after what felt like hours, their bodies warmed up and normality returned. When they looked out in the morning, the snow had miraculously disappeared, the sun was shining and the smell of eggs and bacon being cooked by the scout leaders under the make-shift kitchen lean-to drifted through the air. Jack smiled to himself, stood and walked towards the nearest stove, no longer thinking about the pain in his arm, he held out his tin mug for a refill.

An hour later the mist had lifted, and looking across the fields, Sergeant Roberts could see the short spire on one of the churches at Duncton.

"That's a lot clearer now," he said, turning to speak to Sergeant Roberts.

A few minutes later, Major Foster gave orders to get ready.

"Twenty minutes," he said to those near him, "We'll be off in twenty minutes."

The message was quickly passed around and men packed equipment into the backs of trucks and readied themselves. Each unit knew exactly what was expected of it and where to go, as officers had spent the last hour relaying the major's instructions to all leaders. The one thing that was clear from the start was that no one was going to advance straight across the open fields in front of them. Instead, they were going to advance on both the east and west flanks, with the light tanks up front and the Bren-gun carriers and the infantry following behind. As the sounds of the tank engines spluttering into life broke the relative quiet of a winter's morning, on the other side of the fields, the German scouts watched for a while and then turned and hurried back to report what they had seen to their commanding officers.

Jack walked with the leading group of men with the units approaching Duncton on the west flank. Captain Blake rode in one of the Carriers and Sergeant Bennett walked with the main group of men just behind Jack. There were five light tanks making good progress spread out ahead of them. As the first of the village houses came into view, the sun appeared in a small patch of blue sky, low and almost directly in front of them, peeping across one side of Duncton Hill. The first tank to reach the hedge on the south side of the field, pushed through a half open wooden five barred gate; it's partially rotten main hinge post tipping forwards as it did so. Several rifle shots could be heard ricocheting harmlessly from the armour-plated tank. The tank proceeded through the back gardens of the first row of houses and the other tanks followed. Individual rifle shots rang out above the sounds of the engines of the tanks and Carriers as the men reached the gateway. They stopped and crouched behind the hedge, looking out to see if they could make out where the shots were coming from.

"Off to the right," one of the soldiers shouted as he pointed, "From that small brick shed over there."

A split second after he spoke, another shot rang out and a British soldier near the gateway fell to the ground. Everyone ducked down lower. A dozen men, half doubled, moved as quickly as they could, following the line of the hedge further to their right. One of the Universal Carriers swiveled around, stopped and fired short bursts at the building. More shots were returned and another soldier was hit as he ran through the gateway. Further over, the twelve men reached the corner of the field, climbed over a fence, jumped over a ditch and emerged on the other side of the hedge. They worked their way across some rough ground until they were at right angles to the brick building, its open stable door facing them. The men spread out and started to walk slowly towards the building, all keeping their rifles trained on the stable door.

The Carrier started to move forwards, still firing short bursts and the two German snipers inside the building decided that it was time to move out. As they stepped through the stable doorway, all twelve soldiers fired at them and they crashed to the ground, one of their rifles spinning through the air and landing like a spear in the soft earth some five paces ahead of the fallen men.

Further ahead a heavy machine gun opened up, and at the same time, shooting could be heard on the eastern flank. On the south side of the village, in the shadow of Duncton Hill, the main German defences were readying themselves for the oncoming British. Under heavy fire now, Major Foster and the units on the eastern flank made their way past the Church of St Anthony and St George and spread out to check on the large Palladian house ahead of them and the centre of the village off to their right. Gun fire was coming from the sides of houses along the main road and Foster's light tanks replied; great lumps of brickwork crashing down from the houses. The surviving German gunmen fell back as quickly as they could, the Bren-gun Carriers racing along the road and firing after them.

Jack and his unit pressed on as closely behind the tanks and carriers as they could, passing close to another church; the Church of the Holy Trinity. Sergeant Bennett directed men to check inside; he was concerned that they might miss snipers and then get caught by them later on. They checked as many buildings as they could; finding families huddled together in back rooms, many of them terrified by the sound of war going on all around them. Many windows had been smashed with bullets flying from both sides; fences were being flattened and gardens trampled and run over as men and machines moved forwards.

At the bottom of Duncton Hill and in the hangar woods on the steep sides of the hill the German forces made themselves ready as the gun fire beyond them became closer, louder and more intense. On reaching the last property on the south east side of the village the first tank commander called a halt and the tank stood with its engine idling on the lawn to the side of the house. Mr and Mrs Peters, the elderly occupiers, peered out through the small side window that faced the garden, took one look at the tank, turned and made their way back to the main hallway, where they sat down on cushions under the stairs, holding hands. Outside, the tank commander waited for others to join him before attempting to move any further forward. He knew that the Germans were dug in a short distance ahead and would be waiting.

With all tanks lined up; four to the east and three to the west, they opened fire at the German positions and the German field guns responded in kind. One tank took a direct hit before managing to advance more than twenty yards and immediately burst into flames. No one emerged from its burning hulk. The other tanks moved steadily forward, blasting areas on and around the main road and into the beech trees on the side of Duncton Hill. The Universal Carriers followed, spraying bullets in wide arcs ahead of them. Both sides took casualties, but the onslaught of fire from the British forces was so persistent and heavy that many German soldiers were forced to fall back further up the hill, desperately trying to stay under the cover of the beech trees. Captain Hoffman encouraged his men to retreat up the hill as Weber ordered those around him to hold their positions. Eventually the Germans that remained were totally overrun as an avalanche of bullets whistled through their positions and shells exploded all around them. Captain Weber stood up from behind a pile of shredded sandbags, revolver in hand, firing down the road at the Bren-gun carrier headed straight towards him. He was knocked backwards by a hail of bullets from the Bren-gun and lay lifeless in the middle of the road. Captain Hoffman and what remained of his unit eventually struggled to the top of Duncton Hill and made their way hurriedly across the fields towards Upwaltham.

After quiet had returned, Jack stepped out from behind the low flint wall from where he had been firing and walked along the main road. There were dead and injured German soldiers everywhere that he looked. In the middle of the road was the body of Captain Weber, laying star shaped on his back; his Luger revolver still in his right hand. Jack bent down, eased the gun from his grip and took the spare clips of bullets from Weber's belt pouch. He slipped them, together with the Luger into his back pack. He and others then set to work clearing the road; dragging bodies and sand bags to one side.

"What about the Germans that got away?" said Sergeant Bennett to Major Foster, "Do you want us to pursue them?" "No," replied the Major, "We've bigger fish to fry. Let them go. I don't think that there were many of them left. We can leave our back up teams to clear up here whilst we push on along the lower road, through Sutton and Bignor and on to Houghton Bridge."

The road that passed through the villages of Sutton and Bignor had been there for centuries. It was narrow, cut deep into the rough fields and woods that surrounded it; worn down through constant use by countrymen with their flocks of sheep, herds of cattle, horses and carts and the water that drained from the downs, running incessantly along its chalky floor; often as white as milk. When heavy winter snows came, the road was impassable for days, stacked taller than a man between its flinty banks.

Major Foster and his men pressed on as quickly as they could with three tanks leading the way; stopping every few hundred yards and waiting for those on foot to catch up. The men were tired. They had been on the go for days now and their pace slowed with each mile that they covered. It took them nearly two hours to reach the village of Bury, settled beneath Bury Hill on the eastern side of the main London road.

As they cleared the village, Captain Blake sent a message back down the line that there was only just over a mile to go to Houghton Bridge. Ten minutes later, Major Foster called a halt and stepped up onto the leading tank, looking out over the bank, across the fields towards Houghton Bridge. He waved his radio operator over, and offering a hand to the soldier and helping him up onto the tank, said, "How's the battery power?"

"We've still a bit of juice left Major."

"See if you can reach our boys at the Bridge from up here. There's not much in the way, so with a bit of luck you'll get through."

The operator set his call signal twiddled some dials and tried his luck.

"Blue Seven calling Red Four. Blue Seven calling Red Four. Over."

The operator standing next to Bert Stubbs jumped as his radio suddenly crackled into life. He pulled his head phones down tighter over his ears, lifted the microphone and returned the call.

"This is Red Four to Blue Seven receiving loud and clear. Repeat. This is Red Four to Blue Seven receiving loud and clear. Over."

Bert Stubbs walked quickly to where Commander Henry Clay was sitting with a group of men and waved him over to where the radio operator was.

"There's a message coming through from Blue Seven," he said as they made their way back to join the operator.

Henry immediately pulled out his note pad to check the call sign.

"My God. That's one of the main British Army units. Where are they?"

Commander Clay and his men had remained under good cover, some three or four hundred yards back from Houghton Bridge, back from where the Germans were dug in.

Suddenly the radio crackled again and a long conversation took place between the two operators. Eventually the radio went quiet and the operator relayed the message to Henry.

"Major Foster and his men, including tanks and Universal Carriers, are coming down the road from Bury. There's over three hundred men with them. Major Foster requests that you hold your position and do nothing until he reaches us. He suggests that you meet him at the junction below the George and Dragon pub in about twenty minutes."

"Unbelievable!" cried Commander Clay, placing both hands on Bert Stubbs shoulders and shaking him; a huge smile on his face, "Bloody unbelievable!"

Twenty minutes later, standing in the middle of the road, Major Foster and Commander Clay greeted each other. They quickly exchanged information and Henry explained what he knew of the German positions below them and how he thought it best to tackle them. They realised that by now the Germans would have heard the rumbling of vehicles moving along the Bury Road and would be wondering what was going on, but they were also certain that the Germans would still be expecting the main British force to attack them from the other side of Houghton Bridge.

Word soon spread amongst both groups of men that they were joining forces to attack German positions at Houghton Bridge and Jack suddenly realised that the other group that they were talking about was the Resistance unit from Watersham. Excitedly, he made his way as quickly as he could towards the road junction; pushing past men, machines and equipment that cluttered the Bury Road. On reaching the tee junction, he spotted Alex Miller, leaning against a flint wall, smoking a cigarette. Alex saw Jack coming towards him and jumped up. "Jack. Jack Brown... well... am I pleased to see you!"

"Have you missed me?" shouted Jack as they threw their arms around each other.

"Too bloody right mate!" replied Alex, "What have you been up to? We'd heard that you'd got through the German lines, but we didn't hear any more after that."

"I'll tell you all about it when we get back to Watersham. I expect you've got plenty to tell me too. It's been a hell of a few weeks all around."

Alex's mind rushed. There was certainly plenty to tell. His first thoughts were of the six villagers murdered in cold blood in the square; but now wasn't the time to tell Jack about that. "My God. Janet and the kids will be so pleased to see you safely back home. I saw her the other day by the way. She seemed pretty good."

Jack was about to ask more about everyone else that they both knew, and how life had been in Watersham, when the sounds of tanks arriving at the junction drowned out any possibility of further conversation. They shook hands and both men turned and hurried off to re-join their units.

It had been clear to both Major Foster and Commander Clay that, even though the road was narrow, the tanks and carriers would have to approach the Bridge that way. The surrounding water meadows were just too wet; they'd be bogged down in no time at all. The men however could approach and attack over quite a wide area, keeping well under cover until crossing the fields. In broad terms they agreed that the tanks and Carriers would approach the Bridge along the main road, Major Foster's infantrymen would spread out across the wider fields on the west side, and Commander Clay's men would attack on the narrow east side, between the road and the River Arun.

In their positions, spread out in an arc around the southern end of Houghton Bridge, some of the German soldiers looked back up the road and at the buildings behind them. There was no doubt about the sounds of engines and vehicles on the move, but they had no idea what to make of it. Lieutenant Keller gave instructions to some of his men to reinforce their positions with more sand bags and to focus their attention away from the Bridge. He also told two of the gunnery groups to turn their field guns around and face them up hill, away from the Bridge. As they busied themselves resetting their positions, the sounds of the tanks coming down the road grew louder.

Commander Clay and his men moved as quickly as they could down to the church of St Nicholas and into the church yard; spreading out behind the low wall that gave them a good view of Houghton Bridge, the railway station and the Bridge Inn. Although it was only mid-afternoon and the winter sky was clear, the light was already beginning to fade, but they had a very good view of the German positions. Henry told a few of his men to get down to the river bank. The tide was incoming and the River Arun was rising, but the narrow grass strip between the waters' edge and the raised bank was fairly dry, allowing Bert Stubbs, Alan Benton and Charlie Stewart, keeping low, to work their way about twenty yards further along without risk of being seen. They already knew that not far ahead of them on the river bank was one of the field guns; fortunately, still pointing away from them towards the Bridge.

At full speed, heading straight down the middle of the road, the first tank burst out from cover and fired straight ahead. The pile of sand bags with a German field gun behind it erupted in a great explosion as four soldiers were flung high into the air. Cattle and sheep grazing in the meadows nearby panicked and ran off in all directions. Ducks and geese took off from the river, calling out in alarm as crows and pigeons took off from the fields and wheeled away. The second round whistled down the middle of the road, under the railway bridge, and exploded in the earth bank near to the entrance to Amberley Quarry; great lumps of chalk flying in all directions. One of the other German field guns, already lined up on a point on the road where the first tank had emerged, returned fire. In those first few seconds, the tank had already advanced a further twenty yards towards the Bridge, and instead of hitting it, the shell crashed into the side of one of the Universal Carriers, catapulting the vehicle from the road and into the water meadow; instantly killing the three British soldiers riding with it. Heavy machine gun fire opened up from both sides as the second and third tanks joined the fray.

Bert, Alan and Charlie peered over the top of the grassy river bank towards the German field gun some forty yards ahead of them. The German gunners were frantically turning their gun to face in the opposite direction and removing sand bags from the back wall.

"On the count of three!" Alan said, "One... two... three..."

The three men pulled themselves to the top of the bank, and from their prone positions, fired continuously towards the gunners until there was no more movement. They quickly slid back down the bank, and keeping low, moved along a further twenty yards closer to the Bridge. Shells, mortars and bullets were flying across the water meadows as the British Army and the men of the Resistance totally outgunned the German unit. The three tanks had stopped on the causeway; the first still firing straight ahead, the second to the left and the third to the right as the Bren gunners strafed the meadows. A stray shot from the first tank removed a large part of the roof from one of the outbuildings on the other side of the Bridge. Locals threw themselves on the ground wherever they found themselves; in their houses and workshops, at Amberley Station, in the Bridge Inn. The German soldiers at the station and from further along the railway line, ran to the railway bridge and returned fire from a strong position looking out across the road bridge. In the fields, fire from the German soldiers dug-in there gradually reduced, as more of them were hit from the continuous onslaught, or they dropped as low as they could, hoping that they might survive. Charlie and his men fired at the German soldiers on the railway bridge, and as Major Foster's men advanced closer, across the meadows from the west, they too directed fire towards the railway bridge. A shell whistled over the heads of the German soldiers and exploded three hundred yards behind them in the trees. Keeping as low as they could, the soldiers hurried back to the railway station, out into the back yard, and headed off down the line towards Arundel.

The shooting stopped, engines were cut and relative calm and silence returned to the meadows. British soldiers and the men from the Resistance stood and cautiously walked towards the German positions. The surviving German soldiers threw down their weapons and held up their hands in surrender. Jack watched as the soldiers trudged across the meadows towards the road, supporting the walking wounded as best they could. They looked a sorry sight.

Once Major Foster was satisfied that all the German soldiers had been rounded up and secured in a warehouse by the river; the clean-up operation began. Medics did their best for the wounded as Commander Clay and his men joined in with the regular soldiers and their support teams as they went about the unpleasant task of collecting up the bodies. The men were tired and went about their work in silence, laying out the dead soldiers along the grass verge by the causeway; British and German soldiers together. By the time they had finished clearing damaged vehicles and equipment from the road and the surrounding fields, the men were exhausted and darkness had fallen.

Jack wandered through the railway station and its outbuildings until he found Captain Blake and Sergeant Roberts, in a badly lit room, pouring over some maps of the local area.

"Jack. There you are. Good man," said Captain Roberts as he spotted Jack in the doorway, "Come on in."

The three men talked for a while about the events of the last few weeks, and then Jack said, "Captain. I need to ask you a favour."

"A favour Jack? Of course. Ask away."

"Well," said Jack hesitantly, "I'd like your permission to re-join my old Resistance unit. You know; with Commander Clay and his men, and go back to Watersham with them."

"I'm not at all surprised that you want to do that," replied the Captain, "Of course you can. You've earned it."

He patted Jack on his shoulder and they shook hands. "Thank you, Jack. Thanks for your help over the last few weeks and I hope we can meet up again when this mess is all over. Good luck."

"And that goes for me too," said Sergeant Roberts as he stepped forward to shake Jack's hand, "I'll look you up next time I'm in these parts... Look after yourself mate."

"Well, thanks to you both for looking after me and I hope you both stay safe too. Give my very best regards to Major Foster, Sergeant Bennett and the others. I don't suppose I'll get to say proper goodbyes to everyone before I leave."

"We will," replied the Captain.

Jack stood to attention and saluted, turned, and walked off to find Commander Clay and his men.

In the dark, it took Jack another ten minutes to find them. They had found room in an outbuilding attached to the Bridge Inn where they were trying to make themselves comfortable. "Look who it is!" Alex said as he spotted Jack and stood to greet him.

The two men threw their arms around each other as the others looked on.

Henry Clay walked over and shook Jack's hand. "I'm so pleased to see you again," he said, "I expect you've had a hard run of it?"

"Not half as bad as some of the others. At least I'm still in one piece, apart from a bit of damage to my arm."

Several of the other men walked over to greet him, including: Charlie, Bert and Alan.

"Will you be coming back with us?" asked Charlie. "Yes," replied Jack, "Captain Blake said that I could."

"That's good news," said Henry, "We're planning to stay here the night and then leave at 07:30 hours, just before it gets light. In the meantime, I expect you could do with something to eat and drink? Go with Alex around to the back of the pub. I'm sure that the Landlord will find something for you."

Even though it was fairly cold that night and they had to sleep on the floor, most of the men slept like logs. At 06:30, the early risers lit the stoves to boil water, and as soon as the first signs of steam appeared, men lined up, cups in hand, ready for their morning brew.

At precisely 07:30, having said his goodbyes to the Army Officers, Commander Clay led his men back across Houghton Bridge, heading south towards Watersham. Jack was pleased to be walking with them again. Just in case any of the German soldiers were still about, the men took it in turns, in twos and threes, to scout about two hundred yards ahead, every now and then turning and waving assurances back to the main group. They didn't see any signs of the enemy, and two hours later, they found themselves approaching Watersham.

As they walked down Tye Lane, Henry could see a lone figure standing in the middle of the road, half way along, waiting for them. As they got closer, he realised that it was Julia, and a great smile broke out across his face. She had been on duty again in the hideout the evening before and had picked up the message from Houghton that Henry and his men would be heading home first thing in the morning. She had been waiting there for nearly an hour. "Julia," shouted Henry, "You lovely girl!"

Julia waved at the men and they waved and shouted back at her.

As they reached her, Henry put his arms around her, kissed her on her forehead and whispered, "I can't tell you how great it is to be home. Thanks so much for coming out to meet us." And then as an after-thought, "Are there any Germans still in the village?"

"No," replied Julia, "They've all gone. Gone east they say. It's all quiet here."

One by one, Henry's men greeted Julia, and Alex and Jack put their arms around her and the three of them stood holding on to each other in the middle of the road.

"Welcome home boys," she said.

As they walked further along, people stopped to greet them and villagers opened their doors to watch them go by. Next to the Holly Tree pub, Henry halted and turned to face his men.

"That's it then men. Well done. I'm very proud of you. I'm sure we'll be called upon again very soon, but for now, go home, you've all earned a bit of a rest. Dismiss!"

With that, the men said their goodbyes to each other and set off for their homes.

Alex chatted with Julia for a while, they hugged and then he too, headed home.

Commander Clay, Jack and Julia stood in the road watching the men setting off in all directions.

"Right," said Julia, "Time to get you two home too."

Slowly, they set off together, and one hundred yards further, on reaching the turning that led to Jack's street, they stopped again. Henry and Jack shook hands and Jack and Julia embraced again. Jack then walked away as they watched him go.

"Thanks again," henry called out after him.

Jack turned once more and waved back at them.

Henry looked up at great black clouds gathering in the eastern sky.

"Looks like snow clouds to me."

Julia followed his gaze. "Could well be. All the more reason to get you home then."

They set off again, and on reaching Commander Clay's house, Julia knocked at the door and Margaret opened it to see Julia. Before Margaret could say anything, Julia stepped to one side so that Margaret could see past her.

"Look who I've found!" she said, as Henry walked towards Margaret with his arms held wide open.

Margaret cried out, "Oh my God... Henry... Henry... thank God, you've come home!"

Julia patted them both on their backs, turned and headed home herself.

Chapter 19

HAPPY CHRISTMAS

J ack walked slowly down the road onto Rose Green Estate and stopped by the path that led up to number seven. He was worn out, dog-tired and his arm was aching more than ever. He stood for a full minute staring at the door to his house imagining Janet and the kids on the other side. It was getting darker by the minute and as he looked up at the sky, he felt cold flakes falling on his face.

He held out his hands and muttered to himself in slight disbelief, "It's snowing…?"

Jack smiled, walked up to the front door and gently knocked.

The door opened partially and Janet peered out to see who was there. On seeing Jack, she pulled the door fully open, stepped out into the cold air, threw her arms around him and buried her face into his neck.

"Oh Jack… Jack… bloody hell… thank goodness… you've come back to us…"

"I'm so pleased to be home…" mumbled Jack, struggling

to speak, "I can tell you… there were plenty of times… lots of times… when I didn't think that I'd ever see you again…"

Janet released him and kissed him gently, running her hands up and down his arms.

"Ouch!... Careful…" he said, pulling his left arm away, "I've got a bit of damage there."

Janet took half a step back. "How bad is it? Are you alright otherwise?"

"Not too bad at all," he said, "It'll heal up alright, I'm sure. And no; no other damage to report! Anyway; how are you and the children?"

"We're all just fine. The children will be so excited to see you, safe back home…"

Janet started to cry. "Why… why on earth are we standing out here in the snow?" she said, "For goodness sake… let's go inside!"

In the hallway, Jack dropped his kit bag on the floor, leaned his rifle in the corner and Janet helped him off with his coat and boots.

"We'll have to get you smartened up and smelling a bit sweeter for Christmas," giggled Janet.

"Christmas?" replied Jack, "What day is it?"

Janet smiled at him. "It's Christmas Eve you idiot! Happy Christmas Jack."

For more information on John Charles Hall

Website: www.johncharleshall.co.uk

Facebook: @authorjohnhall

Twitter: #authorjohnhall

Printed in Great Britain
by Amazon